Acclaim for Denise Hunter

"A tender story of faith cast adrift and lives brought together by currents that can only be God-sent, *Barefoot Summer* is a satisfying tale of hope, healing, and a love that's meant to be. Sail away with Denise Hunter's well-drawn characters on a journey that is at once romantic and compelling."

—LISA WINGATE, NATIONAL BEST-SELLING AND AWARD-WINNING AUTHOR OF *BLUE MOON BAY* AND *FIREFLY ISLAND*

"Kick off your shoes and enjoy your time with *Barefoot Summer*! It sets the bar high for this year's vacation read contenders by combining hold-your-breath romance, heartache, and laugh-out-loud conversations between siblings and friends. It's more than a good read. It's a delight."

—LISA T. BERGREN, BEST-SELLING AUTHOR OF *WATERFALL* AND *GLAMOROUS ILLUSIONS*

". . . [A] fast, fun and touching read with the added draw of a first kiss that is sure to make my Top 5 Fictional Kisses of 2012. So saddle up, ladies: We have a winner!"

—USAToday.com REVIEW OF *THE TROUBLE WITH COWBOYS*

"This read will not only have fans cheering the characters on, it will leave them feeling inspired in their own lives."

—*ROMANTIC TIMES* REVIEW OF *THE TROUBLE WITH COWBOYS*

"Hunter's well-developed characters and plot twists make for a delightful and inspirational journey."

—*PUBLISHERS WEEKLY* REVIEW OF *THE TROUBLE WITH COWBOYS*

"The best kind of love story—completely believable, wonderfully real, with a *Sleepless-in-Seattle*-esque vibe that just makes you want to cheer for love's ability to be reborn."

—Susan Meissner, author of *Lady in Waiting*, regarding *A Cowboy's Touch*

"What a tender, touching tale! Another cast of fascinating characters, another compelling storyline, another page-turning plot. All reasons Denise Hunter remains one of my favorite authors *ever*."

—Deborah Raney, author of the Clayburn Novels, regarding *A Cowboy's Touch*

". . . [A] romantic adventure about unconditional love and forgiveness."

—*Library Journal* review of *Surrender Bay*

"Hunter's characters are well drawn and familiar. [W]ill appeal to all women readers with the taste for a good love story."

—*Foreword* magazine review of *Surrender Bay*

"[In *Surrender Bay*] Denise has turned the spotlight on the depth of God's love for His children in a story that will remain with you long after the last page is read."

—RelzReviewz

"No one can write a story that grips the heart like Denise Hunter . . . If you like Karen Kingsbury or Nicholas Sparks, this is an author you'll love."

—Colleen Coble, best-selling author of *The Lightkeeper's Bride*

"In *Finding Faith* Denise Hunter once again brings me to tears with her thought-provoking story. For depth and emotion, this author always hits her mark."

—Kristin Billerbeck, author of *What a Girl Wants* and *She's All That*

Barefoot Summer

Also by Denise Hunter

Novellas included in *Smitten* and *Secretly Smitten*

THE BIG SKY ROMANCE SERIES

A Cowboy's Touch
The Accidental Bride
The Trouble with Cowboys

NANTUCKET LOVE STORIES

Surrender Bay
The Convenient Groom
Seaside Letters
Driftwood Lane

Sweetwater Gap

Barefoot Summer

A CHAPEL SPRINGS ROMANCE

DENISE HUNTER

THOMAS NELSON
Since 1798

NASHVILLE DALLAS MEXICO CITY RIO DE JANEIRO

Published in Nashville, Tennessee. Thomas Nelson is a trademark of Thomas Nelson, Inc.

Thomas Nelson, Inc., books may be purchased in bulk for educational, business, fund-raising, or sales promotional use. For information, please e-mail SpecialMarkets@ThomasNelson.com.

Scripture quotations are taken from Holy Bible New International Version®, NIV®· Copyright © 1973, 1978, 1984, 2011 by Biblica, Inc.™ Used by permission of Zondervan. All rights reserved worldwide. www.zondervan.com

Publisher's Note: This novel is a work of fiction. Names, characters, places, and incidents are either products of the author's imagination or used fictitiously. All characters are fictional, and any similarity to people living or dead is purely coincidental.

Library of Congress Cataloging-in-Publication Data

Hunter, Denise, 1968-
  Barefoot Summer / Denise Hunter.
     pages cm. -- (A Chapel Springs Romance ; 1)
  ISBN 978-1-4016-8700-7 (trade paper)
1. Boats and boating--Fiction. 2. Family secrets--Fiction. 3. Christian fiction. 4. Love stories. I. Title.
  PS3608.U5925B37 2013
  813'.6--dc23
                                    2013000164

Printed in the United States of America

13 14 15 16 17 RRD 6 5 4 3 2 1

"A farmer went out to sow his seed.
As he was scattering the seed, some fell along the path;
it was trampled on, and the birds ate it up.
Some fell on rocky ground, and when it came up,
the plants withered because they had no moisture.
Other seed fell among thorns,
which grew up with it and choked the plants.
Still other seed fell on good soil. It came up and yielded a crop,
a hundred times more than was sown."

LUKE 8:5–8, EMPHASIS ADDED

The Lord is not slow in keeping his promise, as some
understand slowness. Instead he is patient with you,
not wanting anyone to perish, but everyone to come to
repentance.

2 PETER 3:9

CHAPTER ONE

MADISON McKINLEY SCANNED THE CROWDED TOWN HALL, wondering how many of her friends and neighbors she'd have to fight to get what she came for. Half of Chapel Springs had turned out to support the fire department. The faint scent of popcorn and coffee from last night's Rotary club meeting still lingered in the air, and the buzz of excitement was almost palpable.

When she reached the front of the line, she registered for her paddle, then looked for her mom. She spotted Joann McKinley seated on the left, near the old brick wall.

Before Madison could move, Dottie Meyers appeared in the busy aisle. "Madison, hello, dear. I was wondering if I could bother you about Ginger. I found a little knot behind her leg. I'm worried it might be something serious."

Last time it had only been a burr. Still, Madison set a hand on the woman's arm. "I'm sure it's fine, but I'll have Cassidy call you tomorrow and squeeze you in, okay?"

"All right, everyone," the emcee was saying into the mike. "It's about that time."

"Thank you so much, dear," Dottie was saying. "I'm so excited about this year's play. It's called *Love on the Line*. You are planning on coming out again, aren't you? You'll be fabulous as Eleanor."

Auditions were still two months away. "Looking forward to it. See you tomorrow." Madison participated in the town's production

1

every year. She enjoyed the theater, and the proceeds supported the local animal shelter, a cause she was committed to.

She turned toward her mom and ran straight into a wall. *"Ooomph."*

Or a chest. A hard chest.

She looked up into the face of the one man she least wanted to see, much less slam into. She jumped back, looking square into his unfathomable coal-colored eyes.

She nodded once. "Beckett."

He returned the nod. "Madison."

His black hair was tousled. He wore a Dewitt's Marina work shirt and at least two days' stubble. His jaw twitched. She hadn't spoken to him since she'd confronted him two weeks ago—for all the good it had done.

"Please take your seats," the emcee said.

Gladly.

She stepped to the left at the same time as Beckett. He was wide as Boulder Creek and twice as dangerous. She'd always thought so. The incident with her little sister had only confirmed it.

"Excuse me," she said.

He slid right and swept his arm out as if to say, *After you, princess.*

She shot him a look, then hurried down the aisle and slid into a metal chair beside her mom.

"Hi, sweetie. Good day?" Mom's short blond hair and blue eyes sparkled under the fluorescent lights, but it was her smile that lit the room.

"Twelve dogs, seven cats, two bunnies, and a partridge in a pear tree."

Beckett passed her row and slid into a seat up front by his sister. Layla had long brown hair and a model-pretty face. Their mom must've been beautiful, though Madison didn't remember her. Beckett leaned over and whispered something to his sister.

Madison tore her eyes away and loosened her death grip on the auction paddle. She refused to think about Beckett O'Reilly tonight.

The emcee took the podium and spoke about the importance of the fire station and their financial needs, then she introduced the auctioneer—hardly necessary since he also ran the local gas station. Moments later the bidding was under way.

Madison's eyes swung to Beckett's dark head. She could swear he was stalking her lately. He seemed to be everywhere she turned. If anything, the man should be avoiding her. Should feel ashamed of . . . well, whatever he did to Jade.

Madison tracked the auction items, ticking off each one as they sold to the highest bidder. A handmade quilt, piano lessons, pie of the month, a cabin rental at Patoka Lake, and dozens of other things generously donated by the community.

Someone had made a miniature replica of the town's sign. WELCOME TO CHAPEL SPRINGS, INDIANA, it said. PRETTIEST RIVER TOWN IN AMERICA. A writer from *Midwest Living* had used the phrase twelve years ago, and the town had squeezed every last drop from it.

Evangeline Simmons, eighty-five if she was a day, amused all by driving up the bids. It was no secret that the fire department had saved her beloved Persian from a tree last month. So far her generosity had left her with two items she probably had no need for. But money was no object for Evangeline.

People trickled out as the auction wore on. Beckett left after losing a tool kit. Over an hour later, Madison grew tense as her item came up. The auctioneer read from the sheet.

"All right, ladies and gentlemen, this next one's a winner. Dewitt Marina has kindly donated a sailing/regatta package. Lessons taught by sailing enthusiast Evan Higgins. Learn how to race on the beautiful Ohio River, just in time for our 45th Annual River Sail Regatta, and sail with Evan Higgins, winner of the regatta for two years running! Now, who'll give me five hundred?"

Madison's grip tightened on the handle, waiting for the auctioneer to lower the bid. Her breath caught in her lungs. *Patience, girl.*

"All right, a hundred, who'll give me a hundred? A hundred-dollar bid . . . ?"

Casually, Madison lifted her paddle.

"A hundred-dollar bid, now a hundred fifty, who'll give me one and a half . . . ?"

In her peripheral vision she could see her mom's head swing toward her just as Evangeline raised her paddle—and the bid.

"A hundred fifty, who'll give me two, now two . . . ?"

Madison lifted her paddle, keeping her eyes straight ahead.

"Two hundred, now who'll give me two fifty, fifty, fifty . . . ? Got it! Now three, three hundred, who'll give me three . . . ?"

Madison sighed, waited a moment before nodding.

"Three, now who'll give me three and a half, three fifty, fifty, fifty . . . ?"

Evangeline turned toward Madison, her eyes twinkling. She raised her paddle.

Evangeline. Madison hadn't counted on spending so much. Would serve the lady right if she dropped out. Just imagining the spry old woman on the bow of a boat, trying to manage the ropes and sails and whatnot, all four-foot-eleven of her . . . It was tempting.

Madison could, after all, just go down to the marina and buy the lessons, but then she wouldn't be virtually assured of a win, would she? She needed Evan Higgins for that.

"Three fifty, do I hear three fifty . . . ? Got it! Now four, who'll give me four . . . ?"

A murmur had started in the crowd that remained, a few chuckling at Evangeline's antics.

The woman lifted her paddle.

"And now we're at four and a half, four and a half, who'll give me five, five, five . . . ?"

Madison clenched her jaw. She glared at Evangeline's silver head. *It's a good cause. It's a good cause.*

"And we have five, five, who'll give me five fifty, five fifty, five and a half . . . ?"

The rumbling had grown louder, though half the crowd was gone now that the auction was nearly over. The remaining people were being rewarded for their patience with a good show.

"Five fifty, fifty, fifty . . . ?"

Evangeline turned, and their eyes met. Her thin lips widened into a grin, then she folded her hands on top of her paddle.

"I've got five, now, five fifty, five fifty . . . anyone, five fifty . . . ? And . . . sold at five hundred to Madison McKinley."

Madison expelled a heavy breath. She was five hundred dollars poorer, but she had her lessons. She was going to learn to sail, and she was going to win the regatta. For Michael's sake.

Chapter Two

"You want to do what?" Dad stopped the basketball mid-dribble, straightening from his crouch. His short gray hair was tousled and damp with sweat.

Ryan gave up the guard and faced Madison, hands on slim hips, frowning at the interruption. The firstborn of the McKinleys and steady as an oak, he was the sibling they turned to in a crisis.

Madison hadn't planned to tell her family just yet, what with the stress over Jade, but they were going to find out eventually.

"She said she wants Michael's boat." PJ, the baby of the family, flipped her long brown ponytail over her shoulder. She'd inherited her dad's brown eyes and her mom's winning smile—though it was missing at the moment.

"So that's what the sailing lessons are all about," Ryan said.

"You know they actually put the boats on water," PJ said.

Madison swatted her sister's arm.

"Jo," Dad called, his eyes on Madison. "Know what your daughter's planning?"

Joanne set a container of potato salad on the cloth-covered picnic table. "You mean the regatta? I was at the auction, remember? You know the burgers are getting cold, right? Daniel, honey, could you grab the silverware?"

"Sure thing, Momma Jo." Daniel Dawson had been an

honorary member of the McKinley family since Ryan brought him home in junior high. His wealthy grandma had raised him while his parents were off doing more important things. Daniel had recently won the mayoral election in Chapel Springs, following in his grandfather's footsteps.

At the mention of burgers, Dad dropped the ball. It patted the concrete as they walked off the court.

PJ kicked Ryan in the backside for no apparent reason, and he threw her over his broad shoulders just because he could. She squealed and pounded his back, but he didn't set her down until they reached the table.

"Brute," PJ said, giving him a playful shove.

"Brat."

Ryan saved lives, and PJ could feed an army, but when they got together it was like they were twelve. She was home for the weekend from culinary school.

They took their seats at the picnic table. Twilight had swooped across her parents' backyard, but the white lights strung over the patio and along the landscaping twinkled brightly. The mild spring temperature had beckoned them outside for the weekly family meal. Somewhere nearby, a cricket chirped from the flower garden, which was already burgeoning with new life.

Across the yard, the white farmhouse sprawled over the oak-shaded knoll like a plump aunt, arms spread wide for a comforting embrace. Beyond the house, corn grew about half the year on two hundred forty acres of gently rolling farmland. Her dad, proud to be one of Indiana's sixty-one thousand farmers, had never pressured the McKinley kids into filling his shoes, freeing them to find their own way. They were still working on that part.

Once they were seated, Dad said grace and they dug in. Grilled burgers, potato salad, green beans from last year's garden, and of course corn. There was always corn at the McKinley house.

"How's the planting going, Dad?" Ryan swatted a fly. "I can help next week if you want."

"Sounds good. I could use the help." Dad dished out a heaping spoonful of potato salad. "She wants to sail that old broken-down barnacle, Jo."

Madison placed her napkin in her lap, her eyes glancing off Mom. Despite her mother's perpetual smile, sadness had lingered in her blue eyes since Jade's sudden departure.

"Is that so?" Mom's look said more than her words. She knew Madison better than anyone. Knew the turmoil losing Michael still caused, even though Madison hadn't shed a tear, even though she rarely spoke of it. A girl didn't lose her twin brother without repercussions.

"For Michael." Her family stilled, even PJ, and that didn't happen often. "It's important to me."

Michael had been a capable sailor, though he hadn't lived long enough to sail in the regatta. It had been his dream to be the youngest winner ever—the current record holder being twenty-seven. And with their twenty-seventh birthday around the corner, time was running out.

"And you think you can actually win in that thing?" Dad asked.

She hadn't meant to blindside him. "I'm sorry, Dad. I didn't mean to upset you."

"It's a hunk of rotten wood."

He was making it sound far worse than it was. "I'm going to restore it."

Her dad breathed a laugh.

Okay, so it was in rough shape, but Michael had saved for it for two summers. On the doorstep of seventeen, he'd bought a boat instead of a car. She still remembered the look of pride on his face when he'd shown it to her.

"She's all mine, Madders," he'd said, running his hand along the flaking white paint at the bow. "I'm going to be the youngest winner ever, you'll see."

"In that thing?" she'd asked.

"It's just cosmetic stuff. Her bones are good."

"It's still in the barn, honey," Mom said now, setting her hand over Dad's clenched fist.

"Thanks, Mom. It won't be the fastest boat out there, but the race is handicapped, so I have a good shot."

"She can't swim, Jo."

"That's what life vests are for, Daddy," PJ said gently.

Dad's lips thinned. He was torn, Madison knew. Between wanting to support her and being afraid for her.

"I'll be fine. I'll take every precaution. I'm getting lessons, aren't I?"

"Let me know if I can help," Ryan said. "I can, you know, crew or whatever."

PJ nudged him with her shoulder. "You wouldn't know a sail from a bath sheet."

"Oh, and you would?"

"Children. Eat your supper."

A few minutes later PJ launched into a story about a soufflé disaster, lifting the mood. By the time Mom set the apple pie on the table, Dad's expression had lightened, though Madison noticed that Daniel was quiet tonight. She caught him casting a look at the empty seat next to her. She understood. It seemed strange without Jade there.

After supper, Madison helped her mother with the dishes while the others played HORSE. She scrubbed the burger platter while Mom loaded the old brown dishwasher.

Madison loved the little house she rented—which until two weeks ago Jade had shared—but there was something comforting about her parents' home. Something about the predictable squeaks in the old wood floor, the hourly chime from the grandfather clock, and the familiar scents of lemon and spray starch. She rinsed the platter. Even the ancient spray hose, which was more trickle than spray.

After the dishwasher had whirred into action, Mom leaned against the sink ledge. The pendant lights illuminated her face, settled into the laugh lines around her eyes.

"Are you sleeping okay, honey? You look tired lately."

"I'm fine." Madison had never told Mom about the nightmares, and she wasn't about to worry her with them now.

Her mom gave her a long, knowing look. The kind that made Madison realize that she could shutter off her heart to the outside world, but Mom would still see right through.

"You know, Madison . . . if it's peace you're looking for, you won't find it on the regatta course."

Madison put the platter away, the old cupboard giving a familiar creak. Was that what she was after? Peace? Did a person ever find such a thing after losing someone they loved so much? Someone so innocent and undeserving of death?

Mom took her hands, which had begun wringing the towel. "I wish I could help. I can't, but I know Someone who can."

"I know, Mom." She'd heard it often enough. From her parents, Pastor Adams, even Ryan. If showing up at church could fix what ailed her, she'd have been healed long ago. She was as regular as the pianist. All the McKinleys were.

Mom's eyes turned down at the corners and glimmered with sadness.

"Don't worry about me. I'm fine. Really. Learning to sail will be . . ." She squeezed the word past her lips. "Fun."

"I don't know how you'll have time with the play and all. You know how busy you get every summer with all the rehearsals."

"It'll be a lot, but I can handle it." It wasn't like she had a husband and kids. Or even a boyfriend.

Madison hung the towel on the oven door, and they meandered outside and sat on the concrete stoop. Mom grabbed a handful of sunflower seeds from the bag she kept there and tossed them onto the dirt path near the birdbath.

"I should've gotten you a birdfeeder for Mother's Day."

Mom tossed another handful. "This is just as easy."

"It's a wonder you don't have a sunflower forest out there for all the seed you've thrown over the years."

"The ground's too hard. Besides, the birds snatch it up as quickly as I scatter it."

A sparrow fluttered to the ground, picked up a seed, and made off with it.

"See what I mean?"

On the court, PJ whooped. "That's an R. So that's H-O-R for all of you." She might be small, but the girl could shoot. The men groaned as she sank another shot.

"I finally heard from Jade today," her mom said.

Madison turned. "Why didn't you say something?"

Joanne shrugged. "I told the others before you arrived. She only left a message. Didn't say where she was. I don't think she's coming home anytime soon."

Madison's lips pressed together. *Beckett.* What did he do to her? "She didn't say what happened?"

"No. It's been a long time coming, I think. Jade's always been restless, and I've had a feeling she'd leave sooner or later. I just wish I'd said something. I hate the thought of her out there all alone."

Madison put her arm around her mom. "She's an adult, Mom. She can take care of herself."

Neither of them said what they were both thinking. Jade might be an adult—she wasn't even the youngest sibling—but she was the most vulnerable of all the McKinleys.

Chapter Three

Beckett guided the twenty-foot Bayliner *Caroline* into the narrow slip. The river was fast and high today from the late spring rain, but now the sky was clear, the setting sun bright as it dropped behind the hills.

His boss met him on the dock as he tied off the boat. Carl Dewitt was short and thick with a paunch that strained his shirt buttons. "Hey, you fixed it?" he asked.

"Yep."

Carl nodded, his bushy gray brows lifting toward his receding hairline. "Good, good. Our customer will be thrilled. His mechanic in Tampa couldn't figure it out."

Beckett shrugged, handed over the keys. "Been at this awhile." He'd been fixing motors long before he was legally employable, more from necessity than anything else.

They parted ways at the shop entrance, Carl going inside to shut down for the night, Beckett heading for his truck. He turned over the engine, and it purred smoothly. Friday night, thank God. A nice quiet evening with Rigsby and ESPN, a short day tomorrow, and then a day off.

Several minutes later he turned into his gravel drive on the other side of town. The front yard was hardly big enough to host a flea, and the house wasn't much bigger, but it was home. Had been since he was a boy. The backyard was more generous. After saving for years, he'd put up an outbuilding last year. It took up most of the yard, but that only meant less mowing. The building was spacious, heated, and well lit. The perfect place to build boats.

His landline was ringing as he unlocked the door. Rigsby, his black Labrador mix, barreled him over on the threshold. "Hey, big guy." Beckett gave him a quick scratch behind the ears before reaching for the phone.

He shrugged from his work shirt as he answered. "Yeah?"

"Hey, Beckett. It's Evan Higgins." His old friend sounded winded.

He greeted Evan as he flipped on ESPN.

"I'm in a fix," Evan said. "Wondered if you could help."

"Name it." Evan ran a crew for Exterior Solutions. He had helped Beckett put up his outbuilding.

"I donated sailing lessons for that auction last week, but I just found out I'm going to be working a lot of Saturdays. The crew on an apartment complex in Louisville quit, and they were way behind. Left it in kind of a mess, and the owner's ticked. I'm headed there now to straighten it out. Long story short, can you fill in for me tomorrow . . . and maybe a few other Saturdays? Your boss donated rental of a sloop."

Rigsby barked, facing the back door, his black tail nearly knocking over the wastebasket as it swished around. Beckett let him out, turned on the porch light.

"Sure, I don't see a problem, as long as Dewitt doesn't mind me taking time off. I can fill in as much as you need."

"I ran it by him first. He was happy to donate to the cause."

"All right then. What time tomorrow?"

"One o'clock at the marina. Listen, I appreciate this. The package was for lessons with a racing pro, so my options were pretty limited. I think she's a beginner, so you'll have to start with the basics. We're crewing together for the regatta, so teach her well."

Evan, saddled with a beginner. That only upped his own chances at the regatta cup. Beckett chuckled at the thought.

Evan caught on. "Hey. No giving her bad instruction."

Beckett opened the door and let Rigsby back in. "No worries. I like to win fair and square. So one o'clock at the marina. Who am I meeting?"

"One of the McKinley girls—the vet. She's eager to learn and bright, so she should pick it up quickly."

His hand froze on the door. "Madison?" Her accusations from two weeks ago returned with enough force to sting. Last thing he wanted was hours alone on a boat with Madison.

She wouldn't be any happier about the change of plans than he was. But he'd already agreed. Why hadn't he asked more questions first?

"Does she know?" Beckett asked.

"I left her a voice mail. I'm sure it'll be fine. I mean, you're almost as good as me."

Beckett ground his teeth. Well, things just went from bad to worse where she was concerned, didn't they? First the supposed date with her sister, now this.

"Just kidding," Evan was saying.

"Yeah, right, I know, I was just . . . thinking about something else." He squeezed his eyes closed, pinched the bridge of his nose.

He couldn't believe this was happening. How many lessons had he agreed to?

"Well, I'm almost there. Let me know how it goes, and thanks again."

"No problem."

After they said good-bye, Beckett set the phone on the counter and beat his forehead against the tight mesh of the screen door.

Lessons with Madison. Great. Just great. How could he be alone with her, out on the water where he could see her, smell her, touch her?

Why is this happening, God? I promised to stay away from her, and now look.

For the thousandth time he chided himself for his impetuous decision two weeks ago. What kind of fool was he, showing up at Madison's house, flowers in hand, on the night of the Spring Sowers Banquet? What had he been thinking?

He'd had his speech all prepared, but instead of Madison, Jade had answered the door. She took one look at the cluster of pink roses, and a shy smile bloomed on her face. Half a dozen silver rings glimmered in the waning daylight as she brought her hand over her heart.

"It was you?" she said.

He didn't understand, didn't know what to say.

She took in his collared shirt and dark jeans, then smiled, her green eyes sparkling. "The banquet . . . ?"

He felt like a heel. "Jade, I—"

But suddenly she was gone from the doorway. "I haven't been to the Sowers Banquet in forever. I'll be back. I have to change." She was down the hall when she seemed to remember she'd left him on the porch.

She returned, letting him in. "Sorry, sorry! Come in. Let me just . . . you think you could find a vase in the kitchen? They're so pretty, thank you!" Her cheeks bloomed with color.

"Jade, listen, I don't think—"

"Don't worry, it won't take me a minute." And then she was gone again.

Madison's kitchen was meticulously clean and smelled of pine and lemon. He rummaged for a vase inside the maple cabinets. What now? He didn't have the heart to tell Jade the truth. Not after seeing her face light up. Not after she'd scurried to her room to change like she'd waited all her life for this date. Not when she was finally coming alive again after losing Seth.

Stupid. Why didn't you just call Madison and ask like a normal person? Better yet, why didn't you just keep your feelings stuffed deep inside where they belong?

He reviewed Jade's behavior. It was like she'd been expecting him. Well, it couldn't be helped now. He was going out with Madison's sister, like it or not.

He shut a cupboard hard. Opened another.

He'd been reminding himself for years that Madison was beyond his reach. What kind of a future did the son of Wayne O'Reilly have with the daughter of Chapel Springs' most respected family? It just didn't happen. He'd always known that.

What didn't make sense were the moments of insanity today, when he'd convinced himself it was worth the risk. And now here he was, in Madison's kitchen readying for a date with her sister—what was she anyway, twenty-one, twenty-two? He may as well kiss his chances with Madison good-bye.

Not that you had one anyway, O'Reilly.

Could things get any worse?

"Can I help you?"

He pulled his head from a low cupboard to find the object of his thoughts entering the kitchen.

The sight of her stole the moisture from his mouth. She was

all dark flowy hair and big brown eyes. One finely arched brow lifted.

He found his tongue. "Looking for a vase."

Her eyes flickered to the cluster of roses on the counter, then back to him as he rose to his feet.

Her jaw set, she passed him, going to the high cupboard above the stainless steel fridge. She wore a pair of fitted jeans and a white T-shirt—an outfit that promised a comfy evening home on the couch. His source had been right. She wasn't going to the banquet. Especially not with him.

She stood on tiptoe, pulled down a clear glass vase, and handed it to him.

"I'm ready." Jade fairly skidded into the room, having pulled off what must have been the fastest wardrobe change ever. She wore a black gauzy skirt, leggings, and a funky off-the-shoulder top.

"Good, you found a vase. He brought me flowers," she told Madison.

Madison crossed her arms. "I see that."

Beckett squirmed under Madison's stare. He suddenly wanted out of there more than he could say. He ran water in the vase, willing it to flow faster. He could hear Jade whispering to Madison over the rush of water, but couldn't make out the words. Was pretty sure he didn't want to.

He stuffed the flowers into the vase and set them on the counter. "We should get going."

Rigsby gave a sharp bark, and Beckett ran fresh water into his dish, his heart still thudding hard at the memory. He'd tried to salvage Jade's feelings, but in the end he'd done just the opposite. And he was sure, lessons or no, Madison wasn't about to let him forget it.

Chapter Four

Madison stood on the dock at precisely one o'clock, looking everywhere but at the mile-wide stretch of the Ohio River. Kentucky was far away on the other side, its tree-covered hills bright green in the afternoon sun. Between her and the distant shoreline sprawled hundreds of feet of deep, murky water.

She shivered at the thought and swallowed, even though her throat was dry as flour. She searched her bag for her water bottle. Great. She'd left it on the counter. Stifling a yawn, she retrieved her bag of coffee beans and popped two into her mouth, savoring the chocolate coating before crunching into the bean.

Nearby, water lapped at the bottoms of the boats in the harbor's slips. Metal hardware pinged against poles, and loose material fluttered in the wind.

She checked her watch. Where was Evan? She hated tardiness, and it didn't help that her nerves were strung tight as guitar strings.

"Ready?"

She turned at the gruff tone. Beckett O'Reilly seemed in a hurry as he passed, heading down a narrow dock as though he had a hundred things to do.

"What are you doing here?"

He barely spared her a glance. "Giving you a sailing lesson."

She opened her mouth and found it empty of words. Her heart raced toward an invisible finish line.

"Where's Evan?"

"I take it you didn't check your voice mail." He stopped at a boat. "Hop in. He was called into work."

She crossed her arms. "No thank you. I'll wait till next week."

He turned and gave that little smirk of his. She wanted to smack it off his face. "Up to you. But he's going to be working a lot of Saturdays, and he asked me to fill in as needed. If you're a beginner like he said, you'll need all the help you can get."

"You're filling in?"

"As needed."

This couldn't be happening. She looked away, over the rippling river. The whole water thing was bad enough, without the prospect of hours alone with Beckett. He'd always set her on edge, even before the incident with Jade. Through high school he'd gone out of his way to ignore her, as if she carried some rare disease. And then after that night in her sophomore year, things had become even more strained.

He crossed his arms. "What's it going to be?"

His back was up. Maybe from her phone call a couple weeks ago. Maybe from her reluctance today. Maybe both. Still, he was right about one thing. It was going to take all summer to get ready for the regatta. And she *would* be ready for the regatta.

"Fine." She eyed the boat. It was bigger than she'd expected. "Are you sure this is the right boat?"

"What kind did you expect?"

"I—I don't know. Is learning to sail one boat just like any other?"

"Not exactly. There are single rigs, divided rigs, different types of boats in each category."

"Rigs . . ."

He looked skyward in a move just short of an eye roll. "What are you looking to sail, exactly?"

"I have a twenty-five-foot Folkboat."

"Where is it?"

"I—it's not ready yet."

"Then this sloop will work fine."

She hated to admit it, but one sailboat looked just like another to her. She'd have to take his word. He was a capable sailor, after all, perfectly qualified. He'd even won the regatta several years back.

He tilted his head and gestured her aboard.

She gave a mock salute. *Aye, aye, Cap'n.*

The boat rocked under her feet. She sat and gripped the warm railing. Her heart beat like a drum, pounding out a syncopated rhythm.

He showed her how to untie the ropes, then stepped aboard and tossed her a life vest, which she caught against her chest.

The wind pulled at her hair as she buckled the vest. She should've put her hair up, but it was too late now. Besides, that was the least of her worries. She listened as Beckett explained how to start the boat, trying hard to commit his instructions to memory.

But as he moved the boat from the slip, out of the marina, it was hard to focus on anything but the water, deepening each second, rippling under the wind.

You can do this, Madison. You're a McKinley. Made of tough stock.

She continued the pep talk until they were in the open river. He eased off the throttle, and as their forward momentum slowed, the boat began to pitch in the water.

"You gonna sit there all day, or you want to learn how to hoist the sails?"

She lifted her chin, loosened her grip on the rail, and slowly navigated to where he stood, her legs shaky on the moving boat. When she reached his side, she gripped the nearest rail.

"Both the strength and direction of the wind are important in setting the sails and controlling the boat. You can basically sail any direction except directly into the wind—that's called 'in irons.'"

He went into the difference between true wind and apparent wind and started talking about positions.

It was all Madison could do to hang on to his words. That same choking fear she'd experienced on her first-grade field trip rose into her chest, swelling and heavy like a lead balloon.

She wanted off the lurching boat, wanted to plant her feet on still, dry ground. *Come on. You can do this.*

"You're not listening," Beckett said.

"Yes, I am," she said automatically.

"What did I just say?"

She rewound the tape in her head. Nothing. She went back to the last subject she remembered. "You were . . . talking about broad reach . . . and running."

"That was five minutes ago."

"Well, pardon me for dozing off during your scintillating lecture. Are we going to get the sails up or what?"

His lips flattened. "Fine." He approached the mast and began working. After a minute he stopped suddenly, turning. "You coming?"

Madison forced herself to leave the rail. She clutched every handhold in her path as she made her way toward him.

His movements were jerky as he worked the doohickey. A frown furrowed between his brows, and the line of his jaw was tight. It was more obvious by the minute he didn't want to be here.

Well, that made two of them.

"Got it?" he asked after he finished his explanation.

She should be used to him. In high school his gruff behavior had hurt her feelings—even scared her a little, given his reputation for trouble. And though she was now past the petty teenage drama, her nerves had had about all they could take.

"Look," she said, "I'm not happy about this either. I bid on lessons with Evan Higgins, not you. But I need to learn to sail and race, and I paid fair and square, so maybe you can just put on your big boy pants and teach me."

"Maybe if you let go of your white-knuckle grip on the shroud I would."

She automatically loosened her fingers. They ached from clenching them so long.

"Look, this is pointless," he said. "You can't be out here trying to control a four-thousand-pound boat when you're scared to death of water."

So much for hiding it. "I'm going to do this. I have to learn."

"You're gonna hurt yourself or someone else. You lose concentration for one second, that boom'll come flying across the boat, and you're a goner."

"I get it. I do. I'll—I'll get over my . . . my trepidation." *Fear* was such a strong word.

He gestured toward her death grip. "I can't teach you like this."

Her fingers had curled right back around the shroud. And

she couldn't seem to let go. Especially when a passing motorboat sent their boat rocking from side to side. Her breath caught in her throat and her arms stiffened, holding her steady, even as her heart rocked as wildly as the boat.

He turned, undoing everything he'd just done, suddenly all business.

"What are you doing?"

"Taking us back."

"But what about my lesson?"

"It's over."

She thought of the nightmares, more frequent the last year, waking her in a cold sweat, making her exhausted. She thought of the regatta. Of Michael and his dream, already dashed once. She wasn't going to have it dashed again. She'd promised herself she was going to do this.

"Fine. I'll wait for Evan."

"Nobody can teach you under these conditions, lady. Evan will tell you the same thing."

She let loose of the shroud long enough to grab him as he passed. His arm was rock solid, his lips a hard line.

"Please. I have to sail in the regatta. I have to." For Michael. For herself. She couldn't bring herself to tell Beckett that. She didn't want his pity. Just his help. She needed it. Her eyes stung and watered. Stupid wind. She blinked back the dampness, hating how vulnerable it made her feel.

His eyes softened, but the frown between his brows remained.

"Learning to sail is the least of your worries, Madison. You need to get over your fear of water, and that takes time. And winning . . . do you know how many experienced sailors will be there, the kind of boats you'll be racing against?"

"But it's a handicapped race—"

"Aim for next year—"

"No!" She let go of his arm, taking hold of the shroud again. "*This* year. It has to be this year."

Before their twenty-seventh birthday. Besides, she couldn't go another year with this gaping hole in her chest. Another year of nightmares, of this awful . . . disquiet inside her. How many years would his loss haunt her? No, she was going to soothe the pain once and for all.

~

Not the tears. Beckett looked away, clenched his jaw. Tears, any woman's tears, made him feel helpless. But Madison's . . . they were like a sucker punch to the gut. He looked back at her and wished he hadn't. A tear trembled on those thick lashes, and he clenched his fist before he could brush it away.

"I can do it, I know I can. I just need help."

Her voice, all quivery, so unlike the strong Madison he knew and—

Cut it out, O'Reilly. Think. You owe her. You know you do.

But he couldn't help her out here, that much was certain. He wasn't kidding about the danger. He'd never forgive himself if something happened to her.

He knew a little about fear of water. He was renowned for teaching his grandpa how to swim. At age sixty-two, Grandpa O'Reilly had decided he'd been fearful long enough. It was the summer of Beckett's junior year of high school, and he soon had the older man swimming laps—just a year before his grandfather was diagnosed with Alzheimer's.

"I'll do anything," Madison was saying now. "Just tell me what to do."

He was helpless against those wet brown eyes. *Not fair, God. A man can only take so much.*

She looked up at him, hopeful. She was placing her hope in him. What a mistake. And yet, the heady feeling it evoked made something pleasant swell inside. He wanted to live up to her expectations—wanted it bad. Besides, he owed her big. He could never repay the debt, but he could try.

He covered the sail and moved away, passing her.

"Beckett?" she called to his back, a hint of desperation edging her voice.

He closed his eyes, gritted his teeth. He was going to regret this tomorrow. Shoot, he regretted it now.

"Be at Boulder Creek next Saturday, off Trailview Lane. There's a turnout there. Know the spot?"

"Boulder Creek?"

He relaxed his features before he turned. "If I'm going to teach you to sail, you're gonna learn to swim first."

Chapter Five

Madison couldn't find it. She hunted frantically through the cluttered room. Rain pummeled the roof. No—that was Michael, pounding on the windowpane. He wore his white sailing cap, and he was calling her name. She couldn't hear him, could only read his lips. His face was pale and strained through the glass.

She had to find it before the storm came. But the room was so messy. She looked under a table, in drawers, under a chair. Where was it?

Rain pounded the roof now.

"Hurry! It's coming!" She read her brother's lips.

Tears slid down the window, all but blocking Michael's face.

Fire shot through her veins as she scanned the room. She'd never find it in this mess. She could hear it coming now, loud and hungry. A roaring wall of water.

"Help!" she screamed, but Michael couldn't hear her. No one could hear her. Her mouth was stuffed with something like cotton, choking her. Panic surged through her like electricity.

"Help!"

Madison's eyes flew open to darkness. Her heart thudded against the mattress. Her breaths came in shallow puffs. She closed her eyes and ran her hand over her damp forehead. Not again.

When would it stop? The same thing, over and over. What was she looking for? It made no sense. *Make it stop, God. Please make it stop.*

Just as quickly as the prayer surfaced, she pulled it back. He was the cause of this. He could've stopped it all if He'd wanted to. But He hadn't.

She rolled over and pushed the covers down, welcoming the cool air. On the floor beside her, Lulu, her border collie, let out a soft snore. She was glad somebody was able to sleep.

~

Madison didn't even own a bathing suit. Hadn't stepped foot in anything deeper than the tub since she was twelve. So as she made her way through the thick copse of evergreens the next Saturday, it was no surprise that her heart kicked into high gear, that her legs felt as wobbly as a newborn pup's. Dead ahead, the pool of water glistened in the afternoon sun.

Rather than fight her trembling legs, she dropped her towel and sank onto the grass a good ten feet from the bank. Evan had called earlier in the week to find out how her first lesson had gone. She'd explained the slight delay, and he'd told her to call when she was ready to resume lessons.

She looked at the sun-dappled water, her nerves firing off warning flares. Why was she here? More importantly, why was Beckett doing this? The question had rolled around her head all week. This went way beyond the package she'd won at auction. Way beyond helping out a buddy with an overloaded work schedule.

She could figure only one motive behind Beckett's offer: guilt. Whatever he'd done to Jade, he at least had the decency to feel guilty about it. Madison wondered for the hundredth time where her sister was, how she was making her way, if she'd found a job.

She stifled a yawn. The nightmare had kept her awake for

hours. Sleepy, but terrified of the dream returning, she'd gotten up and watched TV, finished a tub of butter pecan ice cream.

Madison pulled her knees to her chest, wondering how deep it was in the middle, how it would feel to be surrounded by water, to sink under it and feel it pressing in on all sides. She shuddered.

It wasn't as if she hadn't tried to swim before. Her dad had tried to teach her when she was little, and then Michael had tried again when they were twelve.

She could still see him now, coaxing her from the creek's shoreline. "Come on, Madders. It's not even deep."

She had followed him in, hating the way the water licked her ankles, then her calves. But she forced herself forward, up to her knees, then her hips. It had rained the day before, stirring up the mud. She couldn't see the bottom, couldn't even see her knees.

"I don't want to do this." The anxiety was illogical, she knew that. But recognition didn't make it go away.

He'd taken her trembling hand. "Doesn't it feel good?"

It was over ninety degrees that day, and somewhere in her subconscious she knew he was right.

"Come on," he said. "I won't let anything happen."

He'd always been her protector. At school, with their siblings. He was her brother, her twin, a part of her. But the panic she felt was stronger than reality.

She pulled away, turning toward dry land. "I can't. I just can't." She splashed toward the shoreline, eager for the familiar feel of solid ground instead of the mucky mud. Onshore, she grabbed her jean shorts, struggling to get them over her wet hips. She didn't even look at her brother as he stepped up on the bank.

"It's okay, Madders. We'll try again another time."

The hum of a vehicle broke through her thoughts. The memory had made her nerves spark to life. She picked at the fray of her cutoffs, her eyes returning to the water. Upstream she could hear it rippling over rocks, surging forward to this spot, where it funneled into a wide, bowl-shaped pool. A concave cliff wall formed the other side of the bowl, trapping the liquid, a clear blue broth. At the other end, boulders forced the water into a narrow stream that trickled forward to the river.

She was seconds from bolting when she heard Beckett's footsteps on the bed of pine needles behind her. Too late.

"Hey," he said, passing her, dropping a towel at the bank.

She frowned at his jeans and work shoes. In all her imaginings of these lessons, he'd been in the water with her. As scary as that thought was, being in the water alone was worse.

"You're—you're not getting in?"

"Came from work." He pulled his shoes and socks off, then off came his jeans. She turned her head, feeling heat that had nothing to do with the sun overhead burning her cheeks.

When he sank onto the grassy bank, she dared to look again. He wore black trunks and a white T-shirt. He stuck his feet in the water and patted the spot beside him.

Madison stood, slid off her sandals, and lowered herself onto the ledge a safe few feet away.

"We'll take it slow," he said. He was being nice today, and that made her suspicious.

She dipped her feet into the water up to her ankles. There. That wasn't so bad. The water was only a foot or so deep here. She could see the sandy bottom. See the little tadpoles flickering around. She closed her eyes and drew a deep breath.

Pine. Loamy earth. Some manly, musky smell.

"I'm impressed. It took me three lessons to get my grandpa this far."

"Really?" He was probably just trying to boost her confidence.

"You'll be swimming in no time."

She huffed. He had no idea what he was working with here. No idea how many times she'd tried.

"How's the clinic doing? Been busy?"

She saw through the ploy to distract her but grabbed at the chance like a lifeline. "Not bad. Helps that it's the only one in town. Haven't seen Rigsby in a while. He must be due for his shots."

"Probably. Almost brought him with me today. He loves the water but—"

She gave a wry smile. Rigsby was an exuberant young male; think bull in a china shop. "Yeah, not the best of ideas."

"My grandpa's nurse said you brought him a cat this week."

Madison took an animal from the shelter to the Countryside Manor one evening a week. The elderly folk lit up when they saw a friendly canine or feline face, and the animals needed the attention too.

"He likes the dogs—the cats, not so much."

"He had a basset hound for years. Grandpa may not remember me all the time, but some part of him remembers Bosco."

Beckett's grandpa had more or less raised him and Layla, their own dad in and out of jail, usually for petty stuff. Beckett had come by the rebel gene naturally. You didn't live in a town as small as Chapel Springs and not know these things.

"Alzheimer's must be tough," she said.

"On everyone." He stood in the water and removed his shirt.

Madison looked away, but not before she saw the rippling muscles of his stomach. His shirt hit the grass beside her.

He took a few steps out, the water wetting the legs of his trunks. His shoulders were broad, tapering down to a narrow waist, his skin coppery under the sun.

"Feel like standing?"

She looked down. The water would be over her calves here, the ground sloping into deeper water. Uh, no, she didn't feel like standing.

"Sure." She scooted toward the edge. "We're taking it slow though, right?" She hated the wobble in her voice.

"Like I could make you do something you didn't want to."

She was on her feet now. Her toes sank into the sloped bottom. The water lapped at her knees.

"How—how deep is it out there?" She nodded toward the middle.

"Not very. Chest-deep, maybe."

"On you or me?"

"You. We won't go any farther than the shore today though."

That thought made her relax a bit. Here it wasn't much deeper than bathwater. If she could just forget about all the water . . . out there.

He gathered water in his hands and wet his arms, then splashed to the middle, stomach-deep. He bent his knees, disappearing under the surface, then came up dripping. Show-off.

"So, tell me about this boat of yours."

"It's old. Kind of in rough shape."

Beckett waded toward her. Rivulets of water ran down his neck, over his shoulders. She wondered if he had to work out or if those muscles came from his work. Then she wondered why she was wondering.

She looked away as he approached. Somewhere in a nearby

tree, a whippoorwill called. A breeze rustled the branches and drew chills from her arms.

"So . . . the regatta . . ." Beckett's eyes narrowed. "You're not looking to win or anything, right?"

"Actually . . . I'm kind of counting on it."

"You'll have your work cut out for you, even with Evan. Lots of stiff competition—including me."

"You just teach me everything you know, and let me worry about the rest."

He sank down, sitting a few feet away, the water reaching his rib cage.

"I suppose that's next," she said.

He shrugged. "If you're up to it."

Like she was going to chicken out in front of him. Her heart accelerated as she squatted. The water closed around her hips. She wet her arms, stalling, her mouth dry, her breaths shallow. When she ran out of excuses, she sat down in the chest-deep water. It pressed against her lungs, its weight crushing.

I'm at home, in my bathtub. I'm just taking a bath.

Except this water was like a living, breathing thing. It licked her arms and tugged at her hair. She forced air into her lungs and back out. In. Out.

"You okay?"

She struggled to act normal and hated that she couldn't fake it. In front of Beckett, of all people.

"Maddy?"

"*Madison.*" The word was forced through her clenched teeth.

Her veins buzzed with adrenaline, leaving her shaky in its wake. She hated this. Hated it. This was why she'd stopped trying. She was suffocating.

"Just breathe. I'm right here."

She focused on the rock wall across the way, where a tree had managed to sprout from a crevice. A blue jay joined the whippoor-will, his cry loud and sharp.

You're fine. It's just water.

She felt a gentle tug, the water pulling her to and fro. She braced her hands on the creek bed, her fingers clutching for a hold in the sand, sinking.

Then a hand settled on her shoulder, weighting her, steadying her.

He was rushing her. He'd said they wouldn't go past the shore, and she hadn't imagined herself chest-deep in that picture.

"You said we'd take it slow." Her teeth started to chatter, and she clamped down on them.

"Doing great. Just keep breathing."

She wanted to tell him to kiss off. She wanted to slap his hand from her shoulder, but she needed it, and that only irritated her more.

Why this? Why him? She'd never felt so vulnerable and was too afraid to hide it. It was one thing to do this with Michael, another thing with Beckett. He was probably over there sneering at her weakness. Big bad Beckett, afraid of nothing. His middle name was Risk, and here she was, sitting in a puddle, scared out of her wits. He must be having a real laugh.

Her eyes stung, but she clenched her jaw. Blast it. He wasn't going to see her cry. She swallowed hard.

He squeezed her shoulder. "Relax. Nothing's going to happen, I promise."

He was closer somehow. Did that make her feel better or worse? She wasn't sure. She breathed in. Breathed out. In. Out.

The warmth of his hand penetrated her skin, warming her to the bone, the weight of it rooting her to the creek bed. She loosened her fingers from the sand, bringing her hands in front of her, pulling her knees up until they peeked above the water. She could do this. Just sit here and relax.

He removed his hand from her shoulder. "See? You're fine."

It didn't sound like he was laughing. His voice was deep and soft, like velvet to her ears. Her heart rate was slowing. Still fast, but better. Maybe she could do this. Maybe it would get easier.

She dared a look at him. Water spiked his lashes, giving his rugged face an appealingly boyish look. His eyes, as dark and enigmatic as a moonless night, stared back. There was no hint of laughter. Instead, they shone with something like concern. It couldn't be that though. More likely he was afraid she was going off the deep end. Literally.

She looked away, recognizing that her heart thumped her ribs again, this time for an entirely different reason. What was wrong with her? This was Beckett O'Reilly. She'd been half afraid he'd drown her himself, and now she was noticing spiky lashes and . . . and muscles. Fear must be making her chemistry go haywire.

The memory of that night so long ago surged into her mind. Plenty of chemistry then. She pushed the thought down firmly, held it underwater until the last stubborn air bubbles popped to the surface.

She looked down at the water, at the chill bumps pebbling her skin. She wanted to be home right now. Or taking a nice, long run with Lulu. But she wasn't. She was stuck here in the water, wondering how much worse it was going to get.

Madison gave him a sideways look. "So what fun do you have

in store for me next, O'Reilly? Chinese water torture? Holding me underwater until I run out of breath? Maybe you can just throw me in the middle and see if I sink or swim."

A blue jay answered, his mocking jeer making her feel worse.

"I'm not a monster, Madison."

Beckett had been in his share of trouble, but true, he'd never hurt anyone—not that she knew of anyway. In fact, she hadn't heard many rumors about him at all the past few years. For all she knew, he'd turned over a new leaf. Besides that, he'd only come here to help her. Guilt pinched her hard.

She swallowed her pride. When a McKinley was wrong, she apologized. "Sorry. I guess fear brings out the worst in me." Might as well call it what it was. She wasn't fooling anybody.

She felt his eyes on her, felt a wave of heat climb her neck at his continued appraisal. She wondered what he was thinking. If he was remembering the night he'd kissed her, or if it had been such a trivial event he'd forgotten it long ago.

"Everybody's afraid of something," he said softly.

Not him. He hadn't been afraid of the teachers or principal in high school. He hadn't feared the police or the juvie center. She'd watched him run speedboats on the river at a pace that made her palms sweat. And he sure wasn't afraid of what people said.

She turned toward him, suddenly realizing how little she knew of grown-up Beckett. "What are you afraid of?"

His eyes fastened on hers. Something flickered there for an instant, something that made her look deeper. Something she was suddenly desperate to understand. But then he blinked and it was gone.

A shadow passed over his jaw as he turned away.

He stood, drops of water falling onto her shoulders. The wave of water pushed and pulled at her torso, and she braced herself.

He was looking into the clear blue sky, squinting at a hawk as it swooped down and landed on a high branch of an oak tree.

"You've probably had enough for today." He stepped onto the shore.

Madison stood, only too glad to leave the water.

He threw the towel over his shoulder and snatched his clothes from the ground. She shouldn't have asked a personal question. But she was feeling vulnerable and wanted company—was that so awful?

"Look," he said. "Maybe this isn't going to work."

Not work? But what about the lessons she'd paid for? He'd said he wouldn't teach her to sail until she was over her fear. *And clearly*, she thought, looking over her shoulder at the water, *I'm not over my fear.*

Who else could teach her to swim? Her friend Cassidy would just tell her to jump in and get it over with. Mom was as afraid of the water as she; Dad had his hands full with the farm; Ryan was helping out every spare moment he had. PJ would be home for the summer soon, but she was flighty and impulsive—not the person Madison wanted holding her life in her hands.

"I know it's a lot to ask, and if you'd rather not . . . I guess I'll just . . . find someone else or something. But you seem to know what you're doing, and I'd really appreciate it if you hung with me a few weeks. I can do this."

She wasn't sure if she was assuring him or herself.

He studied her in that quiet, thorough way of his. His gaze

warmed her clean through. She gathered her towel around her shoulders, making herself hold eye contact.

If she could just put aside their somewhat rocky past and focus on the present, she could get through this, and then she'd have what she ultimately wanted. That was the important thing. She just needed to keep the goal in sight.

He looked away, gave a deep sigh. "All right. See you next Saturday then."

"Okay."

He disappeared into the copse of trees, and then there were only the soft footfalls of his bare feet on the bed of pine needles.

Chapter Six

Beckett had been a senior when he'd first noticed her. It was a chilly September night, and Chapel Springs High School was playing the Columbus Bulldogs. Beckett, somewhat of a loner, had never attended a football game. But tonight his friend, crushing on a new junior, had dragged him along.

He and Pruitt hung out behind the bleachers, trying to decide whether to crash a party after the game or redecorate the old Weineker place with the can of blue spray paint in his trunk. Just before halftime they hit the concession stand for a snack. The crowd cheered as someone made a play, and a cowbell rang out. The air was full of smells—autumn leaves and mown grass—but it was the popcorn that tugged at Beckett's senses now.

He saw her in the concession line, a few students ahead. She was laughing with a friend, a melodic sound that made him wish her friend would say something funny again. Her wide smile displayed a perfect set of white teeth set off by full lips that were made to kiss. She tossed her head, and her glossy brown hair shimmied over her slender shoulders. Her red sweater hugged her frame in all the right places, and a pair of trendy jeans made the most of her long legs.

"Who's that?" Beckett nodded his chin toward her.

Pruitt followed his gaze. "The brunette? You know her—Madison McKinley. She's a sophomore. Turned out pretty hot, huh?"

Beckett frowned. Last time he'd seen little Madison McKinley, she'd been in braces and little girl shoes. She'd grown up. Boy, had she.

He couldn't seem to look away, especially when she laughed again. She had the prettiest smile he'd ever seen. When it was her turn at the window, she leaned her elbows on the concession counter. His throat went dry. He'd have to spring for a pop now too.

"Don't even go there, man. She's a McKinley. Honor student, student council, class VP . . . You don't stand a chance."

"What, did you memorize her yearbook entry?"

He shrugged. "Just sayin'."

Beckett might have a bad rep, but some girls were drawn to him. Probably just the rebellious ones though. Probably not a girl like Madison. Her family was solid. Shoot, her dad was the Charles Ingalls of Chapel Springs.

She stepped aside with her pop, slurped from the straw as her eyes flitted past him, then returned. She released the straw, staring back, and he felt her gaze down to the holes in his socks. She was way out of his reach, just like Pruitt said, but he couldn't bring himself to look away. She held his gaze for one long moment, until her friend elbowed her and whispered something. Madison turned and walked away without a second glance.

Once Beckett had noticed her, he saw her everywhere. She passed him between second and third hours in front of the biology classroom. He passed her locker before lunch, and if he took extra long at his locker before seventh hour, he saw her as she entered the gymnasium. Sometimes she'd see him too, and a pretty blush would bloom on her cheeks.

He didn't know why he didn't just make a move. He didn't get shot down much, and even when he did, he didn't really care.

But the thought of Madison turning up her pert little nose at him made his blood run cold.

One mid-September night his dad announced he'd found them some extra work. A felon, his dad took what he could get, and Beckett pitched in too. He worked on engines sometimes in the summer, but lately he'd had trouble finding part-time work. Seems his reputation preceded him.

When his dad pulled into the McKinley farm early the next Saturday, Beckett froze.

"This is where we're working?"

His dad shot him a glance. "You too good to be a hired hand?"

His eyes scanned the house up the driveway. It was the kind of home you saw in movies, the happily-ever-after kind: a white two-story on a grassy knoll, a wraparound porch complete with a wooden swing and swaying ferns. Shade trees with low, thick branches, heavy with fall foliage, dotted the front yard.

Please don't let her be home.

They worked all day in the hot sun, but he would've worked twenty-four hours straight if only Madison didn't have to see him here working with migrants for minimum wage.

He scoffed at himself as he and his dad returned to their truck at the end of the day. Had he really thought he'd run into her out here? Like she'd be working side by side with the hired hands or something? She was probably in the house painting her nails or polishing up her acceptance speech for the honor society.

A few minutes later his dad turned the truck toward the house.

"Where you going?"

"The McKinleys feed the hired hands supper. Part of the deal—ain't that nice?"

Beckett went cold inside. "Up at the house?"

"Backyard, I guess. Can't fit us all inside, even in that mansion."

Beckett balled his hands into fists, suddenly antsy. "I have to get home."

His dad shot him a look. "Got time for supper. Not missing a good home-cooked meal—and I hear Mrs. McKinley does it up right."

Beckett squirmed in his seat. He was ten kinds of sweaty. He flipped the mirror down. He had corn silk in his hair, for crying out loud. He pulled it out, wiped his face with dirty hands, and slapped the mirror back in place, his breath suddenly ragged.

When they entered the backyard, he scanned it for Madison but only saw the same men he'd worked with all day. Two picnic tables, set with checkered cloths and plasticware, were the nucleus of the yard. Around it a garden flourished with flowers, vines, and evergreens, and a cobbled walkway meandered through. Even in the yard he felt out of place in his muddy boots and dirty clothes.

He sank onto a bench between his dad and a big quiet guy he'd met only today. The screen door squeaked open, and Mrs. McKinley appeared carrying a pot. Behind her flowed other McKinleys. Ryan, the oldest, carrying a larger pot. The two younger girls—he couldn't remember their names—the gypsy girl and the bubbly one with a ponytail.

Please, no. Not Madison. Not here. Not like this.

Despite his pleas, she appeared next, her twin brother on her heels. Beckett barely took in her navy T-shirt and white shorts before he looked away, tried to shrink behind his dad.

Maybe they'd leave the food and go. He watched Madison from beneath his lashes. She set the bread basket on the other table. Mr. McKinley stood, cleared his throat, and said grace.

After the prayer the McKinleys began serving the food. To

his horror, Madison turned toward his table. He put his elbow on the table, cupped his forehead. Maybe she wouldn't notice him. She came around, serving each worker a roll or two.

She was behind his dad now. Beckett was next. His heart beat up into his throat. Someone said something, and he heard her melodic laugh.

Then she was beside him, brushing his shoulder with her elbow. "Would you like a—"

He clenched his jaw. Great. Just great.

He dropped his hand, then turned. He couldn't bring himself to meet her eyes. Heat crawled up his neck. "Two, please." He managed to keep his voice strong. No sign of the tremor that was spreading through his core.

"Hi," she said, all breathy.

He nodded in her general direction, hoping the dirt on his face at least hid the flush.

She paused an awkward second before moving on. He looked nowhere but his plate for the rest of the meal, but he knew where she was every second.

It was a nice bit, serving the help, but it somehow only cemented the fact that she was different from him. He'd been a fool to dream of asking her out. A stupid fool.

From then on he tried not to notice her. But the more he tried not to, the more he saw her. Saw her laughing with friends, helping someone with her combination, giving an eloquent introduction at a pep assembly. And the more he saw, the harder he fell.

Then the next year he'd gone and sealed his fate. If there'd been a glimmer of hope of a future with Madison, it had vanished in an instant that hot summer day.

Chapter Seven

Madison handed the trembling cocker spaniel to the middle-aged woman after she paid Cassidy.

"Bye, Princess," Madison said to the spaniel, then addressed her owner. "Don't forget the cotton balls when you bathe her."

"Will do. Let's go, sweet'ums." The woman made her way toward the door.

"Don't forget this," Cassidy whispered to Madison, handing her the ear drops.

Good grief, she was losing it. She caught up with the woman and handed her the medication. "Let me know if she's not better in a few days."

Princess's mommy said good-bye, then waddled out of the clinic, soothing the dog with baby talk. Her red wavy hair blended in with the dog's shiny coat.

Madison turned to Cassidy. "Thanks. I can't seem to remember anything these days." She lowered her voice. "Dr. Richards asked me to cover for him tomorrow, and I forgot."

"Whoops."

"He saw the schedule this morning, and knew I spaced it. Can you call and reschedule some of my appointments?"

"Sure thing."

Cassidy Zimmerman had been her best friend for as long as she could remember. Today the humidity had caused Cassidy's hair to form a mass rebellion against her straightening iron. She'd gathered it in a ponytail at lunch and now it stuck out like a bushy chow's tail on the back of her head.

"Oh, and my grandpa has an appointment Friday at ten," Madison said. "So when you make the reminder call, don't forget to subtract an hour."

"You and your wacked-out family."

"I never claimed we were normal."

When daylight saving time had been forced on Indiana, Grandpa refused to fall in line. While everyone else set their clocks ahead in the spring, his stayed right where they were. During the winter they all attended the late church service, but during the summer he showed up just in time for the early one. And for some reason, everyone else, including the clinic, accommodated him.

"Your last appointment's in room two." Cassidy put the check under the cash drawer and closed the register, arching a brow. "Guess who?"

"Not Bernie Schmidt . . . ," she whispered. He was fifty-five if he was a day, and he hit on her every time he brought Flossy in—which was way too often.

"Nope."

"Well, long as it's not him, I don't care." Madison took the chart from Cassidy and felt her smile droop as she read the info sheet.

"Uh-huh."

Madison arranged her features in a confident smile. "Good. Rigsby was overdue for his shots."

"You're not fooling anyone, McKinley," Cassidy called as Madison walked away.

Around the corner she drew a deep breath, notched her chin upward, and entered the exam room.

She caught a glimpse of Beckett reading a wall chart on heartworm before Rigsby clambered toward her, claws scraping the tile floor.

"Down, boy!" Beckett grabbed the leash just in time. He nailed her with those dark eyes. "Sorry."

"He's an adolescent male. It's to be expected." Madison gave the Lab mix some affection and began a general exam. Beckett was aloof as usual. He rarely brought Rigsby in and was always late on shots.

Beckett held the dog still as she checked his ears. Rigsby was all wiggles, panting, and drool.

His owner, coming closer as he reached around for a tighter grip, was all musky soap and biceps.

"Sit, Rigsby." Beckett's low voice rumbled in her ear.

She finished the exam as quickly as she could and studied the clipboard like it was her life manual. "He's overdue for his rabies. Is he on heartworm?"

"We're almost out."

"I'll have Cassidy get you some. Be right back."

She was relieved to be out of the room. She didn't know why he affected her so much. She was going to have to get beyond this. Between the swimming and sailing lessons they'd be seeing plenty of each other over the summer. And, except for that one aberration, he'd made it perfectly clear he didn't like her by avoiding her.

Which makes your little attraction pretty pathetic. And don't forget the incident with Jade. She still had no answers about that. Why did she have to keep reminding herself of all the reasons?

She returned a few minutes later with the vaccine, injected 1.0 ml into the dog's muscle tissue, and scratched the friendly mutt behind the ears.

When Beckett released him, he scrambled to stand, tail thumping the wall.

"You're all done," she said to Rigsby. "That wasn't so bad, was it?"

"Sitting still was the worst of it."

Madison gave Rigsby a final pat and opened the door leading to her office. "Cassidy will have the heartworm meds up front. Bye, Rigsby. See you, Beckett."

Madison left the room and slipped into her tiny office, shutting the door behind her. She could hear Beckett and Cassidy talking casually at the front desk. Rigsby barked and they laughed.

She pulled off her stethoscope and slid out of her lab coat. Well, he shouldn't be back for a while, barring illness. Of course, that didn't fix the whole swimming/sailing thing.

She sat down and ran her fingers over the scrolled edges of the antique desk. She loved her desk. She'd found it after vet school at Grandma's Attic, her mom's antique store. The richly stained mahogany wood, the artistic detailing, and the heavy weight of the drawers spoke to her.

There was a tap at the door. "He's gone," Cassidy said. "You can come out of hiding now."

From her seat, Madison snapped the door open. "You know, sometimes I think work and friendship are a bad mix."

"Face it, you'd be lost without me."

"I could do without the commentary."

Cassidy shrugged, all innocence. "I see what I see."

Madison crossed her arms, looking around Cassidy's pretty face to her bushy hair. "It's finally raining then?"

Her friend gave a mock glare. "Low blow, McKinley." She brushed past Madison and perched on the edge of the tidy desk.

47

"So, you ever find out what happened between him and Jade?"

Madison rooted through her purse for her lip balm. "He isn't talking, and she's nowhere to be found."

Her house was so quiet without Jade strumming her guitar, without the heavy footfalls, impossibly loud for her small frame. She was an easy housemate, always tidying up, a good listener. She had an out-of-the-box way of thinking that had helped Madison solve numerous problems.

"But she called your parents, so you know she's okay. And Jade's always been resourceful. You have to give her that."

Fragile but resourceful. That was Jade. She'd worked at the local coffee shop by day and talked the owner into letting her play her guitar on summer weekends for tips. She'd made decent money during tourist season.

"You don't really think he hurt her . . . ," Cassidy said.

Madison tossed the lip balm into her bag and sank into her chair. "Something happened. I know Jade—she wouldn't have left for no reason. And you should've seen her when they left that night . . . I hadn't seen her so happy since before she lost Seth. She'd been getting these secret admirer notes. I guess Beckett sent them."

Cassidy frowned. "I can't see that—her and Beckett."

"Well, he showed up and asked her to the banquet out of the blue. And he brought pink roses, the same kind her secret admirer left her."

Madison remembered seeing Beckett there in the kitchen, the bouquet of flowers on the counter, Jade running around getting ready, a flush on her cheeks. Even now, Madison couldn't deny the tiny stab of jealousy that flared. She was an awful sister. Jade had been discontented for so long, Madison should've been nothing but glad to see her face lit up.

"She didn't say anything when she came home?"

"I'd gone to the video store and stopped by the coffee shop. If only I'd stayed home, she would've talked to me. I would've convinced her to stay."

"You can't blame yourself."

"I don't—I blame Beckett. He's always been nothing but trouble."

"Now, be fair. Maybe he caused his share of trouble in high school—"

Madison shot her a look.

"Okay, and a few years after. But he's not like that anymore. He even goes to my church now."

"Beckett?" She had trouble meshing the two in her mind. Church and Beckett. Not that she had any room to talk. Oh, she went to church—she was a McKinley. But religion hadn't done much good that she'd seen. Especially not for Michael.

"He mows the church lawn every week," Cassidy said. "And he fixed old Mrs. Barkley's Ford in the parking lot after church last Sunday—in the rain—for free."

"All right, all right, he's a paragon of virtue. What do you want from me?"

Cassidy's lips twitched. "An acknowledgment that you might be wrong."

Madison tossed her hair from her eyes. "Impossible."

"Highly unlikely, true. But sheesh—give the guy a chance."

"Maybe I would if he'd tell me what happened."

"It had to be a misunderstanding or something. Maybe it had nothing to do with Beckett at all. Seriously, I can't see him doing anything inappropriate, not anymore. He's a changed man, I'm telling you."

All because of God, she supposed. Madison didn't get that. Her parents got it. Michael had gotten it. Cassidy—and now, apparently, even Beckett—had gotten it. What was she missing?

Nothing. Nothing at all. She was a good person, wasn't she? She volunteered at the nursing home, treated strays for free, helped her neighbors. What did she need faith for when she had herself and her family to count on?

She stifled a yawn, feeling the dregs of too many sleepless nights. What she wouldn't give for a nice long nap.

"You look tired."

"I need to go to bed earlier, I think."

"Good luck with that. Well, listen, I'm meeting Stewie for supper. Wanna join us? He could call Dr. Fabulous and invite him too. Unless you want to change your mind about Beckett."

Dr. Landon was the newest addition to Riverview General's staff. According to Cassidy's boyfriend, he was interested in meeting Madison.

"I really need to take Lulu for a run, then I've got a date with a puppy and a dozen geriatrics."

Cassidy popped off the desk. "Oh, the exciting life you lead."

"You're just jealous. Tell Stewie hey."

"I will. See you in the morning."

After she left, Madison double-checked the lock on the front and went out the back exit.

Chapter Eight

MADISON WAS SITTING CHEST-DEEP IN THE CREEK BY THE time Beckett arrived.

"Look at you," he said.

"Hey." She focused on the still surface of the water.

Lulu ran to him, her black tail waving, and he gave her a friendly pet. The border collie returned to her side, sitting on the grassy shore as Beckett removed his outer clothing.

Madison had been to the creek twice this week, determined to get through this as quickly as possible. She could actually sit in the water now without freaking out. She'd even gotten her hair wet. She had no doubt Beckett had worse torture in store for today.

He waded out to the middle and dipped beneath the surface, his muscular torso glistening like a bronze statue of Poseidon as he emerged.

"Ready to come out a little farther?"

"How much farther?"

He tweaked an eyebrow. "Past the shoreline?"

Her heart picked up tempo at the thought. Lulu lay down and heaved a sigh.

"Maybe."

She imagined herself doing it. Standing up, walking confidently down the slope while the water climbed up her legs, up her torso. Imagined wading out to him, feeling relaxed and calm.

Yeah, right.

Beckett stared at her, hands on his hips, cocked head.

Might as well get it over with. She stood and slowly began the journey she'd imagined, minus the confidence, relaxation, and calm. Conscious of his gaze, she pulled the wet T-shirt from her stomach. It gave a sucking sound as it released.

"Doing great."

The water was to her thighs now, thick and tugging.

"There's a slight drop-off coming." He stepped forward, reached out.

She took his hand, latching onto his strong grip, her feet feeling their way to the drop-off. There. She felt around with her toes, stepped down several inches. The water was almost to her waist now.

She focused on the surface, rippling and glimmering under their movements. She breathed in, blew it out on a shaky breath. *You can do this, Madison. You* are *doing this.*

"Thatta girl." He still had her hand, and she wasn't complaining.

He stepped backward, guiding her into deeper water. The liquid encased her stomach.

"Isn't this far enough?" She hated the thin, reedy sound of her voice. The water was only waist-deep on him, lucky dog. What she'd give to be six inches taller.

"You've successfully reached the deepest part. Congrats."

"So it doesn't get any worse?"

"It doesn't get any deeper."

"Right." Worse would be going under.

"Have a good week?" His tone was low and soothing. Trying to distract her again.

"I guess. Kind of busy." The water stilled around them, going flat and glossy. She looked down and could barely see his feet on the sandy bottom.

"What made you become a vet?"

She shrugged. "I've always loved animals. My dad complained I brought home every stray in the county. I had a whole menagerie."

"It's a long time to go to school—eight years?"

She nodded. "I took classes during high school though—started college as a sophomore."

"Overachiever."

Their hands were still linked under the water. She became aware of his palm against hers, his thick fingers around hers. She loosened her fingers and he let go.

She could do this. The more she pushed herself, the sooner she'd get over this awful fear. The sooner she could learn to sail.

"Where'd you get your dog?"

She glanced toward the shore where the collie basked in the sunshine. "Lulu? I found her on the street when I was in grad school."

"University of Cincinnati."

It wasn't a small town for nothing. "She was limping, had an infected eye. She was my first real patient. I couldn't find her owner, so I kept her in my dorm."

His brows disappeared beneath his wet bangs. "Isn't that against the rules?"

"I am capable of breaking a rule now and then—for a good cause. Unlike some people who break them arbitrarily."

"People change."

She remembered what Cassidy said about Beckett attending church and whatnot.

She flashed him a look. "Maybe." Though it was rare in her

experience. She moved her hands through the water, trying to acclimate to the way they glided, thick and sluggish.

"Bend your knees, sink down a little ways." He did it as he spoke until his chin rested on the water. He was probably in a full squat to manage that.

She bent her knees, and the water climbed over her breasts, her collarbone. When it reached her neck, she stopped. She closed her eyes, caught her breath. She could swear her heart was beating hard enough to cause a tidal wave.

She hated the anxiety that wormed through her, tweaking her nerves. She wanted to stand up, return to dry ground, but he was going to make her do more.

"Doing great, Madison. Good job."

Next he was going to pat her on the head. "I'm not a dog."

"The water is your friend." She heard the smile in his voice and shoved her hand out, pushing a spray of water at his face.

The force of it pushed her backward, and she was falling. She clutched at air, at water, and found no hold.

He reached for her. She grabbed onto him, steadying herself.

Her heart beat against her ribs mercilessly. She opened her mouth to take in oxygen and glared at him.

Water dripped from his nose, his chin. "Tsk, tsk, tsk. Don't bite the hand that feeds you, darlin'."

The endearment, delivered in a velvety smooth voice, did something pleasant inside her. Probably the voice he'd used on Jade just before he did whatever he did to her.

She shrugged from his hold. "I'm not your darlin'."

"More's the pity. You ready to go under?"

Before she could digest the first thought, the second one parted her lips. "What?"

"You've already done it once." He was looking at her damp hair hanging in ropey strings over her shoulders.

"I just dipped my head back."

"Same thing."

"It most definitely is not!"

"We'll take it slow."

"That's what you said last week." And here they were in the middle of the creek about to go under the murky water. She looked down. Maybe she could see their feet, but it was definitely murky.

"If you're afraid, you don't have to."

Why didn't he just triple-dog dare her? She clamped her teeth together to hide the fact that they were clattering like a set of teacups in a moving van.

"I'm right here. Just take a deep breath, and dip your face in the water. You can hold my hands if you want." He reached out.

She started to push them away, remembered her last sudden movement, and changed her mind.

Ignoring his hands, she eyed the water, unclenched her teeth. "Straight down or forward?" Her words quivered.

"Any way you like."

She wasn't going to like it either way. *You can do it, Madison. Just a quick dip. Like you're in the tub. The water is clean, refreshing.* If she thought it enough, maybe it would feel true.

She stared at the water a moment. It wasn't going to hurt her. She was perfectly safe. Finally she took a long, slow breath, held her nose, and dipped down until her head was submerged. Water pressed against her face, filled her ears, made loud gurgling sounds. She popped to the surface, letting out her breath, drawing in a lungful of oxygen.

She wiped her face with trembling hands and met his eyes, glaring. "Happy?"

His lips turned up in a rare grin. He looked proud or something. She tried not to let that look soothe her frayed nerves. She'd rather be angry.

"Perfect. Let's try it again," he said.

CHAPTER NINE

"How are the sailing lessons coming?" Mom passed the platter of burgers to Madison.

Twilight had draped the backyard in shadows, and a breeze wafted though the yard, rustling the canopy of leaves and cooling the air.

Beside her, Grandpa heaped a spoonful of corn onto his plate, then pushed his glasses into place. "Sailing lessons?"

"She's going to sail the regatta this year," PJ said, massaging her temple.

"I'll bring the boat over later tonight if you want," Ryan said.

"Sure. I need to get started on it." Madison looked at Mom. "I'm actually working on swimming right now."

"Swimming?" Dad said. "Never thought I'd see the day."

Mom was staring at her, eyes seeing everything. "You okay, hon? You still look tired."

"I'm fine."

"She's probably afraid to fall asleep," Dad said. "Recurrent nightmares from when she was a baby." He winked at Mom.

At the mention of nightmares, her gaze bounced off Ryan's.

Mom tipped her chin up. "How was I to know she'd pick the one time I laid her on the couch to learn to roll over? Besides, it wasn't a long drop." The oft-repeated defense was useless. Dad would never let her live it down.

"Don't worry, Mom," PJ said, still rubbing her temples. "You only left Madison with a few scars. I'm the one you should feel guilty about. By the time I came along, playing with fire was an acceptable after-school activity. And where are all those pictures of me again?"

"Poor baby," Ryan said. "I wasn't allowed out of the house until I was eighteen."

"You have a headache, hon?" Mom asked PJ.

"For three days in a row."

"Want some aspirin?"

"I already took some. I'm starting to think something's wrong."

On her other side, Daniel rolled his eyes. Their surrogate brother knew what they all did: PJ was always thinking something was wrong.

"Must be a brain tumor," Ryan said.

Mom swatted his arm. "That's not funny."

PJ made a face at Ryan. "You'll feel bad if it really is."

"Didn't you say you were giving up caffeine again?" Madison asked.

"Well, yeah, since Tuesday. But come to think of it, I have been feeling kind of woozy. Maybe I should Google my symptoms."

"You are such a hypochondriac," Ryan said.

"Speaking of caffeine," Mom said. "There's a pot brewing if anyone wants some."

"Oooh." PJ bit her lip, looking at Madison. "You want some, don't you? Then you could give me just a tiny little sip."

"Who'd you say is teaching you to swim, Madison?" Grandpa asked, turning the topic on a dime.

"Um, Beckett O'Reilly." She slathered mayo on her burger, wishing they could go back to the safer topic of brain tumors.

"O'Reilly?" Daniel frowned. "Isn't he the one who chased Jade away?"

Mom set her hand on his arm. "Now, honey, we don't know that."

"I've heard things about him too," Dad said. "I don't know if I like this, Madison."

Madison met her mom's gaze and saw a flicker of understanding in her blue eyes. "People change, Thomas. He's grown up now."

Her dad's frown hadn't softened.

Madison looked away. "He won't teach me to sail until I learn to swim."

"Well, that sounds smart to me," Grandpa said. "Why, in my day, your daddy took you to the swimming hole and tossed you in. You learned to swim soon enough."

Reason number one why Grandpa wasn't teaching her to swim.

"I thought it was Evan Higgins," Mom said.

"It's going to be a team effort—Evan's work schedule picked up."

"Did he ever tell you what happened with Jade that night?" Daniel asked, concern in his eyes. He had always taken to Jade especially, calling her "squirt" and tugging her hair.

"No, but I plan to get it out of him eventually."

"You be careful," Dad said. "I might do a little checking around . . ."

"Dad."

Ryan took a huge bite of his burger just as his pager went off, followed by Daniel's seconds later.

Volunteer firemen, they were on their feet in an instant,

burgers in hand. The family wished them luck as they strode toward their cars. Madison watched her mom's eyes close, watched her lips move in a silent prayer.

~

Two hours later Madison was directing Ryan as he backed the boat trailer into her drive. The fire run had been a minor car accident, freeing him up pretty quickly.

"Left a little . . . a little more . . . three feet. Okay, that's good."

Ryan got out of the truck and bent down to unhook the trailer. "Good thing you have a long driveway."

When Lulu stuck her wet nose in his face, he ruffled her black and white fur.

Madison turned to stare at Michael's old boat. It looked mammoth in her driveway and old under the naked bulbs at the side of her house. Just looking at it overwhelmed her. Aesthetically, the boat was an eyesore, but Michael had said she had good bones, and Michael had surely been right. She hoped.

Madison followed Ryan back to his truck. "Thanks for bringing her over," she said at the window.

"Hope you know what you're doing."

She gave him a wry grin. "Not really."

"Well, if I know you, you'll figure it out. Let me know if I can help."

"Thanks." She leaned her elbows on the window frame. "How's work going? You're not in a hurry, are you?"

"I don't have a date, if that's what you're asking." He gave his charming half grin.

"Who, me?" She'd set Ryan up with a few of her friends. They all thought he hung the moon, but he'd been ambivalent at best. Truth be told, Madison didn't think he'd ever gotten over his ex-wife. Abby had been his high school sweetheart. Sometimes Madison had wondered if their divorce had left his heart broken beyond repair.

His gaze went to her house. He wasn't noticing the newly washed butter yellow siding or the freshly painted blue shutters, but the darkened windows and deafening quiet hovering over the yard.

Twin commas formed between his brows as he looked back to her. "You doing okay?"

She knew her mom's comment about her looking tired wouldn't go unnoticed. She also knew her makeup didn't quite cover the dark circles under her eyes anymore.

"The dreams are coming more often." Somehow calling it a dream softened the effect.

"Same one?"

She nodded. Jade had known she had an occasional nightmare. You couldn't hide something like that from someone who slept in the next room. But Ryan was the only one she'd confided in.

"He's gone, Mad," Ryan said softly. "I know you loved him, we all did, but you've got to let him go."

"Don't you think I've tried? If I could just understand why. It's always bothered me that we don't know how he died."

"He jumped off the cliff, got a concussion. Drowned. It was all in the autopsy report, hon."

"But that wasn't Michael. He was sensible. Can you imagine him doing something so crazy? It's never made sense to me."

"Maybe you should talk to someone, Mad."

"I'm talking to you."

"You know what I mean. Pastor Adams, maybe. He's helped me through a rough time or two."

A pastor was the last person she wanted to talk to, but she'd never tell Ryan that. Besides, the nightmares would end soon. Just as soon as she won the regatta.

"We used to have the same dreams," she said. "Did you know that?"

"You and Michael?"

"Yeah." She smiled. "We'd both dream of flying across a snowy field the same week, or even dream of the same thing on the same night. Once we both dreamed we were wearing purple shoes. It was uncanny."

"A twin thing, I guess. Did you guys ever have this dream you've been having lately?"

She shook her head. "It didn't start until after he was gone."

Ryan settled his elbow on the window frame. "Maybe the stress of Jade leaving is causing it to come more frequently."

"Maybe. I'm worried about her."

"I know. She's a big girl though."

"I never dreamed she'd go off on her own. I mean, where's she sleeping? She must be running out of money. She didn't have much in the bank."

"I've been praying for her. Hope she comes back soon—I can tell it's taking its toll on Mom. Dad too, he just hides it better."

"I wish she'd call me."

"At least she called Mom, so we know she's okay."

Or was a month ago. She knew Ryan was thinking the same thing, but neither of them wanted to say it.

"You be careful too, with O'Reilly. Mom and Dad have enough to worry about without you getting hurt."

"Not you too. I can handle myself just fine." It would be nice if her family gave her a little credit. She backed away from the truck. "Well, I should probably let you go home and shower."

"Is that a hint?"

She shrugged. "I thought it was pretty direct." She teased, but the fact was, he was a great brother, even if he did underestimate her.

"See ya, baby girl. Let me know if I can help with the boat."

"Will do." She thumped the door of his truck and watched his taillights disappear into the darkening night.

CHAPTER TEN

MADISON WAS WAIST-DEEP AND NOT HYPERVENTILATING. The two trips she'd made to the creek this week had paid off. Beckett, her cruel taskmaster, had still challenged her. She'd spent so much time blowing bubbles underwater in the past twenty minutes, her face was probably as wrinkled as one of her nursing home friends'.

"Okay, let's move on." Beckett disappeared underwater and came up dripping.

"So soon?" She watched a droplet make a trail from his shoulder down to the ridges of his stomach.

"How do you feel about floating?"

"About as good as I feel about diving off the courthouse roof onto the front lawn."

"Just lie back. I'll support you."

She looked at the fluid water and frowned. "Sure you will," she mumbled.

"What was that?"

"I have a chill." She rubbed her arms. She actually did. It had come on about the time he'd mentioned the word *float*.

She knew the science—her body was less dense than the water, so theoretically, she should float. Her brain believed it, but looking at the liquid around her, her heart wasn't buying in.

"Just lie back. I got you." He held his arms at water level.

Sure, she'd just lie back and trust him to keep her from drowning—trust Beckett O'Reilly, bad boy of Jefferson County.

You can reach the bottom, Madison. Nothing to fear. Deep breaths. She sank into the water, raised one leg.

Beckett supported her thigh, her back. She stiffened, poised in pike position, clutching his bicep. She was in his arms, against his stomach. It didn't take a genius to see he was doing all the work.

"Lie back. Relax."

Her heart punished her ribs. She glared at him. "Easy for you to say."

"I won't let you drown. Close your eyes. Let your muscles relax."

She loosened her grip on his arm. She wasn't sure which was worse. The insidious fear or the humiliation.

Relax. Breathe.

"Pretend you're in bed. Sink back into the mattress."

"My mattress isn't made of water."

"You can do it." His dark eyes said he believed it. She locked onto them, tried to soak in some of his confidence, but she got distracted by his wet, spiky lashes. Long, dark lashes.

She closed her eyes and forced her muscles to relax, starting with her stomach. Slowly she unfolded, and a moment later water entered her ears, gurgling.

She stiffened as her eyes flew open.

"I got you."

She felt his arms under her back, under her legs, tried to focus on that. She lay back, anticipating the feel of water rushing up to her hairline. *Straighten out, Madison. Come on, you can do this. Children do this every day. You're lying in a grassy meadow. The sun is shining. You can feel the wind cooling your skin. Breathe in. Breathe out.*

Beckett said something, but the water absorbed the words like a greedy sponge.

She let her legs go limp in the water, starting at the hips, working down to her knees, her ankles. Her arms stretched out limply, her elbow brushing his stomach.

She was almost floating. She could feel his arms under her still, but just for extra support. The water tickled her cheeks, her chin.

Stay relaxed. Bodies float. Breathe in. Breathe out.

He said something again, encouragement probably. She *was* doing good. She was doing great.

The water kissed the corners of her mouth. She locked her lips shut, breathed through her nose. Her breaths became shallow, the rush of oxygen drying her throat.

He was talking again, his tone soothing.

Relax. Relax. Relax. Breathe. In. Out. Think limp.

Loose.

Light.

He's right here, holding you up—

Wait, where were his hands? She didn't feel his hands.

She was floating on her own.

And then she wasn't.

He reached for her, but not before water closed over her face, not before she sucked in a mouthful of creek.

She grabbed for him, coughing. Her feet sought firm ground.

"You're okay. You're fine."

Standing now, she pushed at him, hacking. "You're not the one with a lungful of creek water."

"You were floating though. You did it."

"You let go!"

"And you did it. All by yourself."

"Yeah, right before I drowned."

"You didn't drown. You aren't going to drown. Trust me."

She gave a final cough, glaring at him. Trust. She thought of Jade, of all the stunts he'd pulled in the past.

"Well, I don't trust you, okay?" She made eye contact long enough to make her point.

Something flickered in his eyes, and she steeled herself against it.

She was blowing this out of proportion. She knew that. But she didn't like being at his mercy. It wasn't a safe place to be.

"I need a minute." She waded away a few feet, coughed, wiped her face dry. She studied a wispy cloud drifting slowly across the blue sky. A blue jay cried out. Somewhere upstream, water rippled over mossy rocks. She pulled in a lungful of pine-scented air. She could feel Beckett's eyes burning into her back.

She would trust him—maybe—if he'd just tell her what happened with Jade.

She remembered her conversation with Ryan, her resolve to find out what happened. If Madison knew the truth, maybe she could reason with her sister, talk her into coming home—if Jade ever called.

She turned and found him looking at her. "When are you going to tell me what happened with Jade?"

His brows went taut, his lips flattened. "If she wants you to know, she'll tell you herself."

"Well, she isn't here."

"She's an adult, Madison."

Didn't he know how fragile Jade was? Had Beckett only been toying with her feelings? Were those secret admirer notes some kind of game to him? That he could be so careless with Jade's heart made heat flood her cheeks.

"What did you do to her?" Madison asked.

"I didn't do anything." Beckett clenched his jaw, locked it down tight before he said something he regretted.

He'd gladly tell her if the truth weren't so revealing. If he didn't have something personal at stake.

"You did *something*. She wouldn't have left otherwise, Beckett. She was happy when you left for the banquet, and then she was gone. If you don't have anything to hide, just tell me."

He turned away. Did she think it didn't kill him to know he'd hurt Jade? He'd prayed for her every day since she left.

"I didn't hurt her." Not the way Madison thought anyway.

"Then what happened?" Her voice was closer. "Just tell me."

He turned, took in her beautiful face. The way her eyes shimmered. The way her elfin chin lifted. A bead of water trickled down her temple, down the planes of her cheek like a teardrop. He barely stopped himself from brushing it away.

"We should get back to work," he said softly. "I have someplace to be in an hour."

Something flashed in her eyes. A shadow moved over her jaw. Then all emotion was gone, shut down, a proprietor flipping over the Closed sign.

"I'm going to find out. She'll tell me."

The warning hit its mark, but not for any of the reasons she suspected.

And then she was walking away, the water closing in behind her.

He turned and dived into the center, swimming underwater until his lungs burned. He came up on the other side, near the cliff wall. The shoreline was empty, and a few minutes later he heard the sound of her car starting.

He dived back in, surfaced, and treaded toward the shoreline, needing to burn off energy. The last thing he'd ever meant to do was hurt Jade. She'd always reminded him of a wounded bird, though he was sure she wouldn't like the comparison. She went out of her way to dress "different": gypsy skirts, bandannas, rings on every finger. Sometimes her dark hair sported a colorful streak. Someone like that had either a fashion flair, a rebellious streak, or deep-rooted insecurities. With Jade, he'd never been sure which it was.

Beckett came to his feet in the water and slogged the rest of the way to shore. He sat on the grassy bank and toweled off.

Everything about that night made him cringe. The way she'd talked on the way to the dance, excited but shy; the way she'd smiled up at him after they'd entered the town hall, eyes bright like a child's on Christmas morning.

He'd never been to the Spring Sowers Banquet. Wasn't really his thing: the suits, the soft music and fancy tables. But he had to admit the committee had transformed the town hall. White linens covered the circular tables, soft lighting glowed from the wall sconces, and swags of some frothy material were draped artfully from the ceiling. Gone were the usual popcorn and coffee smells, replaced by something sweet and subtle.

He selected a table in a shadowed corner, pulling out Jade's chair, and made small talk with her for a while. A three-piece band struck up a slow tune, and he was grateful for the interruption of the awkward conversation.

It was sinking in that getting through this night was only half the battle. She'd expect another date and then another. How was he going to let her down easy?

His hand faltered on the way to the water glass when he saw Mr. and Mrs. McKinley across the room. A few seconds later he spied Jade's brother Ryan at a table with friends. Great. Just great. The whole family was going to hate him. They'd be relieved when nothing came of their relationship, no doubt, but they'd hate him for hurting Jade.

At the end of the song, the band shifted to another tune. The soft buzz of conversation filled the room as waiters began placing salads. Jade pushed back, her green eyes shining. "I need to use the ladies' room. I'll be right back."

"I'll be right here."

He watched her go, the guilt pressing hard against his ribs, making breathing uncomfortable. Stupid! Why had he ever thought it was okay to ask Madison out?

A moment later his baby sister slipped into the chair next to his, her blue skirt billowing around her. Layla's hair fell in dark springy ringlets, and a hint of makeup complemented her naturally pretty face.

"She said yes! Where is she?"

Apparently Layla hadn't seen Jade yet. He sank deeper into the metal chair. "She didn't say yes. Her sister did."

Layla's fine brows pulled together. "What?"

He told her what happened, watching every emotion register on her face.

"Oh, honey, that's awful. What are you going to do?"

Sidney Blevins grabbed Layla's arm. "Help! My spaghetti strap broke! You have a pin?"

Beckett looked away as his sister dug through her enormous purse.

"I'll be right back," Layla said a moment later.

"Take your time." He wasn't going anywhere.

The band played two more songs before he saw Jade making her way toward him. He forced a smile, but as she neared he registered a change in her stride, in her posture.

Closer still, he saw more changes. Her lips drawn tight, a smudge of black under one of them. She looked at the floor.

"What's wrong?" he asked as she neared.

"Take me home." Gone was the hopeful lilt to her voice.

He stood, touching her arm. "What's wrong? What happened?"

She shrugged away. "Just take me home!"

A pink flush bloomed on her cheeks. Her bloodshot eyes flitted to and fro.

Beckett led her through the maze of tables, his mind turning. What had happened since she'd left? Scarcely ten minutes had passed.

Outside, sudden silence fell around them like an itchy blanket. Should he press her? Leave her alone? He was no good with teary women. Never had been.

The cab vibrated with tension, the silence broken only by her sniffles. He couldn't let her go until he got to the bottom of it.

He pulled onto Main Street, darting a glance at her as she knuckled a tear off her cheek. "Did someone upset you?"

"Just leave me alone, Beckett," she said through clenched teeth.

But he couldn't. He was responsible for her. She was his date, accidental or not. "If someone bothered you, I want to know. Was it a guy?"

Had someone manhandled her? He felt a surge of protectiveness—the kind he'd feel if someone hurt Layla. He stopped at a red light. "If someone hurt you, tell me, and I'll take care of it."

"You can stop with the act already! I know you wanted Madison, not me, so you can just take your false concern and shove it!"

How had she found out? Beckett bit back a word he hadn't said in years. "Jade—"

Jade turned toward her window, wiping tears. "Just take me home! This is the most humiliating night of my life."

The light had turned green. Beckett accelerated. His sister was the only one who knew. Could she have said something in the bathroom to her friend and Jade overheard?

He didn't know what to say. He couldn't deny it, so he said nothing. The short drive to Madison's house took an eternity. He felt only relief when he saw that Madison's car wasn't in the drive. Maybe Jade wouldn't tell her sister that Beckett had come to ask *her* to the banquet. As soon as the thought surfaced, his stomach turned at his selfishness.

He shut off the ignition and reached for the door handle.

"Don't bother," Jade said, then slammed her door.

He'd watched her enter the darkened house, feeling like the mucky stuff at the bottom of the Ohio River. It was the last time anyone saw her.

CHAPTER ELEVEN

THE BASSET HOUND SQUIRMED IN MADISON'S ARMS AS HER heels clicked on the sterile tile of Countryside Manor's hallway. She passed Mrs. Doolittle's station, and the nurse glared at the pup over her bifocals.

"Hello, Mrs. Doolittle."

"*Hmph.*"

If it had been up to the nurse, Madison wouldn't be bringing "filthy animals" into the center at all. Thankfully, Mrs. Doolittle didn't have the final say.

Madison dropped a kiss on the pup's warm fur, and he raised his bright brown eyes to hers. "You're not filthy, are you, sweetie?"

The hound wouldn't be long at the shelter, with his adorable puppy looks and frisky ways. Her elderly friends were going to love him.

She entered the rec room and found her favorite group of ladies in the far corner, their knitting needles flying almost as fast as their mouths. Known as the Kneeling Nanas, they'd started as a morning prayer group that evolved to include evening knitting. Despite their name, Madison was sure a few of them hadn't a prayer of making it to their knees, much less making it back up. Nonetheless, they were a lively bunch.

"Hello, ladies! I brought a visitor."

"Oh!" Mrs. Geiger said. "He's just a pup—aren't you a handsome fellow." She set down her knitting, reached for the dog, and pulled him against her ample bosom. He licked her fleshy cheek, making her laugh.

"Why does she always get to be first?" Mrs. Etter's needles clacked as she worked them with spry fingers.

"Because she sits nearest the door, silly." Mrs. Stuckey poked her plastic-framed glasses into place. "He sure is cute."

"*Achooooooo!*" Mrs. Marquart's needles went flying as she covered her sneeze. "I'm allergic, remember?" Her project fell to the floor as she stood, reaching for her walker. The sneeze had knocked her auburn wig slightly askew.

"Oh, sit down," Mrs. Geiger said, passing the dog on. "You're allergic to cats, not dogs."

Mrs. Marquart frowned. "Are you sure?"

"I'm sure," Madison said, discreetly straightening the woman's wig. "Remember the spaniel? He fell asleep in your lap."

Mrs. Geiger snorted. "Then *you* fell asleep."

"We should've taken a picture and put it on Facepages," Mrs. Stuckey said.

"Face*book*." Mrs. Etter dropped a kiss on the pup's head. "He's darling. Is he spoken for?"

"We're not allowed pets." Mrs. Stuckey had resumed work on an infant sweater, for one of her great-grandbabies, no doubt.

"My grandson Perry is looking for a dog for his kids. I think they'd love this little guy."

"He's available, but not for long, I'd guess," Madison said. "Talk it over with Perry, and let me know soon if they're really interested. He's potty trained and has all his shots."

"Oh, you're just perfect, aren't you, sugar baby?"

"Still no word from your sister?" Mrs. Stuckey asked Madison, her fingers flying.

News about Jade's sudden departure had spread through town. "Afraid not."

"We prayed for her this morning, and we'll keep right on. Praying for you too, dear. How are those swimming lessons going?"

"How'd you know about that?" Apparently the rumor mill reached far and wide.

"We have our ways."

"More important, how is that handsome O'Reilly boy?" Mrs. Geiger wiggled her drawn-on brows. "He has the looks of his grandfather, remember, girls?"

Three heads bobbed.

"That's to say he's quite the dish," Mrs. Stuckey said.

Mrs. Etter gave the pup a final kiss and handed him to Mrs. Marquart, who passed him to Mrs. Stuckey, arms fully outstretched.

"He won't bite." Mrs. Stuckey cuddled the dog. "Will you, precious? Oh, you're a wiggly little thing."

"I should wash my hands." Mrs. Marquart popped to her feet and scooted off with her walker.

"You'd better take him," Mrs. Stuckey said, even as the puppy squirmed from her lap and landed on the floor.

Madison hooked the leash on his collar. "I think he wants to walk. I'll just make my rounds now and let you ladies get back to your knitting."

"Will you bring him by again before you leave?" Mrs. Etter asked.

Madison agreed and headed down the hall. She stopped in to

see one of her favorite residents, whose family lived in Georgia. The old man perked up when he saw he had company. He was in a talkative mood, so she stayed awhile. Afterward she visited a few other residents with out-of-town family. She wished she had time to spend with all of the residents. Some of them were so lonely.

She stopped in the hall to let the passersby pet the pup. It brought her joy to see their faces light with a smile, and the hound was enjoying every moment too, his nose working almost as fast as his little legs.

Her last stop was Mr. O'Reilly. She walked down the hall, pulling up short when she spied Beckett leaving his grandpa's room.

As he closed the door behind him, she pulled on the leash and hugged the wall, going still. It was silly to hide, but she wasn't up to seeing Beckett tonight. Not after their argument at the creek over Jade. It had been eating at her since Saturday.

When he headed toward the exit, she breathed a sigh. She waited until he rounded the corner before she knocked and entered the room.

"Hello, Mr. O'Reilly."

He was propped up in bed. His sparse white hair sported comb marks, and his gnarly hands opened and closed in his lap. The room smelled like antiseptic and Old Spice.

The lines on his forehead deepened. "Who was that?"

"Who just left? That was your grandson."

He narrowed his rheumy eyes. "He's a liar!"

Madison tugged the dog away from the metal wastebasket. "That was Beckett, Mr. O'Reilly. You remember him. He's your—"

His blue eyes sparked. "He's a liar!"

She scooped the hound into her arms. "Look who I brought with me today. He's a basset hound. You used to have one. Do you remember Bosco?"

His hands still worked, and his eyes seemed stuck on the door.

She stepped closer, between him and the doorway. "Look, Mr. O'Reilly. I brought you a friend."

His eyes finally shifted to the pup, and his face immediately softened, the furrowed brows on his forehead smoothing.

When he reached out, she settled the dog in his lap. The hound sniffed the blanket, licked Mr. O'Reilly's hand, and curled into a furry ball.

~

Beckett had been on Madison's mind all day. Hiding in the nursing home hall had been a wake-up call. She regretted leaving things the way she had. Yes, she wished he'd tell her about Jade, but he was doing her a favor, and she'd behaved poorly.

She slowed her pace as she approached the marina, reining in Lulu, whose pink tongue flopped like a loose shoestring. Madison stopped at a puddle to let the dog rehydrate. The sun slipped behind the clouds, offering a brief reprieve, and a breeze came across the river, ruffling her low ponytail.

After catching her breath, she found Beckett on the gas dock filling the tank of a boat. Its owners, the Tacketts, milled around farther down the dock, checking out the other boats.

She gripped the leash tight, giving Lulu little leeway. As she waited for Beckett to finish, she noted the wooden boat he was gassing up. A fishing boat built for two, it had sleek curves, a caramel finish, and silver trim. She'd never seen a boat like it, and remembering the scaly eyesore in her driveway, she knew a moment of boat envy.

She waited until he capped the tank before she spoke. "She's a beauty."

If he was surprised to see her, he gave no indication. "Hey." He replaced the pump, wiped his hands on a rag hanging from his pocket.

"It's almost like artwork."

He looked at the boat. "It's custom made."

Lulu strained at her leash, her paws on the edge of the deck, sniffing the fishy air. Her ears perked at the sound of a nearby splash.

"Well, I don't mean to bother you. I know you're busy."

He wiped a few drops of gas from the deck, petted Lulu, and stood. "What can I do for you?"

She looked across the water at the green hills rising from the river and realized being here didn't bother her as much as it used to. Thanks to Beckett.

"I feel bad about the way we left things Saturday."

He pocketed the rag, not looking away. He had a way of studying her that made her feel naked. She crossed her arms as best she could with the leash.

"Me too." The wind fluttered his hair, carrying the faint smell of gasoline and that warm, spicy smell that was all Beckett.

"Truce?" she asked.

He seemed to weigh her words before he extended his hand.

She reached for it, and his grip enveloped hers, his eyes not releasing her.

"I do appreciate your help. With the swimming thing."

He nodded once, letting go.

"All right then." She backed away, tugging Lulu with her. "I'll let you get back to work. See you Saturday."

As she walked away, she took note of the thumping of her heart, the dryness in her throat, the impression of his warm palm against hers. *Just a little while longer, Madison. And you can go back to your safe little world.*

Chapter Twelve

Her new truce with Beckett was working; they hadn't argued again. But their newfound peace brought other problems. When she wasn't busy feeling indignant, Madison noticed things. Things like his charcoal eyes, his stubbly jaw, his sculpted muscles.

By mid-July she was able to tread water, and Beckett declared her ready to begin sailing lessons. She celebrated the fact that she didn't have to face the water anymore—or a shirtless Beckett. She had her first two sailing lessons with Evan, squeezing them in on a couple of evenings. She'd been thrilled to step onto the sloop without the panic that had assaulted her the first time. The few nerves she'd felt had disappeared by the time Evan hoisted the sails.

With no word still from Jade, she found herself envious of her parents, who seemed able to pray and let it go. She thought of the nursing home ladies and their promise to pray for Jade. The thought comforted her, though she couldn't say why. Her parents had prayed for each of her siblings daily, but what good had it done Michael?

She was between appointments one afternoon, catching up on paperwork, when her eyes began to droop. She looked in her drawer and found her coffee bean bag empty.

She leaned against the chair. She'd close her eyes for a few minutes. She had twenty minutes before her next appointment. A catnap would get her through the rest of the afternoon.

"Dr. McKinley."

Madison bolted upright from the desk. Her blurry eyes strained to focus on the doorway.

Dr. Richards frowned at her. "Your three o'clock has been waiting fifteen minutes."

She scuttled to her feet. "I'm so sorry. I don't know how I fell asleep."

He pursed his lips. "We'll talk about this later."

The afternoon hours dragged as Madison went through her appointments. She'd blown it twice in a matter of weeks. Two weeks ago Dr. Richards had arrived to find the back door unlocked. Madison had been the last to leave the night before.

He wasn't one to tolerate incompetence. What was she saying? Madison wasn't one to tolerate it either. What was happening to her?

Rather than waiting for him to confront her, she knocked on his door after her last appointment. He invited her in.

"I'm sorry about this afternoon. I only meant to rest my eyes, and next thing I knew—"

"Sit down, Dr. McKinley."

Not good. Not good at all. Madison took a seat in the high-back chair in the corner.

"You're a wonderful vet, Madison. And normally, you're thoroughly capable. But lately you're forgetful and unfocused. You forgot you'd promised to cover for me, you're falling asleep in your office and forgetting to lock up. You've made several billing errors lately and, if you'll forgive the personal observation, you look like you haven't slept in days."

"I've . . . had a bit of trouble sleeping."

"It's affecting your work."

She couldn't deny it. "I'll do better, Dr. Richards."

"I'm not one to dole out personal advice at the office, but you might consider seeing a doctor."

"Of course. I appreciate your patience. And I'll be more careful."

"See that you are." He softened the words with a fatherly smile.

Madison took that as her cue to leave and stood. "Thank you."

She went to her office and closed her door, waiting for her heart to settle. That was no fun. She'd felt like a kid in the principal's office, something she was unaccustomed to.

She was grabbing her purse, ready to put the awful day behind her, when Cassidy poked her head into the office.

"Please don't say no . . . ," Cassidy said.

"No."

Cassidy sighed, entering. "You're so contrary. What if I was about to offer you a million dollars?"

"I'd say you need a pay cut."

"It's just a coffee date. Dr. Drew really wants to meet you, and Stewie and I'll be there, so buh-bye first-date awkwardness. Plus, you can stock up on coffee beans while you're there."

Madison set her stethoscope on her desk and shrugged from her lab coat. "I don't know."

"What's the holdup? He's a doctor, he's handsome . . . he's a doctor . . ." Cassidy brushed her hair off her shoulder. Today it lay in obedient curls, framing her friend's face.

"Your hair looks nice."

"Don't change the— Really?" Cassidy turned to the small antique mirror behind her, peering into the speckled glass. "I bought a new curling iron, it has ions or something. But never mind that. Say yes. I promise you won't regret it."

Truth was, Madison didn't know what was holding her back.

Yes, you do, Madison. He was about six-one, with strapping shoulders and smoldering eyes. She had to stop thinking about Beckett. Clearly he wasn't interested in her. He wasn't the one asking her out, was he?

She sighed hard enough to move papers on her desk. "Fine."

Cassidy whooped. "Super! Okay, I have to run. See you in the morning . . . and tomorrow night!" She left the office, calling down the hall, "You won't regret it!"

"I already do," Madison called back.

~

Coachlight Coffeehouse was located in a remodeled Victorian. Originally built in 1907, the brick structure crouched on the corner of Main and Maple, its wide porch and bold columns an open invitation to enter. A gathering place for locals and tourists alike, it featured excellent brews, tasty pastries, and turn-of-the-century ambience.

Beckett, however, came only for the coffee, a dark-roasted Colombian that made Dewitt's coffee-machine brew seem like motor oil. After a busy summer day like today, he was ready for a tall glass of iced coffee as he climbed the wide concrete steps.

His plans for the evening were refreshingly simple. Grab a cup of joe and head for his rock tower. Accessed by a trail behind Riverside Park and a long uphill climb, the rock tower offered an inspiring view of the valley. It was Beckett's favorite spot to escape humanity and enjoy the beauty of God's creation.

The rich aroma of good coffee teased his senses as he opened the door and stepped aside for a couple tourists as they exited.

He crossed the squeaky wood floor and got in the line, which, as usual on a Friday night, was a long one.

He looked over the display case, eyeing the pastries. He'd worked straight through lunch, munching on an apple between repair jobs.

When it was his turn, he ordered coffee and a slice of Dutch apple pie from the cashier, a teenaged girl who smiled at him with moony eyes.

After paying, he stepped aside and glanced around the bustling room. Maeve Perkins and Dottie Meyers sat at a window table sipping tea. He recognized a couple tourists who'd rented a fishing boat the day before. They'd returned with a string of smallmouth bass.

He passed over a table near the door, then his eyes returned to the group as he recognized Madison. She was sitting with Cassidy Zimmerman, Stew Flannery, and a man he recognized but couldn't place. Beckett wasn't sure how he'd missed them when he'd entered.

Two men, two women—he knew a double date when he saw one. Especially when the familiar man set his hand on the back of Madison's chair, his knuckles brushing her hair.

Beckett's jaw clenched as his eyes swung back to her. Dark waves swept over her slender shoulders. The candlelight on the table cast a warm glow over her face and shimmered off her glossy lips. She wore a thin pink sweater over a white top. A silver necklace sparkled against a modest display of her creamy neckline. She laughed at something, and Beckett's eyes swung to her date.

Beckett suddenly remembered the man. He was the new

doctor at Riverview General. He'd rented a fishing boat after he'd moved to town early in the spring.

He had tousled, light brown hair, a perfect set of teeth, and dimples when he smiled—and he was doing plenty of that.

"Here you go, Mr. O'Reilly," the teenager said.

He turned to his plated pie and mug of coffee. Last thing he wanted was to be stuck here watching some guy fawn over Madison.

"Sorry, can I get this to go?"

She smiled charmingly. "Absolutely."

Of course, Madison had gone out with other men before. He'd seen her with dates, but it had been awhile. And that had been before.

Before what, O'Reilly? Before she hired you for lessons?

When was he going to get it through his head that she was off-limits? Their truce was just a ceasefire, not an engraved invitation. Somehow he'd let himself believe there could be more.

Again. *When are you going to get it through your head—you ruined any chance of that ten years ago.*

"Here you go." The girl handed him a sack and to-go cup.

"Thanks."

"Anytime."

He turned, ducking his head, and beat a path for the door. When he'd skirted the last table, he reached for the knob.

"Beckett, my man," Stew said. "Hold up. I was just telling Drew about your custom boats."

Giving up on his retreat, Beckett stepped over to the table.

"He's interested in something like the one you made for the Tacketts."

His eyes went to Madison, and she arched a brow. He'd been gassing it up when Madison had shown up to call a ceasefire. He hadn't claimed it, even when she'd called it "artwork," though the word had made him glow inside.

The doctor reached his hand out. "Drew Landon."

"Beckett O'Reilly." He shook the man's hand.

"How long's something like that take?"

"Depends. On a lot of factors." He'd only sold two, but he found himself reluctant to do business with Madison's date. Beckett put his soul into his boats, and he wasn't sure this guy was worth the effort. Or maybe Beckett just wanted to believe he wasn't.

Drew pulled out his cell. "Why don't you give me your number, and we can talk later."

Beckett rattled off his number, and Dr. Perfect punched it in.

"Great." The doctor pocketed his phone. "I hope we can do business."

Beckett nodded to the group in general, but his eyes went to Madison of their own volition. She picked at a crescent roll, her eyes on her plate.

Chapter Thirteen

Madison set down the electric sander and stepped away from the boat. A cloud of dust hovered overhead, and multi-colored flecks of paint carpeted her gravel drive like confetti. The boat had been at least four different colors in past lives. She was planning on painting it midnight blue—if she ever finished sanding. Her hands were numb, and she'd only been at it an hour.

Across the yard, Lulu chased a firefly in the waning light, snapping futilely. Another lit up nearby, and she launched at it, missing when its light faded. Lulu put her nose in the air, sniffing something that eluded Madison's nose, then shuffled through the grass in search of whatever had piqued her curiosity.

Madison picked up the sander and turned it on. It buzzed to life, vibrating in her palm. She should've taken her dad's advice and bought a mask. She'd probably breathed in half of what she'd sanded away, and she was wearing the other half.

A cool breeze swept through the yard, clearing the dust. The sander hummed, and the musty smell of old wood filled her nostrils.

Her thoughts went back to the coffee shop date that had ended a couple hours ago. Drew seemed nice. He was handsome and attentive, had a good sense of humor. But when Cassidy had mentioned extending the evening with a movie, Madison had declined. She had given Drew her number, though, and if he asked her out, she'd say yes. He was pleasant enough, and who knew? Sometimes the best kind of love grew from friendship. Or so she'd heard.

A shadow fell across the boat. She turned to see a man nearby. She jumped, almost dropping the sander.

Shutting it off, she glared at Beckett, palming her heart as Lulu bounded forward. "You scared me to death."

"I said hello, but you didn't hear." His eyes traveled over the planes of her face, and his lips twitched as he gave Lulu the requisite belly rub. "You should be wearing goggles and a mask."

He would catch her all sweaty and dusty. She wiped her face with numb hands, imagining the colorful freckles she must be sporting.

"What brings you here?"

"Tried to reach you on your landline—figured you were still out with your friends. I was going to leave you a note. I just realized I have to reschedule our sailing lesson tomorrow, and of course Evan's working."

"Oh." She felt a stab of disappointment and realized she'd been looking forward to it. Of course she was. It was the next step toward her goal.

He looked at Lulu, scratching behind her ears while the dog's eyes practically rolled back in her head.

"I have to drive to Indy."

It was no secret his dad was locked up at the Marion County jail. "Well, no problem. We'll just pick up next Saturday, then."

He ran his hand over the unfinished rim of the boat, chips of paint flying off as he went. "So this is your sailboat."

She tried to see the boat through his eyes and didn't like what she saw. "She's kind of a wreck at the moment."

He walked around the boat, taking it in. She remembered the lovely boat he'd made, with its sleek curves and beautiful finish. Madison hated to admit it, but she cared what he thought, and he couldn't be thinking anything good.

"Think she's a lost cause?"

"How's the motor?"

She shrugged. "I haven't had it checked, but Michael said she was mechanically sound."

His hand stopped on the bow. "Michael?"

"It was his. He bought it just before—" She should be able to say the word by now. But Beckett started walking again, sparing her.

"It's been sitting in my parents' barn. He used every dime he saved working at the Dairy Barn for two summers. Didn't even want a car, just wanted this boat."

Silence hung like dust in the air.

"He was a nice guy," Beckett said finally. "We didn't hang in the same crowd, but he was always kind to me."

That didn't surprise her, even as different as they'd been— Beckett the resident bad boy; Michael the golden child. Michael had seen the good in everyone, including her. Was it any wonder she'd felt so alone after his death?

"He had a way about him," she said.

"Not many teens can get away with spouting off about God like he did and still be liked."

And there was the thought that always chafed her like a burr. For all Michael's faith, for all his love of God, where was his Lord that day? Was He busy doing something else? Her grandma had always said, "God's grip never slips." Well, it had slipped that day. She pushed the disturbing thought away.

"Madison, you can't really think you're going to win in this thing."

"I know she needs a lot of work."

He shook his head.

She lifted her chin. "I'll do whatever it takes." Michael thought the boat had promise, so she must. "Besides, it's based on handicaps or whatever, right? And I'll have Evan Higgins helping me. He's my ace in the hole."

"The handicap will help, but there's a lot of work here."

Beckett didn't know her very well if he thought a little work was going to make her quit. "I can handle it."

He rounded the boat and examined the sander. "You need coarser paper. It'll go a lot faster." He handed it back. "I could help if you want."

She blinked at him. The sunset at his back, his eyes darkened to coal. She remembered the look on his face in the coffee shop when Stew had stopped him. He'd hardly looked at her, and she wondered now why that was.

"Why would you do that?" He'd already taught her to swim, on his own free time. Was it possible he—

"I do this kind of thing for fun, remember?" He looked away, ran his hand over the area she'd sanded.

Right. Of course he didn't . . . How silly of her. If he liked her in that way, he'd ask her out, wouldn't he?

She shrugged. "I wouldn't turn down the help. Heaven knows I can use it."

"I can check the motor too, if you want."

He was being awfully nice. It was starting to make her suspicious. Maybe he felt guilty about Jade. Maybe helping her was his penance.

"Or not," he said.

Her every thought was probably written all over her face. "No, I appreciate the offer. Thanks. I can pay you for any repairs."

"Let's see how it goes. It may run just fine. When should I come by?"

"Uh, Monday, after supper?"

"Sounds good."

A cricket chirped from a nearby bush, and in the distance a car door slammed.

"Well, it's late. I should go." He backed toward the driveway.

She didn't want him to leave, she suddenly realized, but she couldn't find a reason for him to stay. "See you Monday then."

"See ya."

She watched him go, with that slow swagger of his, and realized if he'd asked her to a movie, she wouldn't have found an excuse to say no.

Even though he had a shady past.

Even though she didn't know what happened with Jade.

Even though he'd once given her the best kiss of her life and then proceeded to forget it had ever happened.

The dance had fallen on a snowy February night during Madison's sophomore year. Bored and feeling cooped up, the students of Chapel Springs High School had turned out in droves. With a date, in a group, it didn't matter as long as it got them out of the house.

Madison came with a group of friends and danced with the boys who asked her. But mostly she hung in the corner, trying to talk Cassidy into asking Luke Cavendish, her current crush, to dance.

Madison had worn her favorite skirt, a white filmy piece that floated around her knees, and her new blue sweater with butterflies embroidered on the collar.

When Mrs. Pinsky announced a social dancing game over the squealing mike, students began taking the floor.

"This is my chance," Cassidy said when Luke joined the fray. She pulled Madison forward. "Come on!"

Madison followed her to the center of the gym floor where a crowd had gathered, listening to Mrs. Pinsky's instructions. Boys in the inner circle, rotating one way, girls in the outer, rotating the other. She'd blow a whistle, the circles would stop, and you'd dance with the person across from you.

"Great," Cassidy pouted. "What are my chances?"

"They'd be one hundred percent if you'd ask him," Madison said as they formed a circle around the boys.

"Fifty-fifty at best. Did you see who he's been dancing with?"

The music started and the circles spun. The disco ball flashed faint white specks around the room that was barely dimmer than during gym class. The circle went faster, the girls tugging and laughing. The boys were already spinning out of control in the other direction. Michael tugged her hair as he went by, and he was gone before she could retaliate.

A whistle blew. The circles halted.

Madison's laugh evaporated and her smile faded. Beckett O'Reilly stood opposite her. She hadn't even seen him tonight. He didn't attend things like this—few seniors did.

He stared back with his unfathomable expression.

"Lucky!" someone whispered in Madison's ear before she stepped toward her partner.

On her other side, Cassidy paired up with a tall, lanky freshman.

There was no fudging this now with a little shift to the left or right.

Besides, Beckett had already taken a step forward. Madison placed her hands on his shoulders, her heart double-timing the beat of the slow song. She barely reached his chin, and she noticed a tiny cleft there. His jaw was freshly shaven, and a spicy hint of cologne teased her senses.

Kelly Clarkson began the first words of "A Moment Like This."

"I'm Beckett." She hadn't heard his voice before, not like this. It was deep and husky, not like a teenager at all, but like a full-grown man.

"I know. Madison."

His hands burned through her thin sweater at her waist. She remembered the first time she'd seen him, at the football game. You didn't forget eyes like that when they bored into you. But since then, he'd ignored her. And since then, she'd paid attention to all the gossip about him.

He'd been caught putting graffiti on the old lumber warehouse, suspended for fighting, and accused of stealing a class ring from Bradley Moore's locker—all of it since September. The class ring had been all the talk the past month.

She wondered what he was thinking, but not badly enough to look him in the eyes and ask. Her sweater had gone warm and itchy and her face burned, probably making her look like a clown.

His breath stirred the wispy curls at her temple, and she felt it clear down to her toes. None of the other boys she'd danced with had this effect on her, but then, they hadn't been Beckett O'Reilly.

Cassidy caught her eye over Beckett's shoulder and mouthed something she couldn't read, her eyes wide.

Madison focused on the neckline of Beckett's black T-shirt, on the lyrics of the song, on the pinch of her toes in the low heels. Her stomach felt like a popcorn machine, the contents popping wildly inside. Someone had to say something, break this awful tension. Apparently it wasn't going to be him.

"Did you do it?" Of all the stupid things to say! She bit her lip.

"Do what?"

She couldn't think of a different way to answer. "Steal the class ring?"

His muscles went rigid under her hands.

She winced. He must think she was the Goody-Goody Queen of Chapel Springs High.

She could feel his eyes on her. The popping intensified, assault and battery on her ribs. She could've asked after his grandpa or how his classes were going or any number of things. *Stupid!*

"I'm not a thief." Something in his tone surprised her, something sad.

Her eyes went to his, not quite believing what she'd heard. But when their eyes locked, she saw it there for just a second before he blinked it away.

The moment of unexpected vulnerability moved her. Somehow she'd thought Beckett O'Reilly incapable of actual feelings.

"I believe you," she said.

Inscrutable eyes searched her face. He seemed to drink her in, and she let him. He had the longest lashes she'd ever seen on a guy. His nose was crooked at the bridge, probably from some fight. Not the most recent one, not from what she'd heard. There was an alluring dip in his top lip that—

The room went dark. Completely black. They stilled.

Someone whistled, and a few catcalls sounded before the noise level eclipsed the music.

"I guess someone's trying to be funny," she said. She should step away, even if the music played on. She was sure no one was dancing anymore. She could feel the movement of air brushing past them.

"I'll probably get blamed." Her hair stirred as he sighed.

"I'll be your alibi." She hoped he could hear the smile in her voice.

Someone bumped her, making her wobble on her heels. He pulled her closer, his arms tightening protectively. She wondered how a touch at her waist could send a shiver up her arms and make her scalp tingle.

"Most of it's true," he said in her ear.

She didn't have to ask what he meant. What she wanted to ask was why? Why did he do those things? Why did he cause trouble when it was so much easier to follow the rules?

But before she could ask, his hands framed her face. The questions evaporated, replaced with sensation.

The roughness of his hands on her face. The hardness of his muscles against her palms. The spicy smell of him. Her breath filled her lungs and became trapped there.

She felt him coming closer, then his lips touched hers. They were as gentle as a summer breeze and just as warm. He was gone before she could clear the fog from her brain, and she nearly whimpered for another chance. She hadn't even moved! Had stood there like a mindless ninny. She thought of all the girls he'd gone out with and knew her kiss must've been his worst ever.

His thumb brushed her lower lip, making her tremble, making her wish she could see into his eyes.

Then his lips were on hers again, and she was suddenly grateful for second chances. She wasn't going to waste it. She gave back, move for move.

Her response made him bolder. His arms tightened, drawing her closer. His shoulders were hard, his lips soft, an intriguing contradiction. The gym faded away as she floated someplace else, someplace wonderful and perfect.

Her hands slid up his shoulders, her fingers forking into his hair at the nape. It was as soft as she'd always imagined. Softer.

A light flared against her eyelids and the mike squealed. The perfect world disappeared.

Madison jumped back, her eyes flying open, taking in the movement and noise she'd somehow blocked out while she'd been busy throwing herself at Beckett.

Beckett O'Reilly!

They'd barely exchanged two sentences ever. Of course he'd try to make out with her; he was Beckett O'Reilly. But she didn't have to respond like one of his Saturday night flings.

"Settle down, boys and girls," Mrs. Pinsky said. "All right, let's put on another song. And whoever did that . . . you *will* be caught."

A dance song started. The fluorescents were growing brighter by the second. Her face had filled with heat, and she was sure she looked like a clown now. She couldn't bring herself to look at Beckett after kissing him so passionately.

Cassidy grabbed her arm. "Clearly, you need some air," she said to Madison, casting a look at Beckett.

Cassidy didn't have to persuade her to leave the gym or spill her guts once the heavy gym doors clanged shut. But when she'd returned to the dance, Beckett was gone.

And when she passed him at school the next Monday, he didn't so much as look her way. But she still smiled when, later that month, she heard Bradley Moore had found his class ring behind his nightstand.

Chapter Fourteen

Beckett glanced at Madison as she sanded. The goggles he'd brought swallowed her face, but they protected her pretty eyes. They'd been at it for almost two hours, and even with the mask, his mouth had gone dry.

A breeze cut through the yard, cooling his skin. The buzz of the sanders filled his ears, numbed his fingers, as he worked along the grain, paint chips flying.

His trip to Indy Saturday had gone just as he'd expected. His dad had asked after Grandpa, after Beckett's work, then the conversation had dried up. When his dad's last DUI had landed him in jail, Beckett had been almost relieved. He lived in fear his dad would kill someone. It was a miracle he hadn't already. He'd started drinking when Mom had left and hadn't stopped, despite Beckett's and Layla's repeated urgings to get help.

Beckett had driven home, his thoughts heavy as they always were after visiting his father. Dad had lost weight, his bristly cheeks gone hollow, his stomach flat under the beige uniform.

Beckett knew he should visit more, but the way he felt afterward lingered for days, and he couldn't bring himself to go more than once a month. His dad had brought him nothing but shame all his life. Why that should make Beckett feel guilty, he wasn't sure.

"We're losing daylight." Madison cut her sander and pulled off her goggles. With her hair in a ponytail, she looked about eighteen.

"How about a drink?" she asked.

"Sure." Beckett followed her toward the house, Lulu right on his heels. Madison's place was a small Cape Cod on a tree-lined street. It boasted a tidy patch of lawn and a cozy stoop perfect for good-night kisses.

He crossed the threshold, remembering the last time he'd entered her house, with a fistful of flowers and an accidental date. He wondered if Madison was remembering as she turned from the fridge with a water bottle.

"Thanks." He drank his fill and wandered over to the kitchen window. Beyond the gauzy curtains the sun had sunk over the hills, streaking the sky with pink and purple. The house was quiet. Only the hum of the refrigerator broke the silence. He wondered if Madison had heard from Jade, but he wasn't about to bring it up.

"Thanks for bringing the sandpaper. It's going a lot faster." She leaned against the counter and took a drink.

"A lot of old paint on there."

Even in a sloppy T-shirt and worn jeans, with speckles of paint on her cheeks, she was beautiful. Her almond-shaped brown eyes needed no help from makeup, and her lips were perfect, rosy and full. His thoughts traveled back to that dance so long ago when he'd forgotten, just for a moment, that Madison was out of his reach. For that brief moment he'd let himself believe she might care. But that had been an illusion.

He walked toward the living room, stopping on the threshold, taking in the cushy sofas and braided area rugs. He noticed details he'd missed last time: a small built-in bookshelf brimming with books, lacy cloths covering mission-style tables, lamps that gave the room a homey glow. He felt the vast difference between her comfortable lived-in style and his own stark décor. Remembered he shouldn't even be here.

Why do I keep doing this to myself, God? The more reasons I have to stay away—and I have more now than ever—the more time I spend with her. He owed her, for so many reasons, but paying off that debt was going to be the death of him.

"Need another?"

He turned and found her close. A wisp of hair had escaped her ponytail and fluttered in the breeze of the ceiling fan.

He took the bottle, his fingers brushing hers. She smelled like honeysuckle and cedar, an intriguing combination. She had flecks of paint in her hair, on her nose. He pocketed his free hand before he did something stupid.

~

Overhead, the fan clicked as it slowly rotated.

Madison finished her drink and tossed the plastic bottle into the recycling bin. Beckett was quiet tonight, his mood different. Somber. She wondered why. Something she'd said? Something that had happened at work?

She watched him take a drink. His Adam's apple bobbed twice, three times before he capped the bottle, staring at his hands as he did so, his lashes feathering his cheeks.

He had a large flake of neon green paint under his cheekbone. She couldn't let that go. She reached out and brushed at it.

His facial muscles tightened under her thumb as he flinched away. His eyes bounced off hers.

A sting of rejection pierced her somewhere in the vicinity of her heart. She drew back, leaving the flake of paint, letting her arm fall. Heat climbed her neck and spread into her face. When was she going to get it through her head that he wasn't interested?

He cleared his throat and turned toward the door. "I should go."

Lulu, oblivious to the tension, bounded after him, black tail wagging.

"Thanks for the water," he said as he reached the door.

"Thanks for your help."

"See you Saturday."

"See you."

The door whooshed closed, and Lulu trotted back to Madison's side. A moment later she heard his truck start, the tires spin on gravel. Apparently he couldn't get out of Dodge fast enough.

Madison showered and changed into her pj's, her mood soured. She flipped on a TV show but couldn't keep her mind on it. All she could think about was the way Beckett had flinched.

She pulled the chenille pillow into her stomach. She needed to stop thinking about him. There were plenty of other thought-worthy men.

Drew had stopped her at church and asked her out next weekend. She'd promised to check her calendar and get back with him. Maybe she should call him. She wasn't sure why she'd put it off. She was pretty sure he wouldn't flinch away from her touch.

Her landline rang, and she reached for it. Drew? Beckett?

The caller ID listed an unknown area code. She frowned. "Hello?"

There was background noise. Quiet music.

"Madison?" She'd know her sister's voice anywhere.

She sat upright. "Jade?"

"Yeah, it's me."

"Where have you been? I've been worried sick."

"I'm sorry. I left you a note. And I called Mom and Dad."

She drew a breath, reminding herself that her sister was too old to be scolded. "Are you okay? Where are you?"

"I'm fine. I'm in Chicago."

"Chicago?"

"Can you believe Old Faithful made it that far?" Jade's pea-green Ford had been on its last legs for five years.

"But you're okay? Where are you staying? Do you need money?"

Jade breathed a laugh. "No, I don't need money, big sis. I'm fine. I have a job. I'm staying with Izzy from high school. She's been after me to come up here for a while."

"Didn't Izzy get married?"

"No. She has a little boy, but the dad didn't stick around."

"It's such a big city . . ."

"We look out for each other. Don't worry."

But she did worry. What did Jade know of the world? People would take advantage of her naïveté. Of her generosity.

"I wish you'd come home. Mom and Dad are worried. We all are."

"I'm a big girl. I—I need to stand on my own two feet awhile, you know?"

"You don't have to go to Chicago to do that."

"I'm fine. You don't have to worry." But there was something in her voice that made Madison do just that.

"Where are you working?"

"It's like a little coffee shop/café kind of place. I get good tips."

Chicago was expensive. How could she afford her share of rent? Unless she was living in some dive. If Madison could only get the address, she could check it out on Google Earth.

"You left your favorite scarf. I found it behind the dresser. I can send it to you."

"Just hang on to it. Enough about me. How's everything there? Did you win the sailing lessons?"

"I did. They're coming along." No point in mentioning Beckett.

"And the play? Have rehearsals begun?"

"Auditions are this weekend. I'm looking forward to it. I miss you being here."

"The place is a mess, isn't it?"

"Well, there might be dishes in the sink."

"And a layer of dust?"

An easy smile pulled at Madison's lips. Man, she missed Jade. "Possibly."

She caught her sister up on the rest of the family, then Jade broke in. "Listen, I have to go. My break's over. I just wanted you to know I'm okay—and hear your voice."

"Wait, is this the number I can reach you at?"

"It's the café phone. We don't have a landline at the moment."

That was better than nothing.

"I gotta go," Jade said. "Tell everyone I said hey."

"All right. Love you, Jade."

"Love you too."

And then she was gone. Madison turned off the phone and cradled it against her chest. Jade was okay, for now. Although some of the things she'd said weren't sitting right.

After checking the time, she dialed her parents. They'd want to know everything.

Chapter Fifteen

The wind tugged at Madison's hair as Beckett guided the boat back toward the marina. The day had dawned clear and sunny with a bit of a breeze, perfect for her first sailing lesson with Beckett. Having covered the basics with Evan, she'd been ready to start learning some racing techniques. They practiced beating—staying on the wind—and tacking and jibing.

As they approached the marina, her mind turned to her parents. Last night the spirits at her family's barbecue had been up. Hearing from Jade had set everyone at ease. Madison had found the café online after searching for the phone number and had Google Earthed the place. Not that it did much good.

Beckett eased off the throttle. She'd decided to think of him as a friend. Not as the guy who'd given her the best kiss of her life. Not as the guy whose muscles rippled under the sunlight. Not as the paragon of virtue Cassidy had described.

Friends. That was it.

To that end, she'd avoided touching him, looking at him, or even speaking to him unless necessary. To reinforce her decision, she'd lined up a date with Drew for tonight. He'd decided to audition with her for the upcoming play, having done some acting in undergrad school. *Love on the Line* had won the annual contest for best play by an Indiana playwright.

Madison was excited about trying out for the lead role.

Eleanor was a complicated and engaging character, with a compelling story arc.

After the audition, Drew was taking her to a restaurant over the river in Louisville, a fancy steakhouse. He'd already warned her that he was on call. She'd need to get used to that if she continued to see him.

Beckett guided the boat into the slip. When they neared the dock, she grabbed the rope and stepped ashore, feeling only a moment's trepidation. She pulled until the boat was in place and wrapped it around the cleat, using the figure-eight method Beckett had shown her.

"Nice job today," he said, jumping from the boat.

"There's a lot to learn."

"You've come a long way."

She wanted to write down some of his instructions before she forgot. There was more to think about when racing than she'd imagined. Trimming, tacking, jibing . . . so much to remember.

The sun beat down on her shoulders as they made their way up the dock. She checked her watch. She'd have time for a quick shower before Drew arrived.

"Hope I didn't make you late somewhere."

She started to mention the date then changed her mind. "Nope." When they reached Dewitt's, she thanked him and headed for her Saturn.

~

"How was the date?" PJ plopped down beside Madison in the pew the next morning.

"Not bad." Seats were filling fast, as the service was due to start in a few minutes. The pianist hammered away at an old hymn, her silver curls bouncing with each chord.

"That's all I get? I'm your sister." She flipped her brown hair over her squared shoulders.

Madison sighed. "We went to Morton's. All the reviews were right—the steak was superb."

"I don't care about the cut of beef. Did he kiss you good night?"

Madison hiked a brow. "Yes . . ."

PJ smiled.

"On the cheek."

PJ's lips fell. "Well, that's a bummer."

"He's a gentleman. Nothing wrong with that." She waved as Mom and Dad passed, taking their seats behind her brother and Daniel two rows up.

PJ straightened her floral skirt. "Your audition was all the talk in Sunday school."

She'd been pleased by how well it had gone. She'd also been impressed by Drew's acting skills. "Was it?"

"Yours and Drew's both. Dottie was pleased to have such talent this year. I think Drew might play opposite you. You'd get to know him well during rehearsals."

At the mention of the rehearsals, a thread of anxiety wormed through Madison. Maybe her mom was right. Between her job, learning to race, the rehearsals, and her nursing home friends, she was going to be swamped.

"I hope I haven't bitten off more than I can chew."

"It'll be fun." PJ stretched out the fingers of her left hand and balled them into a fist again. She shrugged her left shoulder.

"What's wrong?"

"It's weird. My left hand feels kind of funny. Numb." She looked at Madison, eyes widening. "Isn't that a sign of a heart attack?"

"Yes . . ." Madison reached out and removed the hair band from her sister's wrist. "It's also a sign of restricted blood flow."

"Oh. Whoops."

The music minister came forward to welcome the crowd, and Madison settled in. After singing several hymns and having a time of prayer, Pastor Adams took the podium and began the message.

Madison opened her Bible to Luke, chapter 8. The parable of the sower. The seed along the path, the seed on the rock, the seed among thorns, and the seed that fell on good soil. She'd heard it a dozen times. She stared at the text as Pastor Adams began reading, but the words blurred on the page as her thoughts turned to tomorrow's hectic schedule.

Chapter Sixteen

Madison arrived at Countryside Manor later than usual. The Kneeling Nanas had already disbanded from their knitting circle, so she found Mrs. Geiger alone in her room.

"Knock-knock," Madison said, crossing the threshold.

"Hello, dear. Oh, a tabby!" Mrs. Geiger shuffled over in her fuzzy pink house slippers, taking the cat from Madison. "I used to have one, you know. His name was Oscar, and he had a terrible habit of impregnating all the female cats in my neighborhood."

"Why didn't you get him neutered?"

"Oh, Mr. Geiger would have none of that. Of course, it wasn't his cat having litter after litter. It didn't make for good neighbors, let me tell you."

"I was hoping to make it in time to catch all your friends since I missed you last week."

"Well, I'm the only cat lover, and Mrs. Marquart is allergic." She cuddled the tabby against her bosom, and the cat blinked slowly. "Mrs. Etter's grandson loves that little hound they adopted. He sent her pictures on the computer, but we can't figure out how to open them. Oh well, I'm sure Perry will bring some in soon."

"I'm glad it worked out."

Mrs. Geiger's penciled-in brows jumped. "Oh, I heard about the play! Congratulations on getting the lead again. I can't wait to see it."

"Thanks. We just had our first rehearsal. That's why I'm late. I have a lot of lines to learn."

"I'm sure you'll be just as wonderful as always. You have a lot on your plate with the play and sailing and whatnot. We'll be rooting you on at both events. Now, tell me about Jade. The girls will want an update at prayer group tomorrow. We heard she called . . . true?"

Madison picked up a photo of Mrs. Geiger with her grandchildren and great-grandchildren. "Yes, she's in Chicago."

"Oh my. Well, she's safe and sound anyway. God will look out for her."

"She's staying with a friend from high school. I'm worried about her." Madison set the photo down. "She's so giving, you know that. She'd give a stranger the shirt off her back. I hope she doesn't get taken advantage of."

"We'll keep praying for her, don't you worry. God's going to use that girl and her music talent for something special. You'll see."

After they chatted awhile, Mrs. Geiger gave the cat a final hug and handed him back. "Bye, little darling. I'd better get my shower and get to bed or I'll oversleep and miss prayer group. Mrs. Etter gets so wound up when I miss."

Madison smiled. "Thank the ladies for their prayers."

"I will. And we'll keep praying for you and that handsome O'Reilly boy too."

"I'm actually dating the new doctor in town now—Drew Landon."

"Hmmm, yes, I heard." She pulled Madison into a warm hug. "Now you let us know if there's anything else we can pray about."

"Will do."

Madison turned down the hall, stopping to chat with a couple of residents along the way. She was about to visit with a friend when she heard a ruckus down the hall. She looked both ways, saw no nurses coming, so she followed the shouting.

"I don't want that!" She recognized Mr. O'Reilly's gravelly voice.

Madison quickened her steps.

"Get away from me! Get away!"

She arrived to find Mr. O'Reilly on his knees by the window. Beckett was reaching for him.

Mr. O'Reilly pushed his hand away. "I don't need your help!"

Madison pressed the call button by the bed.

"Come on, Grandpa," Beckett said softly. "Let's get you back to bed."

"Go away! You're a liar! I don't want you near me!"

"It's Beckett, Grandpa. Come on now." He lifted under the old man's arms.

Mr. O'Reilly swung his fists at Beckett's face, making contact more than once.

Madison hurried forward. "Hi, Mr. O'Reilly. It's Madison. Can I help you?"

Mr. O'Reilly, finally on his feet, pushed Beckett away and turned to her. "Get that ugly cat outta here!"

Nurse Doolittle swept into the room, shooting Madison a look over her bifocals. "You heard the man. Now, Mr. O'Reilly, let's get you to bed, all right, sweetheart?"

Beckett stepped away, rubbing the back of his neck.

Mr. O'Reilly scanned the room, looking suddenly lost and confused. His rheumy eyes passed over Beckett and came to rest on Mrs. Doolittle.

The nurse took Mr. O'Reilly's arm and led him toward the

bed. "There we are. Would you like your nice warm socks, Mr. O'Reilly? Your grandson brought them back all fresh and clean."

The nurse whispered something to Beckett, patted his arm. A shadow flickered over his jaw as he passed Madison and walked out the door.

She caught up with him near the nurses' station and walked by his side, saying nothing for a moment.

"Are you all right?" she said after he caught his breath.

"Fine." His voice was flat, like something had caught in his throat, choking off all emotion.

"You're not fine. Come sit down." She pulled him into the deserted sitting room and sat at one of the tables. Behind her, one of the vending machines buzzed. The cat curled in her lap and closed his eyes, purring.

Beckett settled into the chair, palmed the back of his neck, elbows jutting out. Threads of red ran through the whites of his eyes.

"It must be hard," she said.

"It isn't always like that, thank God."

But it would be eventually. Neither of them had to say it. "It's a terrible disease. So hard on everyone."

He stared off into space. "I don't know why he calls me a liar."

"It's the dementia talking. You can't take it personally. He doesn't know what he's doing or saying. He loves you."

Beckett sighed. "I know that." A red blotch from his grandpa's fist spread over his cheek.

Madison's heart broke for him. She couldn't imagine her own grandfather not recognizing her, saying cruel things. Beckett had been so tender and patient with him.

"You take good care of him. Don't they do laundry here?"

"Sure."

"Mrs. Doolittle said you washed his socks."

"They're his favorites—his feet get cold—and they kept disappearing." He shrugged.

"He's lucky to have you. Some of the residents are so lonely. It's sad."

"Is that why you come?" His eyes shifted to hers, locked on, and didn't let go.

"Animals make people happy. Besides, I like the folks here. Older people are storehouses of wisdom. It's too bad people forget that." She stroked the cat, and he purred in his sleep. "You and your grandpa must've been close."

"I was just ten when we moved in with him."

"You and your sister and your dad?"

He nodded. His dad had been in and out of jail a lot through his teen years. She hadn't thought about what had happened to Beckett and Layla when he was away.

"What about your mom?"

He folded his arms on the table, looked at his hands.

"Sorry, I'm being nosy."

"She left when we were young. I saw her off and on. She's somewhere in California now, remarried."

She thought of her own tight-knit family. Sure, they were sometimes in each other's business, they could be a pain in the patootie, but she couldn't imagine life without them.

"Grandpa practically raised us. He was the one who took us to church. Rain, sleet, snow, didn't matter. Nine o'clock on Sunday morning, we were out the door, driving to church in his big brown Oldsmobile whether we wanted to or not."

Madison smiled. "It was the same in our family. If you wanted to skip, you'd better have a fever."

"Know all about that. A thermometer and a glass of warm water will do the trick. Put a little soap in your eyes to make them nice and bloodshot, and it'll get you out of just about anything."

Madison laughed. "You naughty boy."

"He caught on when I was thirteen. Turns out the trick is not using it too often."

"Thanks for the tip."

"I gave him a run for his money, but he never backed down. I'm grateful he made me go now. He did it because he loved me."

"You go to church with my friend Cassidy, I think."

"Riverview Community. Good people. The ladies' group sends cards and homemade goodies to my grandpa, and the men's group visits him."

And Beckett worked on cars for widows and mowed the church lawn. "You've changed a lot since high school."

He smirked. "Go ahead and say it. I was an idiot."

Madison smiled. "You were misguided."

And so had she been, about Beckett. She looked into his eyes and realized she hadn't given him a fair shake. People grew up. Life happened, people changed.

She'd based her belief of what had happened to Jade on ancient history, and that hadn't been fair. Whatever went down that night wasn't his fault—she was sure of it.

"Tell me about your boats. How did you get into that?"

He shrugged his broad shoulders. "Initially I just wanted to build one for myself. Something cheap and serviceable. Once I got going, cheap and serviceable went out the window. I enjoyed the process and decided to build another. Sold it to a tourist, and it just kind of grew from there."

Madison liked watching the way his eyes lit up when he talked about his boats.

"It's just a hobby at this point," he added.

"You should grow it into a business. Start a website and stuff."

"I plan to, but that takes money. If I win the regatta this year, that's what I'm doing with the prize money, get my business off the ground. Someday I hope to build boats full-time."

They each had their goals for winning the regatta, then. It was too bad they both couldn't win. "Who's on your crew?"

"No crew. I sail alone."

"No one else to mess things up?"

"It's cost me the cup twice. Too much at stake this year."

The conversation turned from sailing to Madison's boat. They talked and laughed, and she lost all track of time until Mrs. Doolittle stopped in the doorway, eyeing them over her bifocals, lips pursed.

"What are you two doing? It's way past visiting hours." She crossed her arms, waiting, like they were four-year-olds caught raiding the cookie jar.

Beckett checked his watch, his brows shooting up.

"Whoops." Madison stood, cradling the cat, and pushed in her chair under Mrs. Doolittle's watchful eyes.

"Good night," Beckett told the nurse on their way out.

She could feel Mrs. Doolittle's eyes on her back as they walked down the quiet hall.

"You're a bad influence," Madison whispered.

Beckett spared her a glance, and Madison couldn't hold it back any longer. Their laughter echoed down the hall. She could almost see Mrs. Doolittle's look of disapproval.

Chapter Seventeen

Beckett followed Madison into her house. After her sailing lesson, they'd worked on her boat, and when she'd offered popcorn and soda, he'd seen no reason to turn her down. Their relationship was more comfortable since their chat at the nursing home the week before.

Madison was an astute student, even outside the classroom. She'd had a couple of lessons with Evan since he'd been out with her last. Beckett was amazed at how quickly she'd picked up sailing terms and racing techniques. Looked like she wasn't going to be an Achilles' heel for Evan after all. Beckett had better bring his A game on racing day.

He was enjoying Madison's company and found himself hoping Evan had to work every Saturday. She had an ability to laugh at herself that he found surprising and admirable. Just today she'd tripped over her own feet on the way to her car, landing facedown in the grass before he could catch her. He thought she'd be embarrassed, but she'd laughed until she had tears in her eyes. She still had that same melodic laugh. He could listen to it all day.

"Coke or Sprite?" she asked over her shoulder.

"Coke. I'll get it." He joined her in the kitchen where she handed him the two-liter and two glasses.

"I'll get the popcorn started. I use an air popper. None of those microwave bags for me."

He filled the glasses with ice. "Didn't think they made those anymore."

"It belonged to my parents. They went the microwave route."

"Along with the rest of America."

"Say what you like, air popping is faster and cheaper. Plus, there's no oil."

"We're eating it dry?"

She laughed at the look on his face. "Oh no, I drown it in melted butter. It's much better than oil."

"Had me scared." He poured the soda and waited for the foam to die down.

They'd finished the sanding tonight. Both of them had dust and paint chips in their hair and on their clothes, despite their efforts to brush off at the door.

"What color will you paint the boat?"

Madison entered the pantry. "Dark blue. I'll pick it up on Monday. What kind should I buy?"

"A good metallic primer. Don't waste your money on marine paint. House paint enamel works fine. Get a roller and a good brush. If we work together, we should be able to get a good finish. Soon as she dries up, we'll see what kind of shape she's in mechanically."

"Sounds good."

"Have a name picked out?"

A clatter sounded. "Uh-oh."

He turned to see Madison on tiptoe, the popcorn machine teetering in her outstretched fingertips.

He was behind her in a flash, taking the machine. She fell back on her heels, and he caught her around the middle with his free arm.

She seemed to freeze there, her body all soft and curvy against his. His throat went dry. He caught a whiff of her honeysuckle shampoo, and his grip tightened on the machine.

"Thanks," she whispered, turning in his arms. Her eyes caught and held his. Her bangs fell into her eyes, tangling with her eyelashes. He knew a moment of wanting so intense he felt powerless against it.

Her lips parted. "Michael's Dream."

Her words caught him off guard. "What?"

"The boat—that's what I'm naming her."

Michael's Dream . . .

"He wanted to be the youngest Regatta winner ever—before his twenty-seventh birthday. That's coming up, but I'm going to make it happen in time, thanks to you and Evan."

That's what this was all about? The lessons, the boat, the regatta? He'd assumed it was the competition or the cash prize—same as him, same as many others who turned out for the race.

It wasn't the money at all, but her dead brother's dream. The dream Beckett had stolen.

Thanks to him, she'd said. Beckett had no right to be here with his arm around her. Had no right to be here at all, thinking about the way she smelled, the way she felt against him. Why did he keep forgetting that?

He stepped away. "I'm sorry, I—I need a rain check."

She blinked, her eyes clouding. "But . . . the popcorn will only take a minute."

She wanted to be friends, but he'd been stupid to think that was going to work. Stupid to think he could settle for that. Not with Madison. Not ever.

He set the machine on the nearest countertop. "Sorry. Another time." He didn't even look at her again. One look in those confused brown eyes, and he'd only be tempted to stay.

～

The room went quiet after Beckett left. Coke sizzled in the half-full glasses, the ice cubes crackled. What had happened? One minute things were friendly, they were pouring soda, making plans. The next he was hightailing it out the door. Hadn't something similar happened just a couple weeks ago? She'd thought they'd made big strides since then.

Apparently not.

When she'd felt his hand at her waist, the heat of his body against her back, she'd remembered in a hurry why friendship was so difficult. There were enough sparks between them to start a fire.

At least for her. But he hadn't exactly acted on it, had he?

That's the problem, Madison. Didn't he back away at every turn? When she'd tried to touch him, when she'd stumbled into him in the pantry. Maybe he'd even thought she'd contrived the incident just hoping to wind up in his arms. Was that why he'd practically run for the door?

Her mood at an all-time low, Madison put the popcorn machine on a low shelf and poured the Coke into one glass. She sank onto the sofa, the long night stretching ahead. The house was too quiet.

The thought of facing him again made her face burn. *When are you going to get it through your head, Madison? He's not interested. Not. Interested. So just keep your hands to yourself.*

Besides, she had Jade to consider. Her sister had been happier the night of her date with Beckett than she'd been in months. And

Beckett must have feelings for Jade too. Hadn't he sent those letters? Taken her to the banquet? He *had* sent those letters, right?

She got up and went to Jade's room. The space still carried a hint of Jade's favorite perfume, a soft oriental fragrance. Her sister had shown her the notes as she'd received them. She kept them in her nightstand drawer.

Madison pulled it open, surprised to see Jade had left them.

She pulled out the thin stack and settled on Jade's bed. A pressed pink rose lay on top, its edges brittle. Jade had found the flower on the seat of her car after church one Sunday.

The next was a poem, "She Walks in Beauty" by Lord Byron. She remembered scrutinizing the paper with Jade, looking for clues. It wasn't ordinary notebook paper. The dimensions were smaller, the edges perforated. It was off-white with fine gray lines.

The words were typed on a beige square of paper and centered on the sheet. The entire thing had been folded into neat thirds. She read the lovely verses now and had trouble imagining Beckett choosing the poem. Jade must bring out the romantic in him. No wonder he kept running away from Madison.

Next was a short note that Jade had found on her car after work, handwritten in neat print on the same type of paper, folded the same way. "Your music makes my heart sing." It was one of two handwritten items, but they hadn't recognized the printing. It was easy enough to disguise one's handwriting though.

She opened a red card with a pink heart centered on the front. "Happy Valentine's Day from your secret admirer. XXXOOO."

The others were much the same, giving away nothing about the man who'd written them. Had Jade been as clueless about her admirer's identity as she'd claimed? Had she truly been in the dark until Beckett had shown up on their doorstep?

Madison put the items back in the drawer. What did it matter? The date had been a disaster, and now Jade was gone.

Madison needed to forget about Beckett, just get through the rest of her lessons, and she wouldn't have to see him anymore. The thought should've buoyed her spirits. Instead, they sank even lower.

What was wrong with her? Was she that lonely, that she anticipated time with an uninterested man? A man who was apparently pining for her sister?

Had Madison actually begun to have feelings for Beckett?

She shook her head. It was only chemistry. The memory of that kiss so long ago—so forgotten by him—was toying with her emotions. She needed to forget about it, focus on the regatta and the play. She had plenty to keep her busy, including Drew.

Maybe she should have him over for supper. They could run lines. Heaven knew she needed the practice. She looked around the house, trying to envision him here in her space.

Newspapers littered the antique coffee table, this morning's coffee mug still sat on the oak end table, and across from her, the sofa pillows were in a jumbled pile on the recliner. She hadn't noticed how much tidying Jade had done around here until she'd left.

The wall clock ticked off the time, and the refrigerator hummed. She dug for her script under the newspaper and worked on memorizing her lines for an hour. When she was finished, she turned on the TV, longing for noise to fill the quiet. An old sitcom appeared on the screen, filling the room with chatter and fake laughter. But inside, that familiar hollow spot refused to be soothed by the noise.

Chapter Eighteen

BECKETT SCREWED THE LEG OF THE ASSEMBLY JIG TO THE transom, pressing the drill with more force than necessary. His neighbors probably weren't happy about the noise. He'd tried to sleep. But every time he closed his eyes, he saw Madison, looking up at him, hopeful. Thankful.

He drove the screw home and reached for the next leg. If she only knew.

The memory haunted him still. Followed him like an ominous shadow, creeping up behind him when he least expected it. Like tonight. He tried to push it away, but it came upon him, consuming him.

He'd been swimming at Turner's Bend as he often did on sweltering Saturdays. Shaded by the jagged cliff wall, the river was moving slow and lazy as it curled through the bend, the water clear and refreshing.

He had to get home and shower for work soon, but he was reluctant to leave. He plunged underwater and stayed down until his lungs felt like bursting.

He surfaced to find Michael McKinley kicking off his Nikes onshore. Beckett scanned the area, hoping Madison had tagged along, but Michael was alone. Probably for the best. Ever since he'd kissed her at the dance last year, he'd done his best to ignore her, which had become pretty easy since he'd graduated. But that didn't keep him from thinking about her.

Michael beamed his trademark smile. "Hey, O'Reilly."

Beckett nodded and went under again. He wasn't up for company, had come here to get away from everyone. His dad had started drinking at nine this morning. His grandpa and sister were gone for the day, and Beckett had no desire to hang around and watch him get drunker by the hour.

He surfaced as Michael was splashing in. A basketball player, Michael had been the star of the team last season, even though he'd only been a junior. He had a tall athletic build and eyes the same color and shape as Madison's.

Beckett pushed off toward the cliff wall with long, punishing strides. Madison again. Why couldn't he forget about her? Even after all the girls he'd been with since, she hovered around his mind like a pesky mosquito.

When he came up for air, Michael was nearby in the shade of the cliff wall.

"Man, this feels good," Michael said. "Gotta be ninety-five today."

"Or hotter." Beckett kicked to stay afloat, one hand on the jagged cliff wall.

"Makes me wonder how bad August will be. Should be working on my boat, but the barn's too hot. Not a breeze to be found today."

"Our air conditioner's broke."

"Bummer." Michael looked up the fifteen-foot cliff where a blue jay squawked from a high branch. "They say it's too shallow to dive off, but I've often wondered."

Beckett looked up the wall. "I did it once." He'd practically been on a death mission, his dad just arrested the night before on the corner of Main and Oak for driving through a red light, drunk.

"I don't believe you."

If anybody else had said it, Beckett might've put a fist into his face, but Michael had a way about him. Besides, he was Madison's brother.

"Last summer. River was lower than it is now."

"No way."

Beckett studied him a minute. "I'll show you." He swam toward the bank, pulled up onto the shore, then started up the steep path to the side of the cliff, water running down his legs in rivulets. Weeds tickled his calves even as roots and stones cut into the soles of his feet.

"Hey, I don't know if that's a good idea," Michael said as Beckett reached the top and approached the ledge.

"Anchors aweigh." Beckett pushed off, diving, sailing down. He broke the surface and went under. He turned up sharply and kicked to the surface.

When he came up he drew a breath and slung his wet hair from his eyes. "See? Plenty deep."

"Wow, you had me worried."

"Your turn."

Michael chuckled. "I don't know. Maybe later."

Beckett laughed and messed with him a bit before leaving Michael to swim laps along the shoreline.

Beckett floated down the river for a while, then headed back to shore where he shook off and draped a towel around his neck.

"See ya," Michael called.

Beckett lifted his hand, not looking back. Not seeing the last smile Michael McKinley ever gave. When he heard the sirens later, he hadn't known who they were for. But when he'd heard Michael had been found dead, he hadn't needed the autopsy report to confirm how he'd died.

That night he'd wept in his dad's arms for the first time, the only time he could remember, guilt making words spill from him like water bursting through a dam. He hadn't been able to bring himself to attend the funeral.

Now he drove the screw until it sank deeply into the wood. Only then did he stop to wipe the beads of sweat from his brow.

No, he had no right to touch Madison, no right to care for her, no right even to think of her. But if she needed to win the regatta for Michael, he was going to do everything in his power to help her. It was the least he could do.

Chapter Nineteen

"I'm off to meet Stewie for supper," Cassidy said from the office doorway.

Madison looked up from the paperwork. "Have fun. Don't forget the new printer's coming between eight and nine."

"I'll be here, and I'll get those reminder cards out in the mail tomorrow. You have a date with Drew tonight, right?"

"A picnic at Riverside Park. Mom's packing us a feast."

"Good ol' Momma Jo. You have the best family."

"Don't I know it. They're helping me with the boat too. Between them and Beckett, it doesn't look like the same boat any-more—and that's a good thing."

Cassidy cocked her head. "Beckett's helping with the boat?"

"The sanding and stuff." Madison bent back over her paperwork.

"You still have a thing for him."

"Do not."

"Do too. I remember that kiss . . ."

Cassidy's memory was far too good. Helpful on the job, not so much in Madison's personal life. "One kiss. I was practically a baby, and he doesn't even remember it."

"Really?"

Madison hiked her chin. "Really. I'd practically forgotten it myself until you just mentioned it." She wrote a series of nonsensical numbers.

"Uh-huh. That would explain the sudden flush in your cheeks."

Madison gave a mock glare. "Didn't you say you had some-where to be?"

Cassidy gave an innocent shrug. "Don't shoot the messenger. If you have the hots for him, you can hardly blame—"

"I do not have—" Madison cleared her throat. "He's helping me learn to race. That's all."

"And fixing up your boat."

"Very gracious of him."

"Gracious."

"I'm dating Drew, not Beckett. Remember Drew? The guy you begged me to go out with?"

Cassidy's hands flew up. "Drew's great. I like Drew. And if you like Drew too, we're all good."

"I like Drew."

"Perfect." Cassidy straightened, gave Madison that look that said she wasn't one bit fooled. "See you Monday."

~

Madison packed the last of the picnic while Drew struggled to fold the blanket as it whipped in the wind. The two families who'd been in the park earlier had gone home when the sun had set.

She stifled a yawn and hoped Drew didn't notice. Sleep had been elusive enough lately, but the night before, Cappy Winters had called at midnight. His Saint Bernard had gotten into his neighbor's garage and eaten rat poison. She'd met him at the clinic, induced the dog to vomit, and started him on a vitamin K regimen. Thankfully, Cappy had caught it early, so she expected a full recovery.

The next yawn sneaked up on her.

"Am I boring you?" Drew asked.

"Sorry. Middle-of-the-night canine emergency." The wind kicked up, and she smelled rain. "I hope a storm's not coming in. I need my sailing lesson tomorrow." The regatta was only two weeks away.

"Stew told me you were sailing in the regatta. I hear there's a nice cash prize."

Madison stood and brushed the grass from her knees. "There is, but that's not why I'm going to win."

He dropped the folded blanket on top of the basket. "I like your confidence. So why are you going to win?" His eyes teased.

She wished she hadn't brought it up. "I had a twin brother who died at seventeen. I'm kind of doing this for him—it was his dream."

Drew's countenance fell. "Oh. I'm sorry."

She waved off his concern. "It was a long time ago. It's just something I have to do."

"I hope you win. Do you need any help? I've never sailed, but maybe I could lend some muscle power."

"That's sweet. Thanks, but I have a partner. He's won the last two years, so I actually have a good shot. He's amazing."

He tossed a smile over his shoulder as he walked toward the swing set. "Should I be worried?"

Madison laughed, following. "He's married with three kids, so probably not."

"I'm more a fisherman than a sailor," Drew said. "I've got that O'Reilly guy working on some boat plans for me. He's pricey, but his work is spectacular. I sold my old boat before I left Chicago, and I miss being on the water."

"You'll find the river a lot different than Lake Michigan, but the fishing's good."

"No doubt." Drew held out a swing. "Come here."

The sun had set over the hills, and a streetlamp nearby kicked on. She sank onto the U-shaped seat. The chunky metal links were cool against her palms, and the seat pressed her knees together.

He pulled back and gave her a gentle push, and she angled her feet outward.

"You know how long it's been since I've been in a swing?"

"Know how long it's been since I've been in a park?"

The wind in her hair, the sensation of floating through air, felt good. "I should do this more often."

With her busy schedule, she didn't factor in much downtime. She'd found that time spent doing nothing usually resulted in self-reflection, which tended to spiral down into discontent.

Drew's pager went off. He gave her an apologetic smile. "Excuse me a minute . . ."

"Sure."

He walked away, dialing.

Madison pumped, the motion carrying her higher and higher. At the peak she could see the river over the park's thick hedge. The last light of the day shimmered over the surface.

She wondered where Beckett was, if he and Rigsby were curled up in front of the TV or if he was working on his next boat, maybe even Drew's.

A short distance away, Drew paced as he spoke on the phone. She wondered if he'd have to go to the hospital and found herself indifferent at the thought. Lulu had been cooped up all day, and

Madison felt bad for neglecting her. She'd almost brought her to the park, but Drew had seemed less than enthusiastic.

A few minutes later Drew approached, pocketing his phone. "Good news. It's not appendicitis."

"That is good news. PJ had appendicitis when she was four-teen."

"PJ . . ."

"My sister. The one who's in culinary school in Indianapolis."

"Oh, right. You mentioned her." He sat on the swing beside her. His long legs hampering him, he shuffled back and forth.

Madison tucked her legs, coasting. "Must be hard having your plans interrupted so often."

He twisted toward her. "You get used to it. There are a lot of perks to that one drawback."

"What do you like the most about your work?"

"Helping people," he said without hesitation. "Finding the problem and fixing it."

"What if you can't fix it?"

"Then it's hard, but I try not to dwell on those."

She drifted in silence for a few minutes while he drew in the wood chips with the toe of his Top-Siders.

"Rehearsal went pretty well last night," he said. "I'm really enjoying the theater here. Nice people, all of them. I love that they include Elliot."

"He's great." Elliot was in his early twenties and was mentally impaired. He helped with the lighting.

"Are you getting excited for opening night?"

It was only a month away, but she had her lines memorized and most of the blocking down.

"I'm good with most of it, but I'm struggling with the final scene. Once I get that down, I'll be okay."

"I thought you did pretty good. We'll get there."

"I had it down, then Dottie added the blocking, and now I'm having trouble thinking about what I'm saying, how I'm saying it, where I'm standing, and where my hands are supposed to be."

She dragged her feet in the chips, coming to a stop.

"We could run through it a few times."

She looked around. "Here?"

He shrugged. "There's no one around. Not like at rehearsal."

"Good point. Well, all right." She stood and found an open grassy area near the park entrance. Surrounded by the hedge, they had plenty of privacy.

"I'm having trouble understanding the emotion Eleanor's feeling in that scene," Madison said. "What's your take on it?"

"Well, remember, she's in love with Lucas, but he's hurt her before, so she's afraid to trust her feelings."

"So should fear be her primary emotion? He's grabbing for her, but I don't want it to seem like she's afraid of him, because he's never physically hurt her."

"Right," Drew agreed. "He gets physical, but only because he's desperately afraid of losing her. It's passion, not aggression. She's not afraid of him, but of her own weakness toward him, her own feelings."

"How do I convey that?"

"The body language Dottie taught you. It's about self-preservation. The words sound angry, but the body language says fear."

"That makes sense. Let's run through it a few times."

~

Beckett wiped his hands on the dirty rag and checked his watch. Later than he'd thought. But the Sea-Doo repair was finished for pickup tomorrow as promised.

He grabbed a drink from the fountain, locked up, and headed toward his truck behind the marina shop. The breeze felt good on his damp neck. The air carried the fragrance of honeysuckle, reminding him of Madison.

He'd see her tomorrow, if the weather held. And he prayed it did, since they were running out of time. He couldn't deny that he was looking forward to seeing her. Which was foolish, considering Madison was a dead end. Considering that it was torture to be with her.

His thoughts went back to the moment in her pantry the week before. She'd felt so good in his arms. Too good. He had no right thinking of her that way. Her face would turn all kinds of red if she knew that the scent of her so close had sent a shiver down his spine. Or that he'd wanted to pull her closer and feel her heart against his.

You've really gone off the deep end now, O'Reilly. Best that the regatta's almost here before you go and make another mess.

He was reaching for his truck door when he heard something over the wind. A woman's voice, raised in anger. The nearest house was a couple blocks away. Too far to be coming from there, and besides, he thought, turning his head, the voice was coming from the direction of the park.

He listened a moment, registering another voice, male, angry. He pocketed his keys, walking toward the disturbance.

It took less than a minute to reach the line of shrubs edging the park. He continued up the sidewalk toward the entrance, the voices growing louder. His feet picked up pace.

"I said no! How many times do I have to say it?" Madison's voice.

A shot of adrenaline propelled him forward.

"You don't mean it. You know you don't. Don't walk away from me!"

Beckett reached the entrance, his blood pumping hard.

"Leave me alone!"

"Come here!" Drew was grabbing Madison's arm. He spun her around.

Something red and hot exploded in Beckett's head. He shot forward, reaching Drew in a blink. Beckett grabbed his shirt, spinning him. His fist connected with the man's jaw in a satisfying pop.

Drew flew backward, staggering.

But Beckett wasn't satisfied. He grabbed Drew's shirt, shoved him against a thick tree. "You wanna push someone around? Huh, punk?"

"No, Beckett!"

Drew pushed back, futilely, his eyes wide. "We were acting!"

Beckett jerked him forward, then back, the red-hot fog spreading through him. Drew's head smacked against the tree. "Not so tough now, are you?"

"Beckett, stop!" Madison pulled on his arm. "We were *rehearsing*. We were just rehearsing."

Rehearsing.

The word seeped into the mass of emotion. The fog began to clear. Beckett stilled, his hands still clenching fistfuls of shirt.

Madison shook his arm. "The play. We were rehearsing, that's all."

The play. The hot mass inside cooled. His fists released.

Drew pushed him. "Get off me."

Beckett's hands fell. He stepped back.

The play. Rehearsing. His breaths came in gulps.

The blood that had rushed through like a flash flood seemed to pool into a chilly sludge in the center of his gut.

Drew rubbed his jaw, shooting daggers at Beckett. "I should sue you for that."

Madison's hand fell from Beckett's arm. "He didn't mean . . . "

As the adrenaline petered out, something new was moving in. Something that made him wish he could puddle right into the soil. "Sorry . . ."

Madison touched his arm. "It's okay—"

Drew nailed her with a look, gave the hem of his shirt a sharp tug.

"I mean—"

"I should go." Beckett backed away, lifting his hands. "I'm sorry." He turned and strode toward the exit.

"Are you okay?" he heard Madison asking Drew. He didn't wait for an answer.

Stupid! He was a fool, rushing in like that, busting a guy's jaw. Not just any guy—Madison's date. Had he thought himself a knight in shining armor? What a joke. He was the last person to save Madison—if she'd needed saving—and she hadn't.

Did you ever think to stop and ask a question, O'Reilly?

He'd done just as he would've in his younger days, rushed in, acted on impulse. His old nature, rearing its ugly head.

And look where that had gotten him.

Chapter Twenty

Madison stepped aboard the boat, waiting for Beckett. She'd slept late after tossing in bed for hours, the night replaying in her mind like some hideous movie. By the time Drew had walked her to her door, he'd sported a puffy red bruise on his jaw. Looking at the tender flesh, she felt bad, and for so many reasons. Bad that he'd been mistaken for a bully, bad that she'd asked if he was okay so belatedly.

But she'd also felt terrible for Beckett. He'd charged into the park like an avenging angel, fists flying. To protect her. She couldn't forget the look on his face when he'd realized his mistake. The hard planes of his face softening, his eyes shuttering. It was that look, if she were honest, that kept playing in her mind.

And that only made her feel worse. Shouldn't Drew be the one drawing her sympathy? It had been the guilt that prompted the quick kiss at the door. Not the best reason for a first kiss.

She turned her head at the footsteps on the pier. Beckett approached, his face inscrutable.

She braced herself for awkwardness. "Hi there."

He stopped at the bow cleat, rubbed the back of his neck. "I don't even know what to say, Madison," he said finally.

His voice, deep and quiet, made her want to ease his conscience. "You meant well."

He untied the boat and stepped aboard. "I feel like a jerk."

"You couldn't have known. It was kind of sweet, you coming to my rescue—don't you dare tell Drew I said that."

His laugh was a mere exhale. "Don't think he'll be talking to me anytime soon."

Beckett's actions had probably cost him a boat order. But he obviously hadn't been thinking about that when he'd rushed at Drew.

"He's okay?" Beckett asked.

"He's sporting a bruise, but he didn't think anything was broken. I'm sure he didn't mean it about the lawsuit."

"Doubt I have anything he'd want anyway."

"Except maybe your right hook."

"Funny."

Madison smiled. "Just thought I'd bring a little levity to the situation."

Once they were out on the water, they hoisted the sails, the moment of awkwardness passing. Madison worked the sheets, trimming the main, adjusting the traveler.

"Okay, let's talk line bias," Beckett said, back to business. "A good start is critical, and knowing what position to take is crucial. The starting line will be slanted, with one end closer to the first windward mark. First off, whatever you do, don't be over the line when the horn blows. You'll have to sail back and cross again—hard to recover from that. Now, line bias. Which side gives you the best line for the first mark?"

"The closest end?"

"Well . . . depends."

"On the wind?"

"Exactly. Let's say you start on the north end of the line. You might be closer to the mark, but if the wind is stronger on the south end, the boats down there will be sailing with more speed. Also, you have the right-of-way on a starboard tack and have to give way if you're on a port tack."

"So it's a race-day call?"

"That's where good tactical thinking and prerace preparation come in. Most likely Evan will be out on the water early, deciding on the preferred side. But you should understand what's going on."

He ran through various possibilities, illustrating the best starting positions in each instance and why. Then they sailed both sides of the river, assessing the conditions. With the wind coming from the north side, that was the preferred start side today.

"Okay, let's do a dry run on the first mark. It's three boat lengths ahead," Beckett called. "Give me something," he reminded her as they approached it.

"Boat four on starboard tack," Madison called. "We're not crossing."

"Continue on port tack."

"Roger that. No ease on the jib."

As soon as the jib started to back, she flipped the port sheet loose and pulled in the starboard sheet.

"Nice job," he called after they rounded the imaginary mark. "Let's do it again, only a little smoother this time."

~

Cappy's Pizzeria was a hole-in-the-wall disguising the world's best pizza. Beckett took a whiff of garlic as he navigated full tables toward an open booth in the back corner. The green overhead pendants were always dim, and little light permeated the tinted windows. Probably to hide the fact that the place wasn't exactly sterile.

He slid into a red vinyl booth. TVs blared from the walls, and in the back room a rowdy game of pool was under way. Through the kitchen window he saw Cappy lumbering around, giving orders to frazzled teenagers, his bald head catching the glare from the kitchen fluorescents. A rumble of thunder sounded, barely audible over the chatter, the televised game, and the clattering of forks on plates.

Beckett pushed the menu aside and ordered drinks when the server came by. A few minutes later he saw his sister skirting the deserted salad bar—a place where few dared to eat.

Layla slid into the booth, tossing her big silver bag into the corner. She brushed the raindrops from her arms. "Sorry I'm late. It's cats and dogs out there."

He was glad he and Madison had gotten the lesson in before the storm hit. "You're not. Just ordered you a root beer."

"Perfect. Let's order the Whole Shebang. I'm starving."

"Sounds good." He was hungry himself, having worked through lunch.

"I went to see Dad this morning," Layla said a few minutes later after the server took their order. She brushed her damp hair over her slender shoulders and took a sip of her root beer.

"How's he doing?"

"You know Dad. He didn't have much to say. He's working his way through his Hemingway novels, hoping to get paroled."

Beckett started to ask when, then changed his mind. Sometimes ignorance was bliss.

"How are rehearsals going?" he asked. His sister had a bit part in the production.

"Not bad. Dottie's a good director. Kind of demanding though. It's eating up a lot of my time."

"What else do you have to do?" Beckett asked.

"Oh, I don't know. Work, volunteering, VBS . . ."

"Poor baby."

She cocked her head. "You better stop or I'm not paying."

"It's my turn anyway."

Layla's face lit up. "Oh yeah. Rats. I knew I should've ordered breadsticks."

"Too late."

"It's never too late for breadsticks."

"You'll be lucky to finish your half of the pizza, little girl."

"I can hold my own just fine, thank you." Layla tucked the menus into the holder and put the paprika shaker in the metal cubby. "Oh, meant to tell you . . . I ran into Drew Landon at the pharmacy this morning. You know, he's the guy who—"

"I know who he is," he said, his tone gruffer than he'd liked.

She hiked a brow. "Okay, then. Well, anyway, his jaw was all black and blue and puffed up. Looks awful. I hope it heals in time for opening night. A patient must've gotten hold of him or something."

Beckett looked down at the paper place mat. Straightened it. Brushed a few crumbs from the table. He took a sip of Coke, trying to ignore the heat climbing his neck.

"Beckett . . . it was a patient or something, right?"

"Or something."

Layla's mouth dropped open. "You didn't."

"It was an accident."

Layla smirked. "You accidentally clocked the guy."

He explained what happened in the park the night before, finishing with, "You could've told me Madison and Drew were lovers in the play."

She snorted. "So this was my fault?"

"I didn't say that."

She stared at him until he looked away. His sister had a way of looking into his eyes and reading his every thought. It was annoying.

"I didn't think you'd want a play-by-play," she said when she'd finished dissecting his brain. "But I have noticed them getting pretty friendly at rehearsals."

Something twisted inside. Stupid play. Bad enough the doctor was going out with her, and now all this time together practicing at being lovers . . .

"If you're going to make a move—finally—you'd better do it soon, bro."

"It's not like I haven't tried."

"Taking her sister to the banquet and breaking her heart doesn't really count."

"Low blow."

She shrugged. "I call it like I see it."

Deep down he guessed he'd thought, with them working together on this sailing thing, that if it was meant to be, it would somehow happen. He hadn't counted on Dr. Perfect showing up and sweeping her off her feet.

Layla set her hand on Beckett's arm. "I think you should go for it. I know you get hung up on the person you used to be, but you've changed, Beck. You have a lot to offer. I mean, I know I'm just your sister, but you're a good man. You're loyal and fun. You can even be charming when you decide to smile. And I've heard other women say you're nice-looking." She put up her hands and settled back in the booth. "I don't see it, but whatever."

He gave a wry smile. He wasn't sure his sister was right about any of it, but she didn't have all the facts. He'd never told her about his part in Michael's death. There was only one person who knew, and he was in jail.

Layla squeezed his arm. "Seriously, it's now or never. I mean, you know I think you're tops, but a *doctor*, Beck. In single-girl world that carries a lot of weight. And he seems like a nice guy too. I won't mention how I feel about his dreamy good looks because that would just be mean."

He narrowed his eyes. "Yes, it would."

Layla took a sip of her soda. "So how did Madison react last night when you pummeled her date?"

"It was one swing."

Layla made a face. "Impressive. So did she get mad at you and fawn all over her fallen hero or what?"

He thought back, skimming the scene in his mind, something he'd avoided all day. "No, she just, I don't know. She wasn't mad exactly. And she was pretty cool about it this morning."

"You talked to her? Good job." Layla patted his hand as if he were a child.

"We had a sailing lesson."

"Oh. Well, at least she's not mad."

"She even joked about it a little."

Layla smiled. "I like this girl."

"She said it was sweet that I came to her rescue, or something like that."

Layla pressed her hand to her heart, smiling. "Awww. She felt protected."

"From her innocent date."

"Still. I'm sure she didn't approve of you, you know, beating up her date and all, but a woman does love a protective man."

"Sounds old-fashioned."

"Not old-fashioned, timeless. Trust me. So pray about it, okay? 'Cause I think she'd make a great sister-in-law."

"You're jumping the gun, little girl." But he couldn't deny the tiny thrill that coursed through him at the thought.

The server slid a piping hot pie onto the table. "Enjoy!" she said before sashaying away.

Beckett served Layla the first slice, then took one of his own, the fragrant smell of garlic and oregano teasing his nose.

"So you'll pray about it?" Layla asked again after he said grace.

"You're a pest."

"That's not an answer." She took a big bite from the end of a slice, wiping the tomato sauce that dribbled down her chin.

"Fine. I'll pray about it."

She shrugged. "All I'm asking."

Chapter Twenty-One

Play rehearsal was canceled on Monday due to an electrical problem, and Madison found herself with a rare free night. The long night stretched ahead like a deserted country lane. Instead of relishing an evening of relaxation, she found herself weighing options to occupy her night and finally settled on a jog. Not wanting to fight with the leash, she left Lulu at home, feeling a tug of guilt as she strode down her drive. The evening air was cool, a nice breeze blowing in off the river. The sun dipped low in the sky.

Ever since Jade had left, a night at home meant quiet. Quiet led to thinking, and thinking led to feelings. Feelings she was tired of shoving down. Even sleep was no escape. Once or twice a week the nightmare intruded, waking her in a cold sweat. Then she'd lie there, unable to shake the awful panic.

Just two more weeks, Madison. Then the nightmares will be gone. She'd win the regatta, achieve Michael's dream, and she'd finally have peace, finally move on with her life. Finally replace the bad dream with a good one.

Even so, the dark feelings pressed heavily on her. They'd been coming more often lately, she realized, despite her busy schedule. Maybe because of the upcoming race. It was making her think of Michael more. She just needed to stay busy and on task. When she won, the rest would take care of itself.

She picked up her pace, wanting to clear her mind. She wished she could fast-forward to race day. She was eager to put it behind her. She ran faster, as if she could speed time along as easily. Her feet pounded the pavement in rhythmic thumps, her breaths came more quickly, making her lungs burn.

A few minutes later she was ripping through Riverside Park. Halfway through, she saw Beckett on the concrete basketball court. He dribbled in for an easy layup, catching the ball after it swished through the hoop.

As he turned with the ball, he spotted her. Madison slowed and walked toward him, huffing. He met her at the edge of the court.

"Hey there . . . just out for a jog." Duh. She winced.

"I thought you were being chased by the hounds of hell for a minute. That's quite a pace you set."

She shrugged. "Working on your game?"

"Not really. Just clearing the cobwebs." He dribbled the ball three times, then held it. "How's Drew?"

She frowned, then realized Beckett was talking about his jaw. "He's fine. Just fine." Several had commented on his bruise at church, and Madison had squirmed as he'd sidestepped the question.

"I should let you get back to your run," he said. "Target heart rate and all that."

She glanced in the direction she'd been headed, realizing the jog was doing nothing to clear her mind or change her emotional state. The realization made her shoulders slump and she pressed her heels into the concrete. Sometimes she wished she could run away from herself.

"You okay?"

She looked at him, ready with an easy answer, and found herself falling headlong into his dark eyes. The easy answer dissolved from the tip of her tongue.

"No." It was the most honest thing she'd said all week.

His face showed no surprise as he held her gaze for a long minute. "Come on. I want to take you somewhere."

He took a few steps backward, and she followed, surprised when he passed the park's walkway. He headed toward the wooded hillside behind the court, turning to make sure she followed. Their feet swished through the overgrown grass, then they started up a trail.

"Where we going?" she asked when they were well into the shadowed woods.

"You'll see."

The pace was easy after her hard run, and the cooler air felt good. She breathed in the loamy fragrance as they wound their way up the hill. Brittle leaves crunched and twigs snapped under the weight of their feet. Overhead, a leafy canopy blocked out the last of the day's light. A chickadee began a string of clear, two-note whistles.

It was a beautiful property. "Who owns this?"

He held a branch for her. "It's part of the state park."

"Lulu would love it up here."

"So does Rigsby, but he comes back covered in burrs."

The terrain grew rockier as they climbed. They crossed over a dry creek bed and a fallen tree. Awhile later Madison saw a patch of light ahead and knew they were nearly to the peak. When they stepped from the woods, Beckett began climbing a tower of boulders.

She followed, taking his hand when her shorter legs made the next step difficult.

Her fingertips gripped a ledge as she pulled herself up. "You're trying to break my leg so I'll have to forfeit the race."

"You're on to me."

A few more reaches and they came to the top. A flat rock the size of a shed roof jutted out over the other side of the hill.

She meandered to the ledge, but the steep drop into a pine-filled canyon made her retreat. Across the way, the sun hung low on the horizon, streaking the sky with vibrant pinks and purples. Across the valley she spied the old white chapel and the nearby site of the spring for which the town was named. They were on top of the world.

She placed her hands on her hips, let out a breath, and stared in awe at the beautiful scene. "How did I not know this was here?"

He sank down onto the rock, a good distance from the edge, facing the sunset. "Pretty nice, huh?"

The perfect spot for a romantic picnic. She'd bet Beckett had brought his share of women here. Maybe all the girls he'd dated in high school.

She sank down beside him. The rock, having soaked in the heat of the day, warmed the backs of her legs. "Your own little Inspiration Point?"

"Nah, like to keep the place to myself."

He was sharing it with her though. She cocked a brow at the realization.

He rubbed his jaw, looked away. His face had taken on a golden glow under the sunset, softening his rugged features, making him appear almost vulnerable.

He seemed content in the quiet. Madison breathed in the scent of pine, decaying leaves, and a hint of Beckett's spicy cologne. She closed her eyes and listened as a bird tweeted from somewhere nearby. The breeze rustled the leaves and caressed the bare skin on her arms and legs.

"How often do you come up here?"

He settled back on his elbows, the position straining the material of his T-shirt. "Sometimes I do my Bible study up here. Sometimes when I need to do some heavy-duty thinking—or praying."

"Is that what you think I need?"

"Does it matter what I think?"

She glanced at him. His own eyes were closed, as if soaking up nature. Or praying.

She wished she could unload her burden. Tell him everything she felt about Michael. How much she missed him. How much she longed to be free of him, and how guilty she felt about that. Yet how desperate—how utterly desperate she was for peace. For sleep.

He would listen, she knew that. And he wouldn't judge her. He was all too familiar with being judged.

She suddenly remembered that night they'd danced her sophomore year, how he'd told her he hadn't stolen the class ring, as if what she thought actually mattered to him. It was a small moment in light of all life had brought since, but it had seemed significant at the time.

Especially the kiss. It had become the kiss she'd compared every one after it to—the one that made all others pale in comparison.

She gave a rueful smile. Pretty lame, considering Beckett didn't even remember it.

"When I sit up here," he said, his eyes open now, "I'm just blown away that God even notices us, you know?"

She looked at the hills and valleys, at the river snaking through them, the hundreds of rooftops of Chapel Springs far below, sheltering families just like hers.

Did God really notice them? Each and every one of them? Did He notice her? She found it hard to believe. It was a big thing, being noticed. Part of what Jade struggled with, she'd always thought. It was hard finding a spot in the big world, hard even in a big family. There'd been plenty of times she'd felt a little lost in the chaotic shuffle of the McKinley household. But she wouldn't have traded her large family for the world. She wondered if Jade felt the same.

"Some people spend their whole lives trying to be noticed," she said.

She felt his eyes on her for a moment before he spoke. "You?"

She lay back against the rock, cupping her head in her palms. "Sometimes."

The sun was sinking lower in the sky, the streaks of pink growing more vibrant.

"I noticed you a long time ago."

His words made her heart thump against the rock, even as she recognized the irony. Beckett may have noticed her briefly, but he'd forgotten her quickly enough.

"No, you didn't," she said. "Not really."

The kind of noticing she meant entailed more than a passing glance. It meant being seen. Being remembered. People wanted significance. She did, Jade did, everyone did.

"You were wearing a white skirt that twirled around your knees . . . and a blue sweater with tiny butterflies around the collar."

She drew in a long, quiet breath as she turned. He remembered what she'd worn to the dance all those years ago?

He returned her gaze. There was something in his eyes she couldn't define, though she desperately wanted to.

"You remember?" Her voice was so quiet, she wasn't sure he'd heard.

"I remember everything about you."

It seemed impossible. He'd been so busy getting into trouble and going out with other girls. Other than that one kiss, he'd never so much as hinted at any interest.

And then, recently, there was Jade.

"You wrote those notes to my sister . . ."

He rolled to his side, shifting his weight to one elbow. "What notes?"

She'd read them herself. Had felt the sting of jealousy when she'd realized who they were from. The same sting of jealousy she'd felt when Beckett had shown up at their door the night of the Spring Sowers Banquet.

"I didn't write any notes to your sister."

Could it be true? She'd just assumed, when he'd shown up at the door in a suit coat, with a fistful of flowers for Jade . . .

Or . . . *had* he come for Jade?

She sucked in a breath, and everything inside froze. Her skin went hot as her eyes locked on his. She'd been in the bedroom changing clothes when he'd arrived. Jade had answered the door, and in light of the recent anonymous notes . . .

"You came for me," she said. Another dot connected. "That's why Jade was so upset that night."

His lips parted and closed again. But he didn't have to say anything. She saw the truth in the softening of his eyes. In the brief flicker of unease.

"Why didn't you tell me?"

He brushed a stray hair from her face, and all thought ceased.

"I was afraid," he said.

"Why?" she whispered.

Their gazes tangled and melded. She forgot the question, forgot everything but the desire reflected in the shadowed pools of his eyes.

He leaned forward and brushed her lips. Something unfurled slowly inside at his touch. Something warm and delicious, intoxicating.

He paused for the barest moment, his lips a breath away. She sensed a decision was being made, and her heart stopped, afraid he'd pull away. Or worse, apologize.

But he closed the gap, and her heart beat again, harder, faster.

"Maddy," he whispered against her lips.

She cradled the back of his neck, and he deepened the kiss, drawing a sigh from the deepest part of her.

She'd wondered, over the years, if time had embellished the kiss. Or if adolescence had inflated the impact of his touch.

But no.

No.

It was just as she remembered. As if somehow, in this great big world, he was her perfect fit. The one who could make her feel like she really was on top of the world.

His hand burned through the material of her T-shirt as his lips worked their magic. How had she lived all these years without this? How had she worked so closely with him this summer without reclaiming this thing that felt like hers alone?

His jaw was pleasantly rough under the tender flesh of her palm, but she wanted more. She wove her fingers through his hair, down his neck, searched the planes of his shoulders, staking claim.

A moment later he ended the kiss. Their breaths came in shallow puffs. Her eyes clung to his as he pulled away, but he was so hard to read.

"Mercy, woman."

It wasn't just her. A smile tugged her lips as he tucked her hair behind her ear. He caught her hand and kissed her knuckles.

"You're right about this place," she said. "I feel better already."

He smiled.

She suddenly thought of Drew and the sympathy kiss she'd given him Friday. Just as quickly, she pushed the thought away, unwilling to tarnish the moment. The exit of adrenaline had left her pleasantly languid.

Beckett's eyes left hers, scoping out the sky, and he squeezed her hand. "It's getting dark."

The sun had sunk below the horizon, leaving the once-vibrant clouds ashen blue. Twilight had dropped its curtain on the final act.

He gave her a hand up, and she followed him across the gentle slope of the rock. Descending the rock tower was slower than the ascent, and twice he caught her at the waist and lifted her down. Each time she braced her hands against his shoulders and hoped there'd be another kiss, and soon.

Chapter Twenty-Two

Darkness was falling fast, the trail becoming difficult to follow in the fading light. Beckett slowed the pace to accommodate, his thoughts rehashing the previous hour. He hadn't meant to kiss Madison. Had only taken her up the hill to soothe the sadness in her eyes.

But then he'd said too much and she'd figured it out, that night with Jade. He hadn't known how she'd respond, but then that look came into her eyes . . . There'd been no stopping things after that. The boulder had been pushed down the hill, and there was only one place for it to go.

He wasn't sorry either. How could he be? He tightened his hand on hers as he held back a low-hanging branch for her. Almost back now, and good thing, because he could barely see the ground.

Moments later, when they stepped from the woods, Beckett offered her a ride home. In the quiet of the cab, he wondered what she was thinking. Had she come back down to earth?

Was she thinking about Drew Landon? Beckett was. He was wondering if the doctor had kissed her. If she'd responded the same way to him. And he was wondering other things too, like if she regretted Beckett's kiss.

She was still Madison McKinley after all, and he was Beckett O'Reilly, son of the town drunk and worse things she wasn't aware of.

He pushed the thought away. He wasn't going to think about that, about any of it. If he could be fortunate enough to hold Madison in his arms, he wasn't going to regret or second-guess it. He was going to enjoy it.

When they arrived at her house, he walked her to the door. Darkness had fallen completely, and the cicadas had begun their nightly chorus. She opened the front door, flipping on the porch light, and Lulu bounded out like Madison had been gone a year, making them laugh.

"Go potty," Madison told her, and the collie trotted down the porch steps and into the yard.

Madison pocketed her keys, crossed her arms. Then uncrossed them and leaned against the screen door. The look on her face reminded him of their hours in the creek, when her fear had made her vulnerable. She was a strong woman. He loved her for that.

Love?

The word streaked across the path of his thoughts like lightning across a stormy sky. He watched her now, watching Lulu, watching a moth flutter under the porch light, looking anywhere but at him, and sudden warmth flooded through him, making his knees weak.

Yes, he loved her.

He'd tried not to. But now here he was. On her porch, watching her watching a moth, and realizing he was the moth and she the light. It would always be this way.

A certainty surged through him, strengthening him. He placed his palm against the door above her shoulder.

Flecks of gold danced in her wide brown eyes as they met his. "You're quiet," he said.

A lock of hair had fallen over her delicate brows, and he ached to brush it back. Even more, he ached to feel her lips on his again, to feel her respond so unabashedly.

"Thoughtful," she corrected.

He wasn't sure of the difference and didn't much care. He drew in a breath of her—fresh air and honeysuckle. He was noticing her perfect little nose, the way it tapered down to her sweet, rosy lips. And suddenly he wanted to taste them again more than he could say.

"I'm going to kiss you again."

She returned his gaze. "I'm going to let you."

He leaned in and collected on the promise. Her lips were soft as a butterfly's wings and warm as the heat flooding his limbs. She placed her hand on his shoulder, and he pulled her closer, loving the way she fit against him. The way she felt so small and delicate in his arms. He wondered if she could feel his rapid pulse.

A car turned into the drive next door, gravel crunching. The headlights swooped across the porch.

He pulled back, and a moment later the engine shut off. A car door slammed shut, then another and another. Voices carried across the yard, kids, their words indistinguishable.

"The Waverlys," she said. Her hand slipped down to his chest.

"They have bad timing."

Her lips twitched. "Yeah."

"Hi, Miss McKinley!" A kid of about five or six waved, and Lulu went to collect some attention.

"Hello, Oliver," Madison said.

Beckett took pride in the breathless quality of her voice.

"I lost a tooth," the boy said.

"Be sure and put it under your pillow."

"Come along, Oliver," his mom said. "Sorry!" She gave

Madison and Beckett a droll grin and ushered the kids up the porch steps.

A baby cried out, a light came on, and Beckett heard the fumbling of the family as they funneled into the house.

Lulu trotted up Madison's porch and wedged between them, her backside wagging. Madison set her hand on the dog's head.

Beckett stepped back, hating the loss of her touch. "I should go. We both have early mornings."

"Thanks for showing me your hideaway."

"You're welcome back anytime."

"I might take you up on that."

He hadn't even left, and he couldn't wait to see her again. "Come over tomorrow night."

"I have rehearsal."

"Afterward. A late supper. I'll order pizza."

He hadn't realized he was holding his breath until her answer slipped through her lips. "All right."

He drove home in a daze. He could hardly remember what day it was, and couldn't bring himself to care. He'd held Madison McKinley in his arms, and it had felt right.

Right? Merciful heavens, it had felt perfect. He could never go back to dating Cara Meyers or Jessie Brooks or any other woman again—not that there was anything wrong with them. It's just—he was . . .

In love, O'Reilly?

Oh yeah. Totally and thoroughly. And though the realization loosened a thread of trepidation, it was overwhelmed by all the good stuff bursting open inside. Joy and satisfaction and bliss. Bliss, a good word for it. He was downright heady at Madison's response.

He pulled into his drive and got out. He couldn't wait to see her again. He didn't care how late rehearsals lasted or how much sleep he missed. She was like oxygen to him.

He didn't notice the house lights were on until he was on the stoop. The faint sound of the TV filtered through the window-panes. He never left lights on, and he hadn't turned on the TV after work.

Beckett twisted the doorknob and Rigsby barreled into his legs, but he didn't look at the dog. All he saw was the back of the plaid chair, the head of thinning gray hair, and the three amber bottles on the floor at his side.

All the good feelings inside settled into a pool of sludge as the chair swiveled around, knocking over the bottles in a series of pings.

"'Bout time you got home."

Beckett shut the door, a weight pressing hard on his shoulders. "Hi, Dad."

Chapter Twenty-Three

MADISON CARRIED THE LAST CHART TO THE FRONT DESK and jotted a note about the aggressive cocker spaniel. The dog didn't seem to like anyone except her mommy. A problem, with seven-month-old twins crawling around her house. The nearest trainer was quite a drive, but Madison promised to get back to the dog's owner with a list of recommended books.

"Okay, what gives?" Cassidy said.

Madison continued writing. "What do you mean?"

"Come on. I'm wearing a new shade of lipstick—and it's pretty hot, if I do say so myself—I spilled iced latte on your office rug, my hair has gotten bigger with every moment of this humid day, and you haven't noticed any of it."

"There's a stain on my Persian rug?"

Cassidy cocked her head, crossing her arms.

So she'd been a little distracted. Madison had been on auto-pilot today, treating infections and allergies, giving vaccines and potty training tips. She'd been up half the night, wondering if Beckett would call, anticipating tonight. It felt like high school all over again.

Cassidy cleared her throat. All that was missing was the tapping foot.

Her lipstick *was* nice, a shade of rose that set off her beautiful skin. Madison's gaze traveled up several inches to the hair. "Oh my goodness."

Cassidy scowled. "Don't change the subject. What's going on with you today?"

Madison caught her lip between her teeth. In the grand scheme of things, she was surprised she'd made it all day.

"He kissed me, all right?"

Cassidy smiled coyly. "Well, it's about time . . ."

"Um, not Drew. Beckett."

Cassidy's brows popped. "Oh!"

"Yeah. Oh."

Cassidy propped her chin on her palm. "Hmmm. Not entirely unexpected."

"It was unexpected to me."

"Well, you're somewhat oblivious in that department."

"Hey."

Cassidy lifted her shoulders. "Just saying. So, do I get any details or are you going to keep it all to yourself?"

Madison smiled. "All to myself."

"Be that way. Just remember, when you're a couple years out in a stagnant relationship, see if I offer you a little vicarious romance."

Madison thought Cassidy and Stew were great together. "Stagnant?"

Cassidy waved her away. "Bad choice of words. So what are you going to do about Drew? He really likes you."

Madison winced. They'd only gone out a few times, but they'd seen a lot of each other because of rehearsals.

"It was only one kiss," Madison said. "And Drew and I are hardly exclusive . . ."

"But . . ."

Cassidy could see right through her. "But I really like Beckett."

Regardless of what came next, her heart was too full of Beckett to date anyone else. It was frightful how many times she'd reviewed not only his kiss, but his words.

"Remember that dance back in high school—when Beckett kissed me?"

"Of course."

She gave Cassidy a meaningful look. "He remembers what I was wearing."

Cassidy sighed, a dreamy smile curving her lips. "No wonder you've been walking around in a fog all day."

"Yeah."

~

Rehearsal was rough that night. Madison forgot her lines twice, and Drew had to cue her. She found it difficult to look him in the eyes, play the part of a besotted woman when she'd been in someone else's arms the night before.

As eager as she was to get to Beckett's house, she'd asked Drew for a private word after rehearsal and waited now by his white Saab in the empty parking lot. Dottie had kept him after to review the new blocking. Rehearsals were about to become very awkward, but she didn't feel right about proceeding with Beckett until the conversation was had.

When Drew came out, approaching with that confident stride of his, she stirred up a smile. "Congratulations. You made it through the whole night without being paged."

"Wonders never cease." As he neared, she saw guardedness in the rigid line of his shoulders, in the way his smile didn't quite reach his eyes.

She'd tried to act normal, but he was discerning. The lone parking light hummed above them and cut harsh shadows across his face.

"Thanks for sticking around a few minutes." She fought for the right words. She hated this. Maybe if they sat down, had a conversation. "Want to sit in my car or something?" she asked.

His lips turned up, not quite a smile. "Just break my heart right here, Madison."

She winced. "Is it that obvious?"

"You're not great at hiding your feelings."

"I'm sorry. It's not you—"

"—It's me." He touched her arm, softening his response. "Is there someone else?"

There was no point in lying. "Yeah. We haven't gone out yet or anything, but . . ." She shrugged, hoping he wouldn't ask who. There was no delicate way to admit it was the guy who'd decked him.

Drew looked across the empty parking lot toward the river. The humid day had given way to a mild evening. Above, the stars were out in force, creating a twinkling canvas.

"It's okay, I get it." He looked back at her and seemed to smile with effort. "If things don't work out with this other guy, give me a call. You're a nice girl, Madison."

And he was a classy guy. Just not the right one for her. "You're very gracious."

He gave her a hug and a parting wave, then she made her way to her car, relieved to have that over.

She forced the conversation behind her and shifted her thoughts to Beckett on the short ride to his house.

A few minutes later the gravel popped under her tires as she pulled into his drive. His white bungalow sported black peeling shutters, a generous picture window, and a crooked stoop. There was a patch of well-groomed lawn and bushes edging the front of the house. But the best feature of the property was the thick oak tree, perfect for climbing with low, thick branches that forked out in all directions. She'd bet he'd spent a fair share of his childhood up there.

He answered the door wearing a pair of faded jeans and a time-softened black T-shirt. Rigsby wiggled between them, nudging her hand until she gave him his due.

"Sorry I'm late."

He kissed her hand, then drew her into the kitchen. "Just in time. Pizza just got here."

The scent of garlic and oregano filled the small space. The box sat on an old drop-leaf table set to accommodate two. Standard salt and pepper shakers served as the centerpiece.

"Mmm. Cappy's."

The fridge door bumped the table when he opened it. "Coke? Sprite? Water?"

"Water would be great." She squeezed past him and served up the pizza on the plates he'd laid out.

"I thought we'd eat in the living room. More room in there."

"Sounds great."

The living room glowed under the light of two lamps. An old Foreigner song played from a radio under the TV.

She followed him to the sofa, taking the center. He pulled a scarred coffee table closer, and she set down her water. As she settled back in the seat, he took her hand and said grace.

She was used to grace at the McKinley house, but not on a

date. As his words rumbled in her ear, she decided she liked it. And she especially liked it when he squeezed her hand and smiled afterward.

She caught him up on rehearsals, then told him about last year's play in which they'd raised a record amount of money for the animal shelter. He told her about finding Rigsby there as a pup. The dog had taken a playful bow when Beckett had walked into the room, his rump sticking in the air, tail wagging. Beckett had been sold at first sight.

Madison shared how her heart had broken each month when the shelter put out its flyer of available animals and how she'd decided to start bringing them as part of her nursing home visits.

When "Desperado" came on the radio, they talked about their favorite classic songs and discovered they both listened to the same oldies station.

Then the conversation turned to church. "So I've been wondering . . . how exactly did you go from Bad Boy Beckett into the paragon of virtue you are today?"

"First of all, paragon of virtue—no. But the summer I was twenty was a turning point. I'd made some . . . bad choices. One night a friend and I were trying to hotwire a car that had been sitting at the Gas 'n Go for days. The cops showed up and I took off. I'd already been in a lot of trouble and knew this would put me in jail. It was Rick's first offense. He'd get off easy—that's what I told myself.

"I ran all the way home, but I didn't go in. I knew my grandpa would see right through me. I ran straight to the shed and sat there in the dark, feeling like a pig. I mean, I'd done bad things before, but I thought I was basically a good person. Not the kind who'd desert a friend like that. I saw myself the way I really was, and it wasn't pretty."

He paused then. The pizza was long gone, their plates on the coffee table. She hardly remembered finishing it.

"What happened next?" she asked.

He shrugged. "I started remembering all those Sunday school lessons I'd sat through, all those conversations with my grandpa, and it suddenly made sense. That faith wasn't something I could just read about and understand. Leaving my friend behind was a lightbulb moment. I knew I was a sinner, that I needed God."

Michael had had a similar story, minus the felony. He'd shared it with her only once, but he'd been so excited. She'd never forget that fervent look in his eyes. His knowing he'd done something important. A part of her had been jealous. Even now, she envied Beckett. For all the rotten circumstances in his family life, he'd still managed to find peace.

"What happened after that?" she asked. "Did your friend go to jail?"

"He didn't—I did."

"You turned yourself in?" She hadn't heard about Beckett going to jail. It would've been sometime after Michael died though, and the world had disappeared for a while.

"It was the right thing. I still keep in touch with Rick. He's married now and living in Tennessee. That was the beginning and end of his career as a car thief."

A car rumbled outside, its headlights cutting through the room. Beckett jumped up and looked out the window, tension obvious in his hurried movements.

He hit the window frame with his open palm.

"What's wrong?"

"It's my dad. I told him to stay out until eleven."

"He's back?"

"As of last night." Somehow that one had escaped her ears today, probably because she'd had her head in the clouds.

A car door slammed.

"Great," Beckett said a few seconds later. He stepped to the front door.

Madison wondered if she should leave. But before she decided, his dad shuffled through the door. He stumbled over Rigsby, muttering a curse word Madison hadn't heard in a while.

Beckett caught his arm. The hard muscles of his jaw twitched. "Let's go, Dad." Beckett pulled him toward a hall.

Mr. O'Reilly spotted Madison. "Heeeyyyyy . . ."

She nodded. "Mr. O'Reilly. Nice to see you." She didn't know if he'd remember her, even sober. "I'm Madison."

"A 'Kinley girl."

"That's right."

"Live in that big ol' fanshy house up on the hill . . ."

"That's enough, Dad." He tugged his dad's arm.

Rigsby got underfoot, nearly tripping Mr. O'Reilly again.

"Move!" Beckett told the dog.

Rigsby lowered his head and trotted to Madison, sitting at her feet. She scratched behind the dog's ears, trying to ignore the noises from down the hall. Mr. O'Reilly's slurred words, Beckett's short tone.

~

Beckett tossed his dad's shoes in the corner, clamping his teeth down on the words he wanted to say. Words that would be forgotten by morning anyway. He glanced at his dad, eyes closed, a bit of drool at the corner of his mouth, and wanted to shake the man. Instead he shut off the light and closed the door, whispered a prayer he'd stay put until Madison was gone.

He entered the living room and found Madison perched hesitantly on the couch. She looked at him with wide, unsure eyes, and he realized the scene she'd witnessed, so familiar to him, was completely foreign to her.

His face burned as he stopped by the recliner. "Sorry about that."

She waved his apology away. "No, it's fine."

It wasn't fine. It wasn't fine at all. He'd known she'd get a glimpse of his world eventually, but he hadn't wanted it to be so soon.

She stood, hitching her purse on her shoulder. "I should go anyway. It's getting late."

He was torn between wanting relief from the tension and wanting to be with her. But the easy camaraderie was gone, and there was no saving this night.

"I'm sorry," he said again at the door when she turned.

She reached up and set her hand on his cheek, and he read the pity in her eyes before she kissed him.

There was no voice mail at home the next night, and Madison chided herself for being one of those women. She considered calling Beckett herself, but it had only been one day, and they were busy people. The awkwardness of the night before had lingered in her mind all day. She felt bad for Beckett. Was that what he'd dealt with his whole childhood?

She was settling in bed with Lulu and her favorite trade journal when the phone rang. She smiled when she saw Beckett's name on the screen.

"Is it too late?" The low timbre of his voice was heaven in her ear.

"Not at all. Just settling in with a copy of *JAVMA*."

"Come again?"

"*Journal of the American Veterinary Medical Association*. Fascinating reading, I assure you."

"Sounds like the perfect sedative."

"You aren't curious about the risk factors for urate uroliths in cats?"

"What does that even mean?"

"If you've lived this long without knowing, you probably don't need to know." She snuggled down deeper into her pillow, getting comfy, relieved the tension from the night before had evaporated.

"Especially since I don't have a cat. How was your day?"

"Busy. We were booked, then I had rehearsal. I just got home not long ago. Hardly time to breathe. How was yours?"

"Long. I missed you."

Her gut tightened at his honesty. Something warm and pleasant set up camp inside, put a goofy smile on her face.

"That so?"

"You sound awful pleased with yourself."

"It's nice to be missed." And there would be plenty of opportunity for that. Saturday felt like forever away. "What did you do tonight?"

"Went to see Grandpa."

"How's he doing?"

"He recognized me, for a while anyway."

"That's great. Those moments must be precious. Maybe they'll come out with a better med soon. Something to slow things down more."

"At least he's at peace with God. That's a comfort. Can't imagine losing someone to Alzheimer's, not knowing that. Knowing every lucid moment may be his last chance."

She thought of Michael, the last moment she'd had with him. If she'd known it would be her last, she would've done things differently. She'd hardly looked up from her book when he'd said he was going for a swim at Turner's Bend.

She was grateful when Beckett shifted the topic to sailing. When they exhausted that subject, there was a comfortable pause. It was getting late, but she wasn't ready to hang up yet.

"When can I see you again?" he asked.

She loved his directness, and she especially loved that he was eager to see her.

"I have rehearsals Thursday and Friday, and Dottie warned us they'd run late. I'm free tomorrow though."

"I have Bible study." He sighed. "So, guess not until Saturday, then."

They had a few minutes of quiet conversation before calling it a night. Madison turned on the TV and settled back into a happy cocoon of contentment.

Chapter Twenty-Four

Madison woke on Saturday to wind that made the windows rattle. Lulu stirred at her feet and laid her head on Madison's leg. Morning light filtered through the gauzy curtains, casting a golden hue over her quilt.

PJ had spent the night the weekend before, a final girls' night before she returned to college. They'd watched two movies and shared a tub of butter pecan, staying up half the night. Madison missed her already, even more so since both sisters were gone. PJ had promised to come home the last weekend in August for the regatta and the first weekend in September for Madison's birthday.

The phone rang, and she knew who it was before checking her caller ID.

"Hi there." She sat up in bed, smoothing her hair as if Beckett could see her.

"Have you stepped outside?"

"No, but I can hear the wind from here. The weather seems to be conspiring against me."

"It's supposed to be windy tomorrow too."

Lulu jumped to the floor, poking her nose between the slit in the curtains as if ascertaining the weather for herself.

"We're running out of time. The regatta's next week, and I still have so much to learn."

"Maybe we can squeeze in a lesson one evening next week."

"I have rehearsals Monday, Tuesday, and Thursday. Do you have Bible study Wednesday?"

"Yeah. How about Friday?"

"Evan and I are running through the course." It would be their last chance before the regatta.

"Good idea. We could meet before work Thursday morning. Get your boat in the water and do some practice runs."

He'd started the motor the last time he'd been over and said it sounded good. "Sounds good. You sure we can't chance it today?"

"In this wind? No."

"You'd go out if it were just you."

"Well, it's not, so just put it out of your pretty head. Don't worry, I'll make sure you're ready."

Though she was disappointed, his concern for her safety pleased her.

"How's the boat looking?" he asked.

"Good. Ryan and PJ helped me prime and paint. That method you showed me worked great. It almost looks like it was sprayed. And Mom helped me clean out the cabin—took most of last Sunday."

"Color turn out the way you wanted?"

"Perfect. Midnight blue. PJ painted the name in white script. She's good at that stuff."

There was a moment's silence. She wasn't ready to hang up—she'd been hoping he'd ask to spend the day with her.

"Well," he said, "I should get going. I have motors to repair by this afternoon."

She'd forgotten he worked on Saturdays when his boss wasn't letting him off for her lessons. Still, maybe he'd ask her out tonight. Maybe they could go for a bike ride or grab a pizza at Cappy's.

"So, Thursday morning, six o'clock?" he asked. "I'll bring my trailer, and we'll put her in the water."

She swallowed the lump of disappointment. "Sure, see you then."

After she hung up, she tugged the quilt to her chin and reached out to pet Lulu. "Well, girl. I guess it's just you and me today."

Beckett hung up the phone and went back to the Mercury outboard, feeling irritable. He wanted to see Madison today, had wanted to ask her out. If it were a week ago, he could've.

But everything was different now with his dad home. When Beckett had left this morning, he'd been reading *The Old Man and the Sea* and nursing his first bottle for the day. But Beckett knew how that went. By tonight Dad would want to hit his favorite tavern, and Beckett was going to do everything he could to keep that from happening. Or if he couldn't stop it, then he'd insist on driving his dad home.

He'd have to settle for a phone call to Madison—if she didn't have plans. His gut twisted at the thought of her going out with Drew Landon. He'd meant to ask about the doctor, but everything had flown from his mind the minute he'd heard her sleepy greeting.

When four o'clock rolled around, he locked up the building

and headed home. As he pulled into the drive, he spotted his dad working on his old red Mazda.

A savory scent floated in the air, making Beckett's mouth water. "You're smoking brisket."

"Been craving it for months. Should be ready around five."

"Sounds great." Beckett nodded toward the car. "What's wrong with it?"

"Mice chewed up the wires while I was away."

"Need help?"

Dad took a long swig of his beer. "I'm about done."

They had to have the conversation. It had never worked before, but he had to keep trying. Maybe this last stint in jail was enough.

Dad lowered the hood and started the car. It turned over easy. His dad was the best mechanic around, had taught Beckett everything he knew.

He followed Dad into the backyard where he checked the brisket. Beckett settled on the rickety picnic table. He wished he could avoid the conversation. For a moment he envied Layla, who'd had the freedom to get her own place. But Grandpa had signed the house over to Beckett before he'd gone to the nursing home. If he hadn't, it would've gone to pot by now.

Dad closed the smoker and leaned against the table, cradling the amber bottle. He hadn't shaved since his return, but he'd had his salt-and-pepper hair clipped at some point. Fine lines had become deep crevices over the past year, and the jail diet had left his cheeks gaunt. It was hard to believe, looking at him now, but he used to be a nice-looking man.

"When do you start back to work?" Beckett asked, deciding to ease into the conversation.

"Hah! Harvey won't have me back, already talked to him." He cursed. "I'm the best mechanic they've got and he knows it."

Never mind that he was away for months on end or that he didn't always show up at work in the best of condition.

"Dad, we need to talk."

Dad pushed off the table. "Not this again. Why don't you just tape the lecture, and I'll play it every so often."

"Dad. You have a problem."

He threw up his hands, the bottle sparkling in the late afternoon sun. "I shouldn't have driven drunk, I know that. I already served my time—are you going to punish me too?"

"You're an alcoholic."

He laughed, shook his head. "You just don't give up, do you? If I was an alcoholic, I couldn't have gone months without a drink. Did I get the shakes? Did I have sweats or hallucinations? No, I didn't. I did just fine. I don't need to drink, I *like* to drink. There's a difference."

"Just because you don't have withdrawal doesn't necessarily mean—"

"If I was an alchy I'd know it. I couldn't hold down a job or raise a family."

Beckett bit back the retort that balanced on his tongue. After Mom left, Beckett and Layla had raised themselves, with Grandpa's help, while Dad tried to drink away his pain. He was still trying to drink away the pain.

"We can get you help, Dad. It's not too late to make a life for yourself. You could open that barbecue joint like you always wanted. You make the best brisket and ribs I've ever tasted. It would go over big with the locals, with the tourists. But first you have to get sober."

Dad smirked. "You have a bunch of money sitting around someplace I don't know about?"

"We'd need a business plan and a bank loan. I'll help any way I can."

"I'm too old for that."

"You're barely in your fifties. You have lots of life ahead of you. But you have to get the drinking under con—"

"Ahhh! Enough, Beckett!" Dad threw up his hands and walked away. He entered the back door, and the screen door slapped shut behind him.

CHAPTER TWENTY-FIVE

MADISON STARED AT THE NUMBERS ON THE EXCEL SHEET until they blurred together. She reviewed her day, then her mind drifted to the phone conversation with Beckett the night before. It sounded like his week had been as hectic as hers. She hoped he'd call tonight after Bible study.

She thought of the boat sitting in her driveway. Every time she came and went, it beckoned. She was eager to get it on the water and see what it could do.

She frowned at the work on her desk, then began clearing it away as an idea formed. She pulled out her cell phone and dialed.

"You busy?" she asked when her brother answered.

Forty-five minutes later she was sitting in the boat, guiding Ryan as he backed the trailer down the ramp across from Riverside Park.

"Straight back." She hung on to the side of the boat as the trailer tires went down the ramp and into the river. "You got it."

This was much better than sitting at her desk. She wasn't going to sail, just wanted to make sure the boat was in working order before Friday.

The truck tires reached the water line, and she felt the boat lift. "Okay, that's good."

Ryan put the truck in park and got out. "I can't believe the regatta's only three days away. Everyone at the fire station is pulling for you."

"I hope I'll be ready."

Ryan looked toward the setting sun. "I wish you'd wait. It's going to be dark soon."

"I'm just running her out and back. And I'm wearing my flotation device." She'd bought a brand-new PFD last week at Bill's Bait and Tackle.

"You know, boats sometimes give off too much carbon monoxide. You could pass out and fall in."

"Hence the inflatable."

He checked his watch. "Maybe I should stay. I could be a little late."

"Good grief, I'm perfectly capable. Beckett showed me how to do all this. It's not rocket science."

"Beckett, huh?" He put his hands on his waist.

It was probably time to let the cat out of the bag. "We're kind of going out now. Just so you know."

"Mom and Dad know?"

"Not really." They'd just have to adjust. "He's a good guy, Ryan. They'll see that if they give him a chance."

He nodded slowly. "*If* they give him a chance. Start her up, and make sure she's running okay."

She rolled her eyes. "You're such a big brother."

She pumped the primer bulb, throttled to start, and gave the rope a couple quick yanks. The outboard motor started on the third try, roaring loudly. She adjusted the choke until the boat idled smoothly, vibrating gently under her.

"Happy now?" she called over the motor.

"Have your cell?"

"Yes, Mr. Safety. You can go now."

"How'll you get home?"

"I live four blocks away. Go to your meeting, McKinley." She gave him a saucy smile as she reversed the boat slowly past the slips where she'd tie off the boat later, then headed out into the open river.

The sun, low in the sky, glimmered across the water and warmed her skin. The slight breeze from the boat's motion skimmed her hair from her shoulders.

A smile tugged at her lips. She was doing it. She was riding in Michael's boat. Okay, so she wasn't sailing, but it was on the water. She'd refurbished it, made her into the kind of boat he'd wanted. She felt closer to Michael out here, somehow. Could almost feel him beside her in the cockpit, hear his laughter ringing in her ears.

You see us, Michael? Doesn't she look amazing? Madison ran her hand along the white trim as a pang of loneliness hit her so hard her middle ached.

Her eyes burned. *I wish you were here. I miss you. I'm going to win the regatta for you, brother. You'll see. I'll make your dream come true.*

She picked up speed as she left the harbor. The wind lifted her hair and tugged at her sleeveless shirt. Once she neared the middle, she turned downstream, then twisted the handle toward her, making the boat surge forward.

It felt like she was flying. She understood why Michael had loved being out here. It was just you and the roar of the motor. The wind on your face, the sunshine on your skin, and the water rippling away from the boat.

She rode downstream toward Louisville, passing no one on this quiet weekday evening. She wondered how long it would take to reach Louisville, how long it would take to reach Cincinnati, going upstream. She'd like to try it sometime, with the sails up.

Awhile later, the hills along both shores had turned almost

gray in the fading light. She flipped the switch for the navigation lights. Time to head back. She slowed, pushed the handle away, making a sweeping right turn, then accelerated.

The air had cooled, and the wind drew goose bumps on her arms and legs. Now that she was traveling upstream, the going was slower. She twisted the handle, accelerating.

Since the boat was fueled up and in the water, she and Beckett could spend all their time Thursday morning running through the course. She'd squeezed in a good practice with Evan this week. They worked well together, and he'd praised her efficient movements and knowledge of terms. Beckett had taught her well. Plus she'd borrowed a few racing books he'd recommended from the library and had been poring over them until the wee hours of the morning.

Reading and doing were two different things though. Experiencing the tug of the wind and the swing of the boom . . . she was glad she'd have Evan's help on racing day. Still, she needed to know what she was doing if they had any hope of winning, handicap or no. Chapel Springs and the surrounding area had some seasoned sailors.

The sky had darkened, and a few lights peppered the distant shoreline. The sun had sunk more quickly than she expected, but she wasn't far away now. She rounded a bend and, far in the distance, she could see Chapel Springs' marina lights. She steered toward them, running through the next morning's to-do list.

The motor hiccuped.

She looked back at it, frowning.

The motor hiccuped again. Then again. It made a sputtering sound, then it chugged a moment. The boat slowed, despite her grip on the handle.

No, no, no.

The motor gave one last burp and then stopped. Silence rang out across the river as the boat drifted to a stop, and the acrid stench of smoke filled her nostrils.

Chapter Twenty-Six

Madison stood, legs apart and knees bent, and yanked the rope. Nothing. She tried again three times before giving up.

The vessel bounced in its own wake. She sat down, catching her breath, her heart racing. What was she going to do?

Paddles. There should be paddles on board somewhere, right? It would take awhile to reach shore, but she was strong. She would paddle ashore and call Ryan.

She looked under the seats. Surely she'd have seen them when she and Mom cleaned. They'd scoured every inch of the place. Nevertheless, she looked in every cubby. Nothing.

She eyed the shore, maybe fifty yards away. That's when she noticed her boat was drifting downstream. Away from Chapel Springs.

The hills were ghostly shadows against the night sky. The water had turned inky black in the fading light. She wondered how deep it was, her old fears resurfacing as she eyed it.

You can swim now, Madison. And you have your PFD on. You're perfectly safe.

Safe but stuck. She had to call someone, and there was only one person who could get her out of this mess. She pulled out her cell, relieved to see two beautiful bars of reception.

Madison dialed his number and perched on the seat. Two rings, three. *Please answer.*

He picked up on the fifth ring. "Hey. What's up?" Beckett said quietly, and she remembered he had Bible study tonight.

"I'm so sorry to bother you. I, uh, need your help. I'm kind of . . . in trouble."

"Just a sec."

She heard some shuffling. Beckett's muffled voice. Then he was back, his voice louder. "Where are you?"

"I'm sorry, I know you have Bible study tonight."

"We were wrapping up. You okay?"

She gave a wry laugh that sounded choked. "Depends on your definition of okay. I'm kind of in the middle of the river with a dead motor."

Over the line, she heard a door or something click shut. "Your boat?"

"It was running so well, and then . . . it wasn't."

"How far away are you?" An engine started.

"I can see the marina lights." She looked toward them and realized she'd drifted around the bend. "Well, I could a minute ago. The current's taking me farther away." She shivered and crossed her arms against the chill.

"Go ahead and lower the anchor. Remember how?"

"Yeah, just a sec." She set the phone down and lowered the anchor until it rested on the bottom.

"Okay, anchor's down."

"You're downstream then? Toward Louisville?"

"Yeah."

"Sit tight. It'll be fine. Give me ten or fifteen minutes. Make sure your nav lights are on. You're wearing your PFD, right?"

"Yeah." She looked around at the darkness, pressing in from all sides, and wished she'd thought this through. She hadn't minded the water when she could see it. Now she could only hear it slapping the hull, feel it rocking the boat.

"You okay?"

Snap out of it, Madison. "Yeah. I'm fine."

"Want me to stay on the line?"

She was being silly. "No, no. I'll see you when you get here. Thanks, Beckett."

She hung up and cradled the cell in her clammy palms. Her first time alone in a boat, and she gets in trouble.

And the motor—the regatta was three days away, and her motor was dead in the water. Literally. She hoped it could be repaired. She was pretty sure a new outboard motor ran a couple thousand dollars, and she sure didn't have that sitting in the bank. Maybe she could borrow one. But every boater she knew was sailing in the regatta.

Even if the motor could be fixed, how long would it take, and how much would it cost? She'd already spent a pretty penny on the refurbishing.

The oscillating rasp of katydids, hundreds of them, echoed across the water. She huddled into the cockpit, leaning against the bulkhead to shelter her body from the wind. The air still smelled faintly of smoke.

She looked into the distance toward Chapel Springs, though she knew it was too soon to see help coming. He wouldn't even have arrived at the marina yet.

She pulled out her cell phone and opened her e-mails, needing a distraction.

A splash sounded from somewhere nearby, and she jumped. *Just a fish, Madison.* But the reassurance did little to settle her heart or her nerves.

She forced herself to read her e-mails, mostly work stuff.

Mrs. Etter had sent her a photo of Perry's family with the basset hound pup. They looked happy together. Perry stood in the back with his wife. He was wearing his trademark do-rag, and the kids were front and center, the pup wriggling in a little girl's arms, licking her face. Madison sent a reply and checked the rest of her e-mails.

PJ had sent a link about a search dog named Samson from Michigan's Upper Peninsula that had made news for finding a seven-year-old girl who'd been missing a week.

She was finishing the article when she saw a red and a green light in the distance. Beckett? A minute later the lights were closer, and she heard the low hum of the motor as the boat approached.

She stood, ready to flag him down, but he was already headed her way, and it wasn't like there was anyone else out here. He slowed as he neared, and she could see his silhouette beyond the bow light. She'd never been so glad to see anyone in her life.

The motor quieted as he circled her, drifting to the other side. "You all right?"

"I am now. I have the fenders out starboard side. Can I help?"

The boat edged alongside hers. "Sit tight. I got it."

He went to work with the ropes. A spring line led from his bow to her midship cleat, and another from his midpoint to her stern. When he seemed satisfied the lines were secure, he went to the driver's seat.

"Okay, pull the anchor in and tell me when it's on board."

After the anchor was up, she gave the okay.

"Hang on."

She grabbed onto the rail as he slowly accelerated, easing

both boats forward. He progressed slowly, constantly checking the lines.

Madison felt like a heel for taking him from his study, for being stupid enough to test the boat so close to dark. She was not telling Ryan about this. He'd never let her hear the end of it. Bad enough that Beckett knew.

It took over an hour to reach the marina, and by the time both boats were tied up, Madison was just glad to be on dry land again. She approached him on the dock as he finished the knot on the cleat and stood.

The marina lights cast a golden hue on his face. He looked tousled, his hair windblown, his jaw covered with a five o'clock shadow. They started walking down the pier.

"I don't know how to thank you. Talk about up a creek without a paddle."

His eyes crinkled as he gave a rare smile. "Speaking of paddles . . ."

"I'll be buying them tomorrow."

"And I'm sure this goes without saying, but—"

She held up her hand. "I know, I know. It was stupid and reckless, and I should've waited until tomorrow."

His lips twitched. "Then we both would've been stuck on the water. I was going to say, I'll work on the motor first thing tomorrow."

He was always bailing her out lately. "Thanks. I hope it's not too expensive."

He gave her a look. "I'm not going to charge you, silly. It'll probably be an easy fix anyway."

"What am I going to do if it's shot?"

"Let's not borrow trouble." He stopped by his truck, and she realized he'd driven up to the docks, parking illegally on the grass. It warmed her heart that he'd been in a hurry to rescue her.

"I'll walk you to your car."

"That's sweet, but Ryan dropped me. I'll walk home."

"You've had enough adventure for one night." He opened the passenger door. "Hop in."

The cab smelled like him, musky with a hint of spice. She drew in a deep breath. Nice. Manly.

After he got in, he started the truck and eased off the curb. "How far downstream did you go?"

"I'm not sure. I was going fairly fast for about half an hour. She was running really well too." Madison sighed. So close to reaching Michael's dream. Why did these things have to happen? Why did everything have to be so hard?

He nudged her shoulder. "Hey, don't worry. Haven't met a motor yet I couldn't fix."

She shared a smile, and when he looked back to the road, she didn't look away. She'd never dreamed in high school he would've turned out to be a gentleman, but somehow he had, despite his precarious upbringing.

She remembered the things Cassidy had said about him, thought of the things Beckett had told her about church and God. Had God really caused the change in his life? Made such a difference in Michael's life?

Her brother had gone away to youth camp in the seventh grade and returned a different kid. Their parents had seemed so pleased with the changes—and they were good ones, she couldn't deny that. But somehow, she'd felt left out. She kept thinking the spiritual high would wear off, but it never did. From that point on, Michael had been almost too good to be true. Devoted to God, obedient to their parents, kind to everyone.

Yeah, and look what happened to him. Was that what God did to His devoted followers?

"Penny for your thoughts."

Madison realized she'd been staring and looked away. "Sorry I interrupted your class tonight. I didn't know who else to call."

He turned onto her street. "As I said, it was pretty much over. Besides, it's not every night I get to rescue a damsel in distress." He flashed her a half grin.

"Believe it or not, I'm usually pretty self-sufficient."

"Wouldn't expect anything less from a McKinley."

"Yeah, Mom drilled that into us all. Especially us girls."

"That's not a bad thing."

He pulled into her drive and got out. Having him walk her to the door seemed like the most natural thing in the world. Her mind turned back to the week before, and anticipation made her heart race. Should she ask him in?

A cricket chirped from somewhere in the shrubs, and the fragrance of freshly cut grass scented the air. Up on the porch, she opened the door and flipped on the porch light. Lulu accepted a greeting, then rushed out onto the lawn.

The light fell around them like a golden blanket. She turned to ask him in, but he spoke first.

"Can I ask you something?"

She crossed her arms against the chill in the air. "Sure."

"I've been reluctant to bring it up . . . Have you heard from Jade?"

Madison wondered if he missed Jade or if he was just concerned. Then she reminded herself Beckett hadn't written those notes. And she realized that, after all that had happened, she still didn't know who *had* sent them.

"She called about a month ago."

"She's okay then." There was no missing the relief in his voice.

"Seemed to be."

She could tell him more. That she had a job, was staying in Chicago, but she didn't.

His face softened in the golden light. "I should go."

She didn't want him to go just yet. "You could come in for a while."

He glanced at his watch, then back at her, something like regret on his face. "I should get home. Early day tomorrow."

She fought the wave of disappointment. "No early run on the river now."

"You'll have to do that with Evan on Friday. I'll get the motor fixed, and you'll be good to go."

"Hope so. Thank you for tonight." She closed the gap between them and gave him a hug. "I don't know what I would've done."

She felt his hands at her waist, drawing her in, welcoming the embrace.

"Anytime." His voice was low and deep in her ear.

The shiver that went through her had nothing to do with the chill in the air. He was warm, and he smelled so good. Felt so good. The hair at his nape tickled the back of her hand. His shoulder was solid under her palm. She wondered if he could feel her heart thumping against her rib cage.

His hand moved over her back in a fleeting caress, and she arched toward him even as her knees went noodley.

Music intruded, the notes of *Seinfeld's* theme song. Her cell phone.

Reluctantly she pulled away. "That's probably Ryan." Her voice was all air, no substance. "Making sure I made it back."

"Better take it." He was backing away already, reaching for his keys.

"Thanks again, Beckett."

He gave her a half smile and a final wave, then she entered the house and answered the call.

But it wasn't Ryan.

~

Evan's voice greeted her when she answered the phone. "Thank God I caught you."

"What's wrong, Evan?"

"I got a call from my mom in Georgia a couple hours ago. My dad was in a car accident. I'm heading to the airport now."

The regatta, she thought, and immediately felt guilty. "I'm so sorry. Is it serious?"

"We don't know much yet. He's unconscious. Madison, I don't know if I'll make it back for the regatta."

Only three days away . . . What if he didn't make it back in time? She couldn't win the race without him. She'd be lucky to finish at all. And she'd never find a replacement. The sailors had settled their crews long ago.

She pushed aside the thoughts. "Never mind that. You go be with your dad. I hope everything works out."

"I have some numbers for you. A couple of retired sailors who might help you out if I don't make it back in time. I'd suggest Beckett, but I know how he feels about sailing with a crew. And I guess he's hoping to score that prize money. Have a pen and paper?"

She couldn't believe he was thinking about her at a time like this. "Go ahead."

She jotted the numbers down. She'd call them and line something up just in case.

Chapter Twenty-Seven

Madison cleated the bowline and stood, brushing back the hairs that had escaped her ponytail. Evan had called that morning. His father was conscious, and they were awaiting test results. Things looked good though, and he'd booked a flight back late tonight on the nonstop from Atlanta.

She had called the two retirees yesterday. One couldn't sail because of his rheumatoid arthritis, and she was waiting on a return call from the other. But it didn't look as though she'd need him.

Beckett had driven to Louisville for the motor part and had finished the repairs this morning. She'd thanked him profusely. The boat had performed great on the river tonight.

Unfortunately, Madison hadn't. Her dry runs through the course had been difficult—and there weren't other boats littering the water like there would be tomorrow.

"I did awful." She tucked the stern line under the cleat, making it fast.

Beckett hopped from the boat to the dock. "You may as well put your perfectionist tendencies aside now. There's no such thing as a perfect race."

"I'm not a perfectionist."

He shot her a look.

"Okay, maybe a little, but that last turn . . . ugh. There's so much to this—and I'm not focusing well." She followed him up the dock.

"Focus is critical, but it's not supposed to be this breezy for the race. Look, you're going to make mistakes tomorrow. Everyone will. The key is to put them from your mind right away. Don't dwell on them. Keep a positive attitude. You know the basics, and Evan will help with the rest."

"As long as he makes it back."

"You said he booked a flight."

"You're right. I'm just stressing out. What else?" she asked.

"It's not a bad idea to follow a good racer. Do what they do. That's what I did my first several races. I got third place one year doing that, and I learned a lot."

"Who should I follow?"

"Me, of course."

She laughed and smacked his arm. "Something tells me Evan isn't going to be following anyone."

"And doesn't really need to. Just remember, the race is built on handicaps. You won't be in the lead, not with a Folkboat, so don't panic."

Easier said than done. She just wanted to win and have it over. She was ready to move on with her life. Ready to put the regatta—and everything else—behind her. She couldn't believe the race was tomorrow. Her stomach knotted at the realization.

She palmed her stomach as she reached her car. "I'm already nervous."

"You'll be fine."

She turned at her car door. Darkness was falling, and the cool breeze felt good against her heated skin. Beckett's hair was wind-blown, a strand hanging down in his eyes.

"Thank you, Beckett. For the lessons, swimming and otherwise. I couldn't have done all this without you."

"You would've found a way. Glad I could help though."

"At least let me pay you for the motor repair."

He waved her off. "It was a cheap part. Besides, least I could do after whaling on your boyfriend."

"He's not my boyfriend. We only went out a few times, you know." She leaned back against the car door. "Besides, I ended things recently—not sure if you heard."

He leaned forward, his arms on both sides of her, a smug smile forming. "Oh yeah? Why's that?"

She held back a grin. "Well, see, some other guy kissed me, so . . ." She left off with a shrug.

His lips twitched. "And you liked it."

"Maybe."

He leaned closer. "In fact, you liked it so much, you want him to kiss you again."

"I might not turn him down."

He was a breath away, too far. His eyes grew serious, the corners of his lips falling. Then they brushed hers, softly, slowly, stealing her breath, her strength. How could the barest of touches make her insides clench, make her heart skip a beat?

He ended the kiss too soon, but he didn't go far.

"Save a dance for me tomorrow night."

River Sail Regatta ended with festivities at Riverside Park, including a band, dancing, and plenty of junk food.

"Just one?"

"Didn't want to sound greedy."

If she had it her way, she'd be in his arms the whole evening, hopefully celebrating her win. Her mind snagged on the thought.

If she won, Beckett would lose. And with the loss, the prize money he was hoping to use to launch his business. She pushed the thought away.

"You want to come over?" she found herself asking.

He checked his watch. "I'd like to, but it's getting late. And you, young lady, need plenty of sleep tonight."

He was right, but she didn't have to like it. She'd review the racing rules while she waited to hear from Evan. He said he'd call when he arrived in Louisville.

He tipped her chin up. "Well . . . it'll be chaos tomorrow, and we might not get a chance to talk before the race, so . . . good luck to you."

"You too."

He dropped a kiss on her forehead. "See ya." He gave that half smile that made her knees liquefy, and she watched him cross the parking lot.

On the way home, she forced herself to think about something else. Her feelings for Beckett had grown exponentially, but there would be time to reflect on that after the race. She wondered if Jade had feelings for him too. She hoped not. Last thing she wanted to do was hurt her sister. She wished Jade could be here tomorrow. Each member of her family had called today, wishing her luck, telling her they'd be there cheering her on. Everyone but Jade.

PJ had made poster-board signs, and her mom had brought her Michael's favorite hat, a white cap with a blue embroidered anchor. He'd worn it all the time, and Madison was planning to wear it for the race.

When she opened the door, Lulu greeted her enthusiastically, then went to scope out the yard. While the dog was outside, the phone rang.

The caller ID showed Evan's name. She answered and greeted him, hopeful.

"I'm sorry, Madison, but I won't be flying home tonight. My dad took a turn for the worse. His tests are showing some brain trauma, and I really have to stay."

"Of course you do. I'm so sorry." Even while the words came out, words she really meant, she slumped in the kitchen chair, deflated. What hope did she have of winning now?

"I know how much this means to you. I feel terrible." He sounded tired.

"Please, don't give it another thought. Really. I'll work something out."

"Thanks, Madison. If you wouldn't mind, say a prayer for my dad. This might be a long road for him . . . for all of us."

"Will do, Evan. Try and get some rest." In a haze, she turned off the phone and set it in the cradle.

She let Lulu back in and paced the kitchen. Why was this happening? She'd never win without Evan. All her work would be for nothing. She pressed her fist against the ache in her middle. The ache that swelled every time she thought of Michael. It would never go away at this rate.

Stop thinking negatively, Madison. There had to be something she could do. Something more than depend on a Plan B that included a retiree who had probably never even placed in the regatta—not that she'd heard back from him. She ran through all the boaters she knew, ticking them off in her head, but everyone she knew was participating. It was the event of the season.

She found the number for the retiree and placed the call, but it went through to voice mail again. She left another message and hung up.

She wanted to call Beckett, but what good would that do? He had his own boat, his own race to win.

She'd just have to wait for the old sailor to return her call. She had little chance of winning, but what else could she do? She could only hope and pray it worked out somehow.

Hope and pray. She was good at the first, the second not so much. Glancing at the clock again, she made a decision. She picked up the phone and dialed a number, relieved when the feeble greeting came.

"Mrs. Geiger, it's Madison. I wondered if I could ask a favor of you and the ladies . . . I have a couple prayer requests."

Chapter Twenty-Eight

MADISON FOUND HER FAMILY UNDER THE LARGE PAVILION IN Riverview Park late the next morning. They were hard to find among the throngs of people indulging in free hot dogs, compliments of the Chapel Springs Sailing Club.

She gave PJ a kiss on the cheek, having not seen her since she left for college two weeks before. Her sister looked adorable in pink shorts and a trendy white top, a ponytail hanging halfway down her back.

"Hey, sis! Are you excited?" PJ put her hand over her heart. "Oh . . . you're wearing Michael's hat."

"There's my girl," Dad said, handing her a hot dog as she took a seat opposite him at the wooden picnic table. "Great day for sailing, or so I hear. You ready to win this thing?"

"What's wrong?" Ryan asked, frowning as he chewed his last bite of hot dog.

"It looks like I won't be racing today. Evan's still in Atlanta."

"Oh no, sweetie!" Mom curled her arm around her shoulder, squeezing. "I'm so sorry."

Daniel frowned. "I thought he was flying home last night."

"There must be something you can do," Dad said.

"We'll find a substitute," Ryan said.

"Already tried." She'd found out this morning from Dottie that the sailor she'd been trying to reach was out of town.

"Hey, maybe one of us could fill in," PJ said.

Madison tried for a smile. "Thanks, but I'm hardly an expert myself. I really need a pro to have a chance at winning."

"Honey, if you just finish the race, that would be enough," Mom said. "We'd all be so proud of you."

"There you are!" Cassidy reached her side. "Hi, gang, Momma Jo." She gave the woman a hug, then turned to Madison. "I was afraid I wouldn't find you in— What's wrong?"

"Evan Higgins had to bail," Daniel said.

Cassidy's face fell. "Oh no."

"It's fine. There's always next year." Even as Madison said it, the hollow spot inside began aching, the pressure building like a teakettle with the hole plugged. Everyone knew next year was a year too late.

"Is there anything I can do?" Cassidy asked.

Madison gave a wry smile. "Not unless you have secret sailing powers you haven't mentioned."

Cassidy winced. "Sorry . . ."

"Let's just make the best of it." Madison put on a smile as the family proceeded to munch down on the myriad of snacks available. After eating, they bought tickets for the canoe being raffled off and participated in the carnival games that lined the riverfront lawn.

The turnout was good and the event well planned, as always. Tourists had turned out in droves for the festivities, and everyone seemed to be having a great time.

The gutter boat races, always popular with the kids, were fun and exciting. The races consisted of seven-inch sailboats, two lengths of water-filled gutters, and all the lung capacity the kids could contribute. All the McKinley children had participated when they were younger, but PJ had been the only one to win. They'd teased her for months about all that hot air.

When it was nearly noon, Madison excused herself. "I'd better find Curtis and let him know I'm out." She'd been putting it off, she realized. Hoping that some miracle would bring another sailor along.

"I saw him down by the docks ten minutes ago," Ryan said.

"When you're done," Dad said, "meet us on the lawn where it slopes up from the marina."

Madison found Curtis on the docks, surrounded by half a dozen other entrants. She stood in line, waiting her turn.

The docks were a hive of activity, sailors getting their boats ready for departure, messing with each other. The race committee boat was already headed out. On the river, orange and white balls marked the course. Some of the sailboats had already left their slips, heading toward the start line.

She couldn't believe this was happening. That she was going to sit on the hill with her family and watch the race she'd worked so hard to compete in. She'd let Michael down. She felt it all the way down to her bones. She took off the cap and crumpled it in her hands.

"Where were you?" Beckett asked, coming up behind her. "You missed the skippers' meeting."

Obviously he hadn't heard. She gave a resigned smile. "I'm out of the race."

His jaw went slack. "Evan's not back?"

She shrugged. "His dad took a turn for the worse."

"Oh no."

She forced a smile. "I'll be cheering you on though. I hope you win, Beckett." She knew he could really use that prize money.

"No. You can't just quit, Madison."

"I don't have much choice. It's okay. You go win this thing."

Twin lines furrowed between his brows. His dark eyes went intense, boring into hers for a long moment before he turned, weaving through the handful of people near Curtis.

She watched as he gently interrupted a tourist and began speaking with Curtis. The man cast a glance her way, looked down at his clipboard. Shook his head. Beckett said something else, gesturing with his hands before placing them on his hips. They continued talking another minute.

Finally Curtis pursed his lips, nodded once. Beckett headed her way, an unreadable expression on his face.

He pulled her arm. "Come on, we need to hurry."

"Where we going?"

"We have ten minutes to get your boat ready. Hustle up."

She stopped at the boat, frowning. "But who's going to help me?"

He gave her a crooked grin. "Meet your new crew."

"But—but your boat—the prize money . . ."

"You going to stand there yapping, or are you going to help me out here?" He'd already hopped in, started the motor. He tossed her a PFD. "Get your mind in the game, McKinley. We're gonna win this thing."

~

Half an hour later Madison had no room for extraneous thoughts. After Beckett caught her up on a couple of last-minute changes, they'd had a good start. She and Beckett were toward the front of the pack. She'd made some minor errors on the first few legs, but Beckett had helped her through.

Sweat trickled between her shoulder blades as they approached a port tack for the last leg of the race.

"Boat eleven on starboard tack," Madison called. "We're not crossing." The boat was a sloop called *Glory Days*.

"Continue on port tack. Let's dip 'em."

"Roger that." *Okay, Madison, come on. Two boat lengths. You can do this.* "Medium dip. No ease on the jib."

"Got it."

Keep going . . . bow down . . . a little deeper. Okay, come up now . . . They were over target on speed, but not on angle. She needed more helm.

"I'll sheet in to bleed off a little speed."

"Okay," she said a few moments later. "The helm feels good."

Arriving at the last leg, there were seven boats in front of them. Seven! It seemed like so many.

Speed was what mattered now. Staying ahead of those behind them and passing the one directly ahead of them. No easy task, she thought, realizing it was Mrs. Etter's grandson, Perry.

Beckett called out directions. She followed without thought. If anyone could read the wind, it was Beckett. A moment later she checked behind. They were widening the gap, and they were closing in on Perry's boat, *River Rat*. His do-rag fluttered in the wind as he worked the mainsail.

Madison's arms and back ached, but adrenaline gave her added strength and endurance.

"We've got to go faster," Beckett called. "Bow down."

Madison followed through, and the boat caught some air and sped forward. They passed *River Rat* on their starboard side, but Madison didn't even give them a glance. They were fat on the wind, making good time, and gaining on the next one, *Daddy's Pride*, Cappy's boat.

Come on, come on . . . They were so close to the end, and there were still six boats ahead of them.

"We'll never make it!" she called over the wind.

"It's okay . . . remember our handicap."

They sailed on. They were getting good air, closing in on *Daddy's Pride*.

"The race is to windward!" Beckett called as they approached the boat. "Plenty of room leeward."

Madison made the adjustments.

"Good!" Beckett said. "Holding speed now."

They were edging up beside *Daddy's Pride*, a couple boat lengths away. In the distance, the race committee boat marked the finish line, its orange flag barely visible. Four boats had already crossed.

Come on . . . come on . . . They matched speed with *Daddy's Pride*, going neck and neck with Cappy and his wife.

Beckett called out instructions, and Madison carried them out. *Focus, Madison. Focus.*

A moment later they were pulling ahead, bit by bit. She kept her mind on the task at hand, her muscles protesting. She didn't spare a glance at the finish line or at *Daddy's Pride*, remembering Beckett's advice to keep her head in the game.

They had to be nearing the finish line, but she focused on her job. The wind pulled at her shirt and tugged her ponytail as she made slight adjustments to the sheet. In her peripheral vision she saw *Daddy's Pride* slipping behind.

They were making good time now.

Come on . . . come on. Finish strong . . .

And then she saw the race committee boat as they passed, heard the blast from the horn.

Daddy's Pride crossed the line a few moments later. From the deck, Cappy gave her a smile and a salute. Madison returned the favor. *River Rat* was shortly behind them.

When they reached the marina, they guided the boat into the slip. She removed her PFD as Beckett turned off the motor. He approached, all smiles, his hair a mess, his eyes brighter than she'd ever seen them.

"Do you think we have a chance?"

"It's going to be close. We'll have to wait and see, but I'm so proud of you, Maddy. You did great."

He drew her into a hug, kissed the top of her head, and held her tight. Her heart thumped against his chest. What a thrilling ride! They'd done their best. All they could do now was wait.

"Hey, look at that." He pulled away.

Madison looked toward the lawn and only then became aware of the cheering crowd. Then she saw what had drawn his attention. Neon poster-board signs dotted the crowd. They all read the same: *Michael's Dream!*

A lump formed in her throat. She put her hand over her heart as tears burned the backs of her eyes. She picked out faces in the crowd. Dottie Meyers, Maeve Perkins, Pastor Adams and his wife, the Kneeling Nanas, their faces wreathed in smiles. Everyone clapping, not only for the exciting regatta, but for her. For Michael.

She spotted her family heading down the sloped lawn toward the dock, PJ leading the way.

"I'll finish up here," Beckett said. "You go on."

"You sure?"

He nudged her shoulder. "Go on. I'll see you at the yacht club in a little while."

Madison hopped off the boat and hurried toward her family. She was swallowed up with hugs and congratulations. Never mind that she hadn't won anything—yet. She still had her fingers crossed.

She hung with her family, filling them in on all the details of the race. It had been fun and exciting, she was surprised to admit. She'd made her share of mistakes, but they'd done well. Maybe well enough to win.

The minutes dragged as she waited for the awards ceremony. When the time finally arrived, Madison and her family joined the throng of people on the yacht club lawn. The Club Commodore stood on the deck of the club at the podium and thanked everyone for supporting the regatta. Daniel was behind him, dressed in khakis and a polo in his official role as mayor.

By the time he was ready to announce the winners, Madison's nerves were stretched as taut as they could be.

Beckett appeared at her side and took her hand, the gesture ushering in a moment of tension. Word had spread that they were dating, but her family hadn't seen them as a couple until now. Surely he'd earned some respect with the sacrifice he'd made on her behalf today.

"Good luck," he whispered.

"Here goes nothing," she said.

The crowd hushed. Madison's heart fluttered in her chest.

"In third place," the Commodore said, "with a corrected time of forty-seven minutes and nineteen seconds, is *Bluegrass Baby*."

The crowd cheered, and the team went forward to collect their trophy.

After they left the stage, the Commodore continued. "In second place, with a corrected time of forty-six minutes and twelve seconds, is *Daddy's Pride*."

Cappy had come in second. *Good for him.* She smiled and applauded. They'd beat Cappy, but how did the handicap play into it?

"Breathe," Beckett whispered in her ear.

Madison realized she'd been holding her breath. Her palm sweated against his. What if they didn't win? What if it was all for nothing? Finishing second or third would've been better than not finishing at all. The cup winner was all that remained. It was all or nothing now.

"And finally," the Commodore said, "the winner of the River Sail Regatta, with a corrected time of forty-five minutes and fifty seconds, is . . ."

Beckett squeezed her hand. Madison's breath caught in her lungs, refusing release.

"*Michael's Dream!*"

Her lips parted, her heart raced. Had he just said—

Beckett let loose a cry of victory, and Madison's whoop joined the cheering crowd. She followed him through the crowd, accepting pats on the back along the way.

Madison's mind was in a fog as the Commodore presented them with the regatta cup and a check from the sailing club. The crowd cheered for so long, it brought tears to Madison's eyes. When the Commodore finally closed the ceremony, the crowd began to disperse.

Beckett drew her into a hug. "You did it, Maddy. You did it."

"*We* did it." She hung on tight, her heart thumping against his chest. "I can't believe it. I just can't believe it. Thank you so much. I couldn't have done it without you."

"My pleasure," he whispered.

His arms were tight around her, his breath on her temple stirring the hairs that had escaped her hat.

They'd done it . . . they'd won! Madison turned her face toward the sun, closed her eyes a moment, and smiled, catching her breath. *We did it, Michael. We did it.* It was over now. She could rest, knowing her brother's dream had been reached.

And then, because the moment didn't seem complete without it, she whispered a prayer. *Thanks, God. Thanks for hearing me.* Something welled up inside. Gratitude mixed with something else she couldn't define. Maybe God did care. Maybe He did want her to find peace after all.

"Congrats, Madison!" Her parents appeared at the base of the deck, followed by the rest of her family.

"Let's see that thing," Dad said, sparing Beckett a stiff smile.

Beckett handed over the cup.

"Such an exciting race!" Mom said. "That was so nice of you to fill in for Evan."

"I couldn't have done it without him. Not any of it." She beamed at Beckett.

Dad nodded once and handed the trophy back to him, then turned back to Madison. "Your brother and sisters are holding us a spot at the pavilion."

"You go on," Beckett said. "I told Layla I'd meet her after the ceremony."

Chapter Twenty-Nine

Madison lay in bed with the lamp on, letting the day's excitement rush over her. It was almost midnight, but she was grateful for the adrenaline that still coursed through her. She shifted and gave in to a grin.

The awards ceremony was a moment she'd always remember. Wearing Michael's cap, holding up the regatta cup, Beckett at her side. Her heart was still warm from all the people who'd sought her out to tell her how proud Michael would've been of her today.

When the light had begun to fade, a local band, the Cornhuskers, took the stage and began playing some favorite tunes. The grass on the town square became a makeshift dance floor, and the white lights strung across the park twinkled above like stars against the black velvet sky.

Madison danced with so many partners, she was hard-pressed to name them all, but Beckett had claimed her every chance he got. Drew had asked her to dance once, surprising her, but he'd danced with other women too, and he'd kept plenty of space between them.

Beside her, the phone on the nightstand pealed, making her jump. At the foot of the bed, Lulu's eyes opened, then drifted shut again.

"Hey, sis." Jade's voice only widened Madison's smile. "Sorry to call so late."

"Jade. It's so good to hear your voice."

"You don't think I'd miss your big day. How'd it go?"

"We won. We actually won. Can you believe it?"

"I knew you could do it."

"We were in eighth coming up the last leg, but somehow we did it."

"I'm so happy for you. Michael's smiling down on you today."

"I know. I can feel it."

Madison realized she'd left out Beckett's name on purpose. Maybe it was time to find out how Jade felt about him. "It was crazy. Evan Higgins had to leave town on a family emergency, and I thought I wouldn't even be able to compete. But then Beckett offered to be my partner."

"Beckett?"

Was there a twinge of heartbreak in her tone? Or was Jade only embarrassed at having mistaken his intentions?

"He's been helping me with sailing and stuff this summer— we've kind of become friends."

"That's—that's great, Madison."

"Really? I thought you might be sore at him. You left so suddenly after your date and . . ."

"That was just a misunderstanding. He's a nice guy."

Madison felt a weight fall from her shoulders. "Well, enough about me. How's everything in Chicago? Do you have a phone yet?"

"No, I'm calling from the café. We just closed for the night."

She hated to think of Jade driving home at this hour. Or worse, taking public transportation by herself.

"So the job's going okay? You're making enough money?"

"Yeah, it's great. I haven't found a place to play guitar though."

"How is Izzy?"

"She's fine. She lost her job, but I'm sure she'll find something soon."

"That's got to be tough, with a child and all. Tell me about your apartment. It must be kind of crowded."

"It's not so bad. Izzy and her son share a room, and mine's the size of a shoe box, but we have two bathrooms and a decent kitchen. It's in Cicero, real close to the El."

"El?"

"The elevated train. Listen, I have to go. My boss needs to lock up for the night, but I wanted to hear how your big day went."

"It was great to hear from you. Call the family soon, okay? Daniel too. He asks about you every time I see him."

"Okay. I gotta run. Love you."

"Love you too," Madison said.

And then Jade was gone, but Madison was still smiling as her head hit the pillow.

~

Madison had no sooner sat in the circle at Countryside Manor than the ladies started.

"Aren't you going to fill us in?" Mrs. Geiger petted the beagle Madison had brought.

"You saw it yourself." Mrs. Marquart edged away from the dog.

"She beat my own grandson! Imagine the nerve." Mrs. Etter gave Madison a mock scowl.

"What I want to know is, how did the O'Reilly boy come into the picture?" Mrs. Geiger waggled her penciled-in brows.

If anyone deserved the details of Saturday's events, it was these ladies. They'd been there for her when she'd been desperate.

"I can't thank you enough for your prayers. Not only did the regatta work out, but Evan's dad is better. He had to have surgery, but he's on the mend, and they're hoping for a full recovery."

"Don't that beat all." Mrs. Marquart tugged her auburn wig into place.

"We want all the details." Mrs. Stuckey took the beagle from Mrs. Geiger and cradled him in her lap.

Madison filled them in, from the moment she learned Evan wouldn't make it back to the moment Beckett joined her crew.

Mrs. Marquart pressed her hands together. "He saved the day. How romantic!"

A smug smile perched on Mrs. Geiger's face. "Two birds with one stone," she muttered.

"What?" Madison asked.

"Oh, never mind, dear. We're just so delighted everything worked out. How does it feel . . . as wonderful as you'd hoped?"

"I'm thrilled, of course," Madison said. She smiled past the feelings that had begun slowly surfacing over the past couple of days. There was something bubbling under the joy of the win that didn't feel right. Something that felt all too familiar. She pushed the thought away.

"Well, you worked so hard. We couldn't be happier for you," Mrs. Stuckey said.

When she'd finished visiting the Kneeling Nanas, she made her rounds. She was in such a good mood, not even Mrs. Doolittle's scowl dampened her spirits.

After returning the pup to the shelter, she realized she had one more errand. She felt for the check in her pocket as she drove down Spruce Street in the waning light. She couldn't deny she was eager to see Beckett. She hadn't seen him since the night of the regatta, and she was planning to invite him to her parents' house Friday. They were celebrating her birthday and the regatta win.

He'd been with her through it all. Through the fear, through the mistakes, through every obstacle. Nobody understood what she'd gone through to get here like Beckett did. And he'd sacrificed his own goal to help her. A celebration wouldn't be complete without him. Still, inviting him to a family event implied a certain level of intimacy. How would he feel about that?

And would her dad behave himself? Would he lay down the rumors of the past long enough to see the person Beckett had become? They'd just have to work through any rough spots.

A light shone through the picture window, but she heard noises coming from the backyard. She followed the curve of the drive behind the house. The night was warm and humid, making her hair cling to the back of her neck. Pine and freshly mowed grass fragranced the air. A radio played softly, intermingling with the occasional whir of a drill.

An outbuilding came into view as she rounded the corner of the house. Just inside the overhead door, a shirtless Beckett stooped over the skeletal hull of a boat, frowning in concentration as he drilled.

Her movement must've caught his attention because he looked her way, a smile curving his lips as he shut off the drill.

"Hey." The word conveyed a tone of surprise. He lowered the drill and dragged his forearm across his forehead.

Rigsby came to greet her.

Beckett glanced at the house. "Did you knock on the door?"

She remembered his dad was home from jail, remembered the scene last time she was here. "No, I heard you back here."

He offered a smile. "Just working on a boat."

Madison tsk-tsked as she approached. "No goggles, no mask . . . what am I going to do with you, O'Reilly?"

Something flickered in his eyes, and his lips twitched. He blew away a tiny pile of shavings from the wood.

The light draped over the ridges of his shoulders like a sculpted cape. She turned her attention to Rigsby, squatting down. "Hey there, fella. Is Daddy giving you your heartworm pill?"

"Yes, he is." His eyes darted toward the house.

She gave the dog a final rub behind the ears and stood. "Brought you something." She pulled the folded check from her pocket and handed it to Beckett.

He opened it, then his face went slack. He handed it back. "No. This is yours."

She pocketed her hands. "I didn't do it for the money, you know that."

He came closer, extending the check. "Neither did I."

Maybe he hadn't helped her for the money, but it was the money he'd been after from the start, the money he'd sacrificed to help her win.

She shook her head. "I want you to have it."

He tilted his head, frowning. "Madison."

"Please. Invest it in your business. Nothing would make me happier."

Slowly, his hand fell. He let out a sigh. "Split it with me then."

"I don't want it. You have a good thing going here. It'll make me feel good to know I had a tiny part in it. Besides, we both know you would've won if you hadn't been helping me."

He considered her until she squirmed. Then he pocketed the check, pursing his lips, letting her know he wasn't comfortable with it.

She ran her fingers along the skeleton of the boat. "Is this Drew's?"

"No, I haven't sold this one yet. Drew never called me back—guess the moral of the story is don't beat up your customers."

"Maybe you can make that your new slogan. Put it on those fancy business cards you order."

"Funny."

"Too bad I didn't take a picture of you in action—would've made a nice visual for your new website."

He gave her a look. "All right, now."

Teasing him felt good. Suddenly, inviting him to the celebration Friday felt like the most natural thing in the world.

"What are you doing Friday night?"

His brows lifted at the shift in conversation. He set his palm on the rough-edged rim of the boat. "Why do you ask?"

"My folks are having a barbecue to celebrate the win. And you *are* half of the winning team."

He shrugged. "Sure. I'll come. What time?"

"Sixish. I'll have to meet you there. You're welcome to bring your dad if you want."

His smile fell. "Oh. Thanks, but he—uh, he probably has plans. Can I bring anything?"

"Just your appetite. And your A game."

He hiked a brow.

"Backyard ball." She faked a free throw. It was only a couple weeks ago she'd seen him practicing layups in the park. "There's always B-ball when we get together. You any good?"

"I've put up my share of blocks."

She smiled. "You're on my team then."

"How do I know *you're* any good?"

She pressed her fingertips to her chest. "I'm a McKinley. Of course I'm good."

He smiled at that, a mesmerizing smile with teeth and everything. The light cast shadows over the planes of his face, highlighting the sharp angles of his jaw.

She watched the smile fall from his face and forced her eyes away.

"Well," she said, backing toward the door, "I should go. It's a work night."

He reached into his pocket. "Are you sure you won't take—"

She gave a mock glare. "*Stop.*"

He mumbled something as she walked away.

"I heard that."

"Good," he said.

She was smiling as she returned to her car. She got in, started the engine, and pulled from the drive, casting a look at the house, watching the TV light flicker against the walls, and wondering about Beckett's dad.

Chapter Thirty

Madison woke in a cold sweat, the remnants of the nightmare hanging on tight. She lay still, her heart pounding her ribs. Darkness pressed in around her, smothering her with its heaviness.

No. No, it couldn't be. She shook her head, willing it to be untrue, trying to shake the lingering panic away. The nightmares were supposed to be gone. She'd won the regatta. Replaced the bad dream with the good one.

Only she hadn't.

Make it go away, God!

She shoved off the covers and sat up, shaking. She ran her palms over her face, brushing her hair back at the temples where it was damp with sweat.

The clock read 4:17, but sleep was only a finger beckoning her to torture.

~

"I smell rain," Grandpa said before he took the last bite of his burger.

"Maybe it'll hold off," Ryan said.

Madison smothered a yawn, the lack of sleep catching up with her. She leaned into Beckett's arm, loving the solid feel of him next to her.

Grandpa engaged Ryan and Daniel in a conversation about weather patterns that Madison knew would probably lead to his story about the worst storm he'd ever lived through. The tornado of '67. They'd heard it a hundred times.

They'd enjoyed an exciting game of three-on-three before supper. She, Beckett, and Ryan had beaten Dad, Daniel, and PJ, though it had been a close game. Her dad seemed to be giving Beckett a chance, though there was no missing the caution in his eyes.

"You could've told me it was your birthday," Beckett whispered in Madison's ear as he set his napkin on his empty plate.

"It's really more a celebration of the regatta," she whispered back after Mom excused herself to fetch the birthday cake.

"Uh-huh."

Fact was, every year Madison wished they'd forget her birthday. She couldn't celebrate it without remembering that her twin wasn't here.

She'd hoped that with the regatta win, it would feel different this time. That she would feel happy and . . . released or something. But as birthday wishes flew across the backyard and gifts were shoved into her arms, she'd found herself feeling the same as always. Like she'd rather be in Dr. Gallagher's office awaiting a root canal.

She'd hoped the celebration of the regatta win would overshadow her birthday, but her family was having none of that. Crepe paper was strung across the yard, balloons bobbed in colorful clusters here and there, and of course the cake awaited her.

She felt a drop of rain on the back of her hand, then another.

"We'd better move the party inside," Dad said.

"Tried to tell you," Grandpa said.

Madison and Beckett gathered the dishes. Dad grabbed the gifts, PJ and Daniel collected the balloons, and Ryan was pulling the tablecloth just as the rain turned to a deluge.

They ducked into the house, sliding off their shoes near the front door so they didn't dirty Mom's shiny wood floor or muddy her antique rugs.

They settled in the living room, loud and boisterous. Beckett was next to her on the sofa, his warm thigh stretched out next to hers the only comfort she felt. Knowing what was coming, the cake, the presents, the memories, she wanted nothing more than to go home and curl up on the couch with Lulu.

She tried to tell herself she was only missing Jade, but it was more than that. It was Michael. Why did she still feel this way? She'd won the regatta before their twenty-seventh birthday. She'd fulfilled his dream. She was supposed to feel better now. It'd been almost ten years. When would she be free of this? At peace? Her eyes found the regatta cup on the mantel, propping up a sign that read *Congrats, Madison and Beckett!* in PJ's lovely script.

Someone turned out the lights and Mom approached, candles flickering atop the rectangular cake, casting a glow over her features.

Dad started the song, singing off-key, and everyone joined in as Mom set the cake on the coffee table. *Happy 27th Birthday, Madison!* the cake said in bold white script. Two flames wavered on white candles in the darkness. One for her, one for Michael. When they were kids, they'd each gotten a cake, their parents careful that neither child felt short-changed. Since Michael's death, there'd been only one cake, but two candles, the meaning unspoken but understood.

The reminder of their loss always saddened her. It wasn't that she wanted to forget him. No, never that. But shouldn't there be some point when she could move forward without the dragging weight of sadness? Some point where it didn't feel like half of her had died with him?

Everyone laughed as her parents finished the last notes of the song with their failed attempt at harmony. Madison's smile felt as brittle as a November leaf.

"Make a wish!" PJ said.

"I wish Mom and Dad would stop trying to harmonize," Ryan said.

"Save it for *your* birthday," Mom said.

"I think Madison got her wish Saturday," Daniel said, flipping his bangs from his blue eyes.

Ryan pushed the cake closer. "I'm sure she can come up with a new one, greedy girl."

Madison leaned over, took a breath, and blew. The flames flickered out, and curly wisps of smoke winged upward.

"Yay!" PJ said. "I'll get the plates. Dibs on the flowers."

"You always get the flowers," Daniel called.

"You don't even like them."

Mom pulled the candles and whisked the cake away with a wink.

"I want ice cream with mine," Dad said, tagging along. "Jo, we got any vanilla?"

"Yes, dear."

"I'll scoop." Ryan followed the gang into the kitchen, leaving Madison and Beckett alone.

"I hope it's not that generic brand." Grandpa's voice carried from the kitchen. "Stuff tastes like cement powder."

Madison traded a smile with Beckett. She wondered if her family overwhelmed him. He probably wasn't used to chaos. She hoped he felt welcome despite her dad's aloofness.

"Well," he said, "this visit has certainly cleared up some things."

She turned to him. "Like what?"

"Where Jade got her musical talent—clearly it was a gift from heaven."

Madison smiled. "What? I think we sing pretty well."

"I could hear Rigsby howling from here."

She swatted him. "We're not that bad."

"Whatever you say."

She listened a moment to the commotion in the kitchen, the laughter and teasing, the clang of silver, suddenly feeling removed from it—removed from her family, like an outsider. Why had everyone else moved on when she couldn't seem to? What was wrong with her?

Not even after the regatta. All that time and effort—she thought it would change things. Would change her. Her eyes found the cup again, a familiar pressure building inside.

Go away. Go away.

"You okay?" Beckett was studying her with those all-seeing eyes. She wondered if he could see right through her, to that ugly thing building up inside.

"I'm fine." She tried for a smile. "Let's have some cake." The sooner they ate and opened presents, the sooner she could go home and pretend it wasn't her birthday. She just had to push these feelings down awhile longer.

The kitchen was a mass of moving, talking bodies. When everyone had a piece of cake, they settled in the living room, where conversation flew at the speed of lightning. If her family noticed Madison's silence, no one mentioned it.

At one point she was so lost in thought that she jumped when Beckett squeezed her hand.

"You're awful quiet, birthday girl," he whispered.

She had to stop dwelling on it. Think of something else. "Hard to get a word in edgewise."

"Present time!" PJ declared, setting the gifts on the coffee table.

Madison did her best to fake joy as she opened presents, even managing a real smile when she opened Ryan's card.

Beckett tweaked a brow at the colorful scrawling on the inside.

"I got Ryan this card when he turned—what was it, Ryan? Twenty-two?"

"Something like that."

"The next year for my birthday, he scratched out my name and regifted it."

"That's how cheap he is," Daniel said.

"It's been going back and forth ever since," PJ said.

"Except that one year Ryan couldn't find it," Mom said.

"Thanks, Ryan," Madison said, holding up the greeting card and gift card to the Coachlight Coffeehouse. "Until next year."

She tore into her presents, eager to be finished. Daniel and PJ had gotten her season one of *Gilmore Girls*. Grandpa gave her a tool kit—she was always borrowing his.

Her parents' gift looked and felt like a book. She tore open the floral paper to find a leather-bound journal.

"It's a prayer journal," Mom said.

Madison ran her hands along the smooth cover inscribed with her name. "It's beautiful. Thanks, Mom and Dad." She remembered the one Michael had. He'd always left it lying around, and one time she'd taken a peek.

Michael had caught her, snatching it from her hands. "Hey, that's personal!" But he wore his good-natured smile.

"Then maybe you shouldn't leave it lying around the living room," she'd said, walking away. She turned at the threshold, wearing an innocent smile. "And by the way, Lacey or Tricia . . . God probably doesn't care either way."

Michael threw a pillow that caught her in the stomach.

"Madison?" She realized Mom had tried to get her attention twice.

"Sorry. What was that?"

"Momma Jo was saying she'd noticed my journal and asked where I got it," Daniel said.

"We ordered it from the same place in Chicago," Mom said.

"The cover was handmade in Italy."

"I know how you love good leather. You used to journal when you were a teenager, remember?"

Madison ran her fingers over the journal again, nodding. "Feels like butter. Thank you." She held it out to Beckett.

"Good stuff," he said.

She placed the journal back in the box and helped gather trash. She needed to leave, and soon. The pressure was building, bubbling up.

When the room was picked up, Madison announced she was calling it a night.

"Already?" PJ asked. "I thought we could play Catch Phrase or something."

"I'm really tired," Madison said. "Maybe tomorrow . . . you can spend the night. We'll watch *Gilmore Girls* and share a tub of butter pecan." Madison didn't know if she'd be up for company, but she had to get out of there.

"Take some cake with you." Mom started toward the kitchen.

"That's okay, Mom. You guys can finish it." She tried for a smile when a crease marred Mom's forehead. "It was delicious though. Thank you."

She hugged Mom and Dad, then the others, trying to hurry without appearing to rush.

As she was slipping on her shoes, Dad asked Beckett a question about pistons. Any other time she would've been thrilled at her dad's softening, but now, she only wanted to go. She knew she should wait on Beckett—he was her guest. But she had to leave. Thank goodness they'd driven separately. She didn't think she could hold it together much longer. She thanked Beckett for coming and ducked through the drizzle, slipping into the quiet of her car.

Chapter Thirty-One

Madison turned on the radio, cranking up the oldies station. The haunting melody of "It Must've Been Love" filled the car, the bittersweet words making her ache. She turned the station and accelerated down her parents' drive. Maybe if she could turn it up loudly enough, it would drown out the awful pressure building inside.

She breathed deeply, holding it in as she flipped on her wipers and turned onto the road. She just needed to keep it inside. Push it down. There was no reason to let it out now, all these years later. It would go away if she just pushed it down far enough.

Really, Madison? Isn't that what you've been telling yourself for years?

No matter how long she pushed, how hard, it always seemed to surface again. The nightmares, this terrible disquiet inside.

I won the regatta, Michael. We achieved your dream. That was supposed to fix it. Why do I still feel like this?

She pounded her fist on the steering wheel. She was so angry. So tired. Why couldn't she move on? Everyone else seemed to be able to.

A few minutes later she turned into her drive, shut off the engine, and ran into the house. The sky wept, droplets falling onto her head, trickling down her face. She opened the door and pushed it shut behind her. Her breaths came shallow and loud. Sweat beaded on the back of her neck. Her fingers gripped the keys until their serrated edges cut into her palm.

She nudged Lulu aside and sank onto the rug in front of the sofa, not even bothering to turn on the light. She heard the quiet patter of rain on the roof, felt a breeze from the open window. The rain was probably coming in, but she didn't care.

Her cell phone rang, and she turned it off without looking.

The pressure inside built, getting heavier, louder, stronger. It was too big, too powerful to be let out. She didn't want to cry. Didn't want to open the floodgate.

She gulped deep breaths of air, pushing, pushing it down. But the pressure refused to be put back in its place. It rose, choking her throat, filling her face with heat. A wave of nausea passed over her. The backs of her eyes burned. She blinked against the pain, but they filled with tears anyway, spilling over.

Why, God? Why did You take him? She pounded the floor with her fist and clamped her lips, afraid to go any further.

She thought of her parents' gift and let loose a crazed laugh that turned to tears. A prayer journal. What would she say to God? She could fill every page with her thoughts, but they weren't things He'd want to hear. Her parents would be appalled if they knew what she'd say.

The tears flowed like rivulets of rain. She tried to choke back a sob, but it was coming out whether she wanted it to or not. The sobs broke forth in wrenching waves, making it hard to catch her breath.

It's not fair. She sniffed back the tears, sucked in a gulp of oxygen. *He was my brother, my twin, a part of me. If You're so good, why did You take him? He didn't deserve it!*

A tap on the front door made her jump. She stilled, the sob

catching in her throat like a lump of wet coal. If she were quiet, they'd go away, whoever they were.

A knock sounded again. "Madison?"

Beckett.

She closed her eyes and felt more tears squeeze out. She just wanted to be alone. Was that too much to ask?

He knocked again, louder. "I know you're in there, Madison."

She should've shut the window when she'd had the chance. Couldn't a person fall apart in private anymore?

"Go away, Beckett."

"Not until I know you're okay."

She wasn't okay. Anyone could see that. She couldn't even pull it together enough to defend herself.

The door squeaked open, and his darkened form filled the doorway.

"I want to be alone." She hoped he couldn't see her in the dark. Then she realized the lights of his truck streamed through her window. How had she missed the headlights?

"You forgot this." He set something on the end table. The journal, she thought.

An involuntary sniffle wracked her. "Thanks."

He came closer, and she turned away. "Go away, Beckett." She meant to sound firm, but her voice wobbled and cracked.

He slid down to the floor beside her, his knee brushing hers, his body making the space seem tight.

She felt his eyes on her as her teeth began to chatter with the effort of holding back her emotions.

She knew how she looked when she cried—it wasn't pretty. The last thing she wanted was company. This big, ugly thing was coming out whether she wanted it to or not, and she didn't need an audience.

"What is it?" he asked. "Tell me what I can do."

"Go away—that's what you can do."

He touched her shoulder. "Not till I know you're okay."

She brushed his hand away. "I'm not okay! I haven't been okay for a long time, and I don't see an end to that, so unless you want to move in here and wait it out, you may as well leave now."

The burst of anger loosened everything up inside. It bubbled up from someplace deep and dark, dredging the bottom of her soul, and spilled out in violent sobs.

She drew her knees close and covered her face, wracked with pain built up over years. "Go away! Just go away."

Beckett drew her into his arms. She pushed against him, fighting, but he wouldn't let go. Finally she gave in.

~

Beckett held Madison tight, stroking her arm, pushing the hair from her face. Her sobs broke his heart, scared him. Was she ill? Was there some awful secret she was keeping? She buried her face into his shirt and let it all out, while he murmured words she probably didn't hear.

It was awhile before she let up. Finally her sobs slowed, her breaths coming in involuntary shudders. Still he held her, stroked her arm, kissed the top of her head.

"Talk to me," he whispered after a minute of silence.

"I thought—" Her breath stuttered. "I thought it'd be better. I thought winning would fix it."

"Fix what?"

"All this—this pain—inside. About Michael, his dying. I don't understand why—I never did and I never will. He was so good. So good! Why did God take him like that—why did God take him instead of me?"

"You?"

"He should've taken *me*!" She thumped her fist against his chest where a jagged rock had settled.

"No, honey."

"Yes, He should've! What did Michael ever do? He was the good one. How could God take him instead of me?"

Words, God. I need words.

"I'm so tired of this, so tired of the nightmares, so tired of being tired all the time. It was all supposed to go away when I won, but it didn't, and now I'm going to feel like this forever."

"Like what?" he asked, not sure he even wanted to know.

"Like I have a gaping hole inside me. It hurts as much now as it did then, and I can't live this way anymore. I'm too tired."

Beckett closed his eyes, set his chin on her head. "Oh, honey. I'm sorry." In more ways than she could know. It was all his fault. Michael wouldn't be dead if it weren't for him.

Madison gave an involuntary shudder.

He had to put aside his guilt and help her. But how? *Help me say the right things, God.*

"I can't sleep for the nightmares."

He tightened his hold, wishing he could somehow protect her from the pain. "God loves you, Maddy. He wants you to have peace, to give this to Him."

"What does that even mean?" she cried, thumping her fist again.

He was messing this up. He didn't want to give her platitudes. He kissed her temple, thumbed away the tears on her cheek. "I don't know exactly how you're feeling, and I've never lost a twin. I don't think there are any easy answers. I don't know why Michael died—" He swallowed his own remorse, which was welling up hard and fast. "But when something awful happens, it helps to know there's a God and that He knows what He's doing. That He has a purpose we might not see, might never understand."

He realized he was talking to himself as much as to her. He hoped the words were soothing her wounded spirits more than they were soothing his guilt.

"I think it helps, too, to know our loved one is in a better place. Michael wouldn't come back now even if he could. And someday you'll be with him again."

She burrowed deeper into his chest. He threaded his fingers through her silky hair, cupping the back of her head.

"I know you miss him. I know you're hurting."

"Our birthday is always hard, but I thought the nightmares would go away if I just won the regatta for him."

He brushed her hair back from her face. "Tell me about them."

She paused so long, he wondered if they were too hard to talk about. Then she started talking, describing the dream and the panic she felt when she woke. How she'd stay up as late as she could to avoid sleeping for fear of its return. His heart ached for her. No wonder she was tired all the time, popping those coffee beans like candy.

"I wish I could fix it," he said numbly, the weight of his guilt pressing hard.

If only he hadn't gone swimming that day. If only he hadn't felt the need to show off. If only he hadn't left Michael alone at the river.

But he had. And look at the pain he'd caused.

Help her, God. Help her where I can't. Heal her heart, make the nightmares go away. Give her the peace she needs.

"Just hold me," she said.

He pulled her onto his lap, cradling her like a small child, feeling like he was betraying her. He didn't deserve to hold her. She'd suffered all these years because of him, was still suffering. He'd had no idea the extent of it, but he knew now. He was holding the proof in his arms.

How could he keep his secret now? He couldn't. He had to tell her. She deserved to know what had happened that day, and so did her family. He'd been a coward for keeping it from them all these years.

"I'm glad you're here," she said. "I feel better when you're holding me."

He winced. How could they have any kind of relationship with this between them? And yet, how could he tell her when it would only hurt her more? He couldn't bear the thought.

The two thoughts circled in his mind until he was dizzy with indecision. There was no good answer. Either way led to pain and loss on both sides.

He wasn't sure how much time had passed when he realized she'd gone limp in his arms. Her breaths were deep, her hand slipping down his chest until it rested in her lap.

He held her awhile longer, relishing the weight of her, the feel of her hair brushing his bare arm. It was getting late, but he didn't want to waken her.

He adjusted her weight in his arms, stood, then found her bedroom down a short hall, past a nightlight. Lulu followed, her nails clicking quietly on the wood floor.

Madison's bed was made, so he laid her on the quilt. She barely stirred, poor thing. Just worn out. He slipped off her sandals and covered her with a blanket from the foot of the bed.

He stared down at her moonlit face. *Sweet dreams, Maddy.* He left quietly, locking the front door, wondering if love was strong enough to survive the kind of secret he held.

Chapter Thirty-Two

THE NIGHTMARE CAME IN THE MIDDLE OF THE NIGHT. Madison flew upright in bed, her heart pounding, her pajamas damp. She crawled from bed, wandered into the living room, and flipped on the TV. Around four, after an hour of infomercials, she broke out the new tub of butter pecan and ate until she felt sick.

She was relieved when seven o'clock rolled around and she could get ready for work. On her way there she popped coffee beans to combat her fuzzy brain and tired body, her thoughts going back four nights to when she'd broken down in Beckett's arms. She'd been embarrassed when she woke the next morning. She'd completely lost it in front of Beckett. But then she'd realized he'd tucked her into bed, and the knowledge soothed her.

That had been her best night of sleep in weeks, and she hoped that, somehow, the breakdown had healed the broken part of her. But obviously not.

It didn't help, either, that Beckett had seemed different since that night. They'd talked on the phone twice, and he'd come over the night before. He was still attentive, still affectionate. But there was a distance or something . . . she couldn't put her finger on it.

She'd asked twice if everything was all right. He'd said it was, offering her a smile and apologizing for being distracted. She wondered if it had to do with his dad. It had to be stressful, living with an alcoholic father.

Once at the clinic, Madison fell into the routine of her workday as the caffeine perked her up. Her full schedule became jammed when Mrs. Tackett's toy poodle decided to break into the woman's chocolate stash. Madison induced vomiting, and once the dog was on the mend, she returned to her scheduled appointments.

She tried to make up ground, but the clients, the human ones, were irritable from a long wait, and their pets responded with anxiety.

She skipped lunch in favor of a handful of coffee beans, but by three o'clock the beans were gone and so was her energy. And she was still behind. Cassidy was also busy and stressed from dealing with impatient owners, and Madison was beyond ready to call it a day when she entered the room of her next-to-last patient.

She pasted a smile onto her face and gave Opus, a basset hound, a scratch behind the ears. "Sorry about the wait, Mr. Campbell."

As Madison read the chart, he complained about the wait and having to bring his wife's dog into the vet. Her eyes blurred with fatigue, her mind muddled as she tried to listen to the man and read the chart simultaneously.

When she finished, she questioned Mr. Campbell about Opus's symptoms, then examined the dog. His skin infection wasn't responding to the antibiotic she'd put him on three weeks ago.

After informing Mr. Campbell of their options, she left the room and returned with a syringe of Convenia.

"Okay, Mr. Campbell, if I could have you hold Opus still . . ."

He did as she asked, grumbling all the while.

Madison picked up the syringe.

Cassidy burst through the door, her eyes a little wild. "Sorry to interrupt, Dr. McKinley, but I need to speak with you."

Madison's hand continued its path to Opus. "Be right with—"

Cassidy grabbed her hand. "Now. Please."

Frowning, Madison set down the syringe and gave the owner an apologetic smile. "Excuse me, Mr. Campbell. This shouldn't take long."

He let out a loud sigh as Madison left the room. In the hall, Cassidy pulled her around the corner and whipped around. "Was that Convenia?"

"Yes, for a skin infection—"

Cassidy's hand tightened on her arm. "Madison, that dog is allergic to cefovecin. He experienced anaphylaxis last year, remember? It's on his chart."

Madison's thoughts tumbled. A dog allergic to cefovecin shouldn't receive Convenia. She knew that.

"Are you sure? I didn't see it."

"I'm positive."

Madison palmed her forehead. "I can't believe I almost did that."

Dr. Richards turned the corner and came up short. "What's going on?"

Cassidy shifted in front of her. "I was just updating Madison on a patient's chart."

He ignored Cassidy, and his laser blue eyes zeroed in on Madison. "What did you almost do?"

Madison straightened. She'd nearly made a mistake that could've taken a beloved pet's life. She wasn't going to compound the infraction by lying.

"I must've missed an allergy on a chart. Fortunately, Cassidy caught it in time."

He asked for the details of the case, including the previous allergic reaction, and Madison filled him in, leaving nothing out.

He looked between the women, his fatherly frown creasing his forehead. "I'll finish the appointment, Madison. Please wait in my office."

Cassidy shot her an apologetic look before scrambling down the hall. Madison took a seat in Dr. Richards's office and let her head fall back against the chair. Her heart raced from her near mistake. She could've killed poor Opus. Mrs. Campbell would've been heartbroken.

How had she missed that allergy? Dr. Richards wasn't going to let this pass, nor should he. It was inexcusable.

It was the fatigue. She knew how critical sleep was to brain function. She'd been having difficulty focusing, difficulty remembering things. Coffee beans only went so far.

It had been relatively small errors up until now. The last thing she wanted was to endanger animals. But she needed her job, and the clinic was the only game in town. What would she do if Dr. Richards fired her?

Her nerves were frayed by the time Dr. Richards entered the office. He sat behind his desk and passed her the chart.

"As you can see, the allergy is noted clearly."

It was right where it was supposed to be. "I'm so sorry, Dr. Richards. I looked at the chart . . . I don't know how I missed it."

"You're normally very competent, Madison, as I said a couple months ago. I was hoping to see an improvement, but—"

"I know."

"You continue to be unfocused and disorganized, and frankly, you look like you haven't slept in days."

"I'm having some personal problems, but I—"

He held his hand up to stop her. Madison's mouth closed. She'd said it all before. What excuse did she have, when it came right down to it?

Dr. Richards removed his glasses and pressed his temple. "I want you to take a leave of absence."

Leave of—but what about her patients? And what good would a leave do? She wasn't going to suddenly start sleeping because she wasn't working.

"If I could just—"

"Take some time. Do what you have to do to get your life together again. See a doctor, a therapist, whatever. I hate to do it, Madison, but I can't have you jeopardizing the lives of our patients."

A sinking sensation hit the center of her stomach. "No, of course not."

"I can only do this alone for so long, you understand."

"How long do I have?"

He shrugged his burly shoulders. "A month. Six weeks at most. You're due two weeks' paid vacation. I wish I could pay you beyond that, but . . ."

Madison looked at her hands, clenched in her lap. She'd never been fired. She wasn't being fired now, but she may as well be.

"You're a smart and sensible young woman. Get yourself together. But don't come back until you're ready."

"I understand." Unfortunately she did. She understood that nothing would get better in six weeks. She understood that he'd have to replace her and that there'd be no room for her in Chapel Springs once that happened.

"You go on home. I'll cover your last appointment."

Madison left his office and gathered her things. As she slipped out the back door, she had the overwhelming feeling she wouldn't be back.

What was she going to do? She hadn't a clue how to get her life together. If she had, she would've done it long ago.

Madison started her car and pulled from the parking lot. The late summer day was warm, the air inside her car stifling. She put down the window and turned onto Main Street. The three-story brick buildings seemed to press in from both sides. A plastic bag blew down the street like a Midwestern tumbleweed. The tourists were long gone, leaving the town empty in the midafternoon heat. Desolate. It looked as desolate as she felt.

A moment later she found herself parked in front of her mother's store. Maybe Mom could help her make sense of this mess. Madison had tried to handle this alone for too long, and look where it had gotten her. Her life was unraveling strand by strand, and she was starting to think she'd never be able to weave it back together.

She opened the door, the bell jangling. The antique store was barren of customers. The familiar smell of forgotten treasures and forsaken belongings surrounded her. She wove her way around bruised armoires and rustic chests. Her mother came out of her office as Madison reached the back.

Upon sighting Madison, Mom tilted her head. "Hi, honey. I didn't expect you at this hour."

"You have a few minutes?"

"Of course. Go in my office, and I'll flip the sign—not that I have any customers to keep away."

Madison entered the room, which more resembled a turn-of-the-century drawing room than an office. High-backed chairs flanked a small fireplace that warmed her mom's workspace during the winter. A thick Turkish rug hugged the blemished wood floor and stretched across the space to a medallion-back sofa covered with a soft rose damask. Her mom had acquired the piece at an estate auction several years ago and refused to part with it.

Madison sat in the curved corner of the sofa, and a minute later Mom bustled into the room and sat beside her.

"What's up, sweetie? It's not like you to leave work this early."

Madison breathed a wry laugh. "Well, Mom, long story short, I'm officially on a leave of absence."

Her mom, patient as ever, took her hand and waited for her to continue. Madison hesitated to bring up the subject she'd tiptoed around for years. It wasn't easy to break the habit.

"You can tell me, whatever it is." Empathy shone from Mom's blue eyes. Fine lines sprayed out from the corners of them, evidence of a woman who smiled often. Madison admired that, because she was also a woman who'd lost a lot.

"I'm not doing so well, Mom." Madison toyed with a string on her purse strap. "I've had trouble sleeping for a while. I have— I have nightmares."

"What kind of nightmares?"

Madison watched her hands. "About Michael. Always the same one. I won't get into it, but suffice it to say it's cost me a lot of sleep. I put off bedtime because I anticipate the nightmare, and then I awake with it and don't want to go back to sleep."

Mom touched Madison's face. "No wonder you're so tired all the time."

"It's starting to affect my judgment, my focus. It's getting in the way of my life."

"Is that what the leave of absence is about?"

She pictured Opus, his trusting brown eyes. "I made a mistake today that could've ended badly. Dr. Richards insisted on the leave, but, Mom, I don't see how that's going to help. I've been fighting this for years. I thought it would get better if I won the regatta, if I just achieved Michael's dream. I thought it would go away, and that I could finally feel at peace about his death, but it just didn't work. It didn't work."

"Oh, honey."

"I don't know what to do anymore. I have six weeks to get my act together, and I don't even know where to start. Why can't I get over the loss of him? Why can't I be at peace about this? How did you and Daddy do it?"

"It wasn't easy. I still miss him."

"I know you do, but you've been able to go on. Your life isn't falling apart the way mine is."

"Honey, I just try to depend on God. I try to trust that He knows best, and even when I don't understand the whys, I trust He has His reasons."

"What reason could He have for taking a good seventeen-year-old kid from us, Mom? Michael had the rest of his life before him. It seems so unfair."

"Life is filled with difficulties. This isn't heaven. We have these big mountains, set right in front of us, and we have no choice but to climb."

Her mom looked down, took a long moment, then squeezed Madison's hand. "When you were a little girl, you didn't like going barefoot, you remember? You had such tender feet."

"The grass tickled, and the sticks and rocks hurt."

"Even that time we went to Lake Michigan, you wore your sandals on the beach except when you were on your towel."

"The sand was hot."

"You remember Michael though?" Mom laughed. "Mercy, I couldn't keep that boy in shoes. It was all I could do to make him keep them on at church. I'd come into the nursery and there his socks would be, all balled up in the corner, and him running around barefoot."

Madison smiled at the remembrance. "We were different as day and night."

"But still so close." Mom tucked Madison's hair behind her ear and looked at her knowingly. "Sometimes we have to find the courage to take off our shoes and feel it all. Even the bad stuff.

"Sometimes those negative feelings are so strong, they're overwhelming, and it's easier to just not deal with them. But they always come out one way or another. After Michael died, I was so worried about you. We all handle grief differently, but you . . . never crying, never letting it go . . . and missing him so much."

It was true. Madison had only begun to let it go days ago. And she had a feeling that was only the tip of the iceberg.

"You've always been afraid of feeling, Madison. Sometimes those negative feelings are so strong, they're overwhelming, and its easier just not to deal with them. But death is part of life. Not my favorite part, not by a long shot. But God does not owe us ninety years on this earth. Life is a gift, however long it lasts. It's God's to give and take away as He sees fit. We go through life thinking we're entitled to our ninety, but we're not entitled to anything. All we can do is trust that He knows what He's doing. That He has a plan for all of us, and that no pain He allows in our life will go unused. I suppose realizing that has given me a good measure of peace."

Madison had never looked at it that way. Could she trust God with the future? With the past? She'd been angry at Him for so long.

"I don't know if I can do that, Mom."

Mom squeezed her hand. "You can if you want to, baby. I'm not saying it's easy, or that it's instantaneous, but if you ask God for help and truly seek Him, He'll show you so many things. He can be your soft spot to fall if you let Him. But first you have to invite Him into your life."

Madison had sat through enough sermons to know what that meant. She could've preached it herself. Something always held her back. But she felt that something giving way bit by bit.

"I don't know where to start."

Mom rubbed her thumb along the back of Madison's hand. "What about the prayer journal? Why don't you just start writing out your feelings?"

Madison's laugh contained no humor. "Oh, Mom. God doesn't want to hear what I have to say, believe me."

"Honey. He can handle all your emotions. Every last dark and wretched thought. He already knows about them anyway."

That was disconcerting. Her heart sped at the thought.

"Just write your heart out. Then listen. See what He has to say. What do you have to lose?"

Madison gave a sad smile. "I am kind of at the end of my rope."

"Well, you know what they say about that." Mom pulled her close. "Tie a knot and hang on tight."

Chapter Thirty-Three

Beckett marked his place in the book and appreciated the view. The sun dipped low on the horizon, painting the sky vibrant shades of purple. A soft breeze rustled the leaves and fragranced the air with pinesap. The rock, still warm from the afternoon sun, served as his footstool, the glowing sun his lamp.

His dad might be a wreck, his own heart a tangled mess, but up on this hill, it was just him and God.

His class had recently begun studying Ephesians, and Beckett had admired Paul's persistence and courage so much, he'd bought a book about the man. He continued at the middle of chapter 4 where he'd left off.

When he reached the end of the chapter, a Bible verse caught his eye. He stopped, the words hitting him like a sucker punch.

"Therefore each of you must put off falsehood and speak truthfully to your neighbor, for we are all members of one body."

The words blurred as his thoughts spun. He'd been thinking since Friday about whether or not to tell Madison about his role in Michael's death. It was hard to distinguish between his desire to protect her and his desire to protect himself.

On the one hand, all he'd done was stay silent. He hadn't exactly lied. Was that so wrong? On the other hand, there was Madison's pain and his part in it. If he'd never gone to the river that day, her brother would still be alive.

He read the verse again, letting it soak into his reluctant soul.

Telling her would cause her more pain. He might even lose her. He wasn't sure which thought troubled him most. After hearing her weep, her sobs rising from someplace deep and dark, he couldn't stand the thought of hurting her more.

How would she feel, knowing he was to blame for Michael's death? Would some part of her be relieved at finally having answers? Or would she only feel anger? Betrayal at his silence?

He'd been in denial before, thinking she was over her brother's death, but Friday had opened his eyes. She wasn't even close. Maybe someone never got over the loss of a twin. How would he know? He could only imagine if something happened to Layla, if someone had caused her death . . . He didn't even want to think about it. And Madison was having to live it. All he knew was, he didn't want to mess this up. The consequences were too big.

His eyes traveled back over the verse. He could lose her. He could hurt her even more, and she didn't deserve that. How could he tell her the truth?

His advice to Madison surged to the surface. Hadn't he told her she needed to trust God? They were supposed to do the right thing and trust God to handle the rest.

It was easier in theory, he realized now, but he felt the unmistakable nudging in his heart. He hadn't lied with words, but sometimes the lie was the thing left unsaid.

He shifted on the rock, knowing in his gut what he had to do. He should've done it years ago. Maybe it would've comforted the family to know what had happened. Maybe it would've only given them someone to blame, but they deserved to know the truth.

He'd been young and foolish and wrong. Now time had caused the wounds to scab over, though in Madison's case not heal, and he was about to tear them off.

Chapter Thirty-Four

Madison walked toward the theater exit. Rehearsal had been a disaster. She'd flubbed her lines four times and had walked smack into a lamppost onstage, bumping her forehead.

With opening night four nights away, she'd only made everyone nervous. She wished she could blink and erase the whole day. She wished she could fall into bed and wait for sleep to claim her. But sleep was no oblivion. Hadn't been for a long time.

At least she was seeing Beckett tonight. He'd been encouraging and sympathetic when she'd told him about her leave of absence, and she'd felt better by bedtime. But in the middle of the night, the nightmare had stolen the breath from her lungs, the hope from her heart.

She exited the building, her heart smiling at the sight of Beckett waiting by his truck. When she reached him, he brushed his lips softly across hers. Ah. This part of her life was good anyway. Very good. By the time he eased away, her knees trembled like stalks of wheat.

"How was rehearsal?"

"Ugh. Don't ask. Sorry I'm late."

"You're worth the wait." He gave her a quick peck before he opened the passenger door.

Inside the cab, Madison watched him round the truck, drawing in a delicious breath of spice and musk. She wanted nothing more than to settle into his arms and stay there all evening.

"I hope you don't mind," she said after he got in. "Mom asked if we could give my grandpa a lift home from Bingo. He can't drive at night because of his glaucoma."

"The town hall?"

Madison nodded.

"It's right on the way."

Once downtown, Beckett pulled into a diagonal slot in front of the building.

They were almost a half hour late, but the sidewalk was empty. A puddle of light splashed down from the porch lamp, and metal hardware pinged against the flagpole out front.

"Hmmm. He's usually waiting outside."

"Let's go in."

Madison set her hand on his arm. "He's embarrassed about needing to be picked up. The one time I went inside, he let me have it all the way home."

She glanced at the clock. Maybe he'd gotten distracted with his friends, or maybe Bingo was running long. No one was coming or going from the building.

Next to the town hall, sounds of music and chatter filtered through the walls of a tavern.

"We'll just wait then." Beckett shut off the engine.

She pulled out her cell and turned the ringer back on. "There's a message. Maybe he got another ride." She pushed Play and listened.

"Hey, sweetie," Mom's voice said. "Grandpa needs to be picked up at *nine*, not eight. Sorry for the confusion—I forgot to add an hour to the time he gave me. If that doesn't work out, give me a call and Dad'll get him. Sorry!"

"Well, that explains it." Madison turned off the phone and

filled Beckett in. "I guess he'll be another thirty minutes. I'm sorry."

Beckett settled his arm around her shoulders and pulled her closer. "Oh, man. You mean I have to wait in a parked truck with a beautiful woman?"

She put her hand on his chest and smiled up at him. "Well, when you put it that way . . ." She lifted her lips to his, and he brushed his across them. How could he stir her with the barest of touches?

When the kiss ended, it was only so she could settle in his arms. Contentedly, she watched the streetlamps kick on as dusk began to fall over the town. An eighties song thrummed inside the tavern, and a car pulled in next to them. A couple got out of the vehicle. The woman grabbed her man's hand and gazed at him in adoration. He pulled her closer and kissed her temple.

The tavern music grew louder as a man left the bar and hopped on a motorcycle. The place was doing good business for a weeknight. She wondered what the people inside were seeking. Companionship? Fun? Peace?

She understood the last better than she wanted to. For a moment she was envious of the people inside, finding oblivion for a brief time.

That won't fix your problem, girl.

No, but there were times . . . She stifled a yawn, last night's lack of sleep catching up with her.

Her cell rang, and she checked the screen. "It's Cassidy." Her friend was still reeling with guilt about Madison's leave of absence. "Do you mind?"

"Not at all."

She answered. "Hi, Cassidy."

"Hey, sweetie." Guilt oozed from her tone. "How was your day?"

"Cassidy. Hon. You have to stop this. It's not your fault. It was a long time coming."

"How are you doing?" Cassidy asked.

"I'm okay. Really. I'm sure everything will work out." She wished she felt as optimistic as she sounded.

"You want me to come over? I can stop for butter pecan on the way . . ."

"Actually, I'm with Beckett. Anyway, I'm tired of thinking about work."

"All right. Tell Beckett hey. Maybe we can go out this weekend, a double date? Oh no, you can't. The play."

"Another time though." She slouched into Beckett's side. He was warm and solid and smelled like heaven. She gave a soft sigh.

"What was that? Was that a lovesick sigh?"

Madison smiled. "Possibly."

"I'm happy for you, girl. You make a cute couple. Your kids are going to be gorgeous, and not a frizzy head amongst them."

She was glad Beckett couldn't hear Cassidy's side of the conversation. "I think you're getting a little ahead of yourself."

"Oh, come on, he's loved you since high school. He's waiting for you to catch up."

She was pretty sure she already had. It had only been a few weeks since their first kiss, but Madison's feelings had grown quickly. Love? If she hadn't already crossed that line, she was edging awfully close. And it felt deliciously good.

"Maybe."

"Well, I'll let you get back to Loverboy. Let me know if there's anything I can do."

"Will do." Madison turned off her phone and pocketed it.

Beckett tipped her chin up, a smile tipping his lips after he'd scrutinized her face. "You were talking about me."

Her face warmed, and she was thankful for the dark. "Maybe."

"What did she say?"

"I'll never tell."

"I'll kiss it out of you."

"Go ahead and try."

He lowered his head and gave it his best shot. An admirable effort that left her breathless when he pulled away. The teasing was gone from his eyes now. His face softened as he looked at her, those onyx eyes melting her.

His expression shifted. There was something in his eyes, something serious. No, somber. "Maybe we should talk."

She drew back a little, to see him better. "What is it?"

He seemed to measure her with a look, taking in her whole face. He opened his mouth. Closed it again.

Madison touched his arm. "Hey . . . what's wrong? Is everything okay?"

He looked away, but not before she saw something else in his face. Something that sparked a flare of dread.

"There's something I need to talk to you about. Something long overdue."

"Okay . . . you can tell me anything. You know that." After all, hadn't she spilled her guts to him several days ago? Hadn't he held her in his capable arms, spoken to her so tenderly?

"Madison, it—it's about Michael."

She looked at him. What could he have to say about her brother? "Michael?"

"There's something you don't know. Something no one knows, about the day he . . . died."

She shook her head. "What?"

He settled back against the door. He was distancing himself from her, and she let him go, feeling the need for some space herself. She watched his face, trying to get a read.

His gaze swung over her shoulder, his expression changing. His eyes narrowed. She'd thought he was lost in thought, but then his lips pressed together.

"Great," he said.

She followed his gaze and saw his dad leaving the bar. He wore a baseball cap, and a loose plaid shirt flapped over his jeans. There was a clumsy shuffle to his walk that made it obvious he'd had too much to drink.

Madison frowned as he approached a red car. It was clear he was planning to drive home.

Beckett was out of the truck before she could speak.

His dad turned at Beckett's approach. They had words, but Madison couldn't hear through the windows. A minute later Beckett walked his dad to the truck, a hand on his elbow. Madison scooted over to make room as Beckett opened the door, her mind still on the conversation Beckett had started.

"Hi, Mr. O'Reilly," she said after Beckett shut the door.

He frowned at her.

"I'm Madison, remember?"

Beckett got in and started the truck.

"The 'Kinley girl."

"Right."

He frowned, then his brows popped up. "The twin," he said too loudly.

"Dad, why don't you just lie back and rest." Beckett's voice was sharp.

"My car," Mr. O'Reilly said.

"We'll get it tomorrow." Beckett's jaw muscles twitched as he backed out onto Main Street. "We'll have to come back for your grandpa," he said to Madison.

"That's fine. We still have ten minutes."

Mr. O'Reilly tugged his cap down. "Usta work for your dad shometimes. The McKinleys."

"You did?"

"Me 'n Beckett, in the shummertime."

"Can you put his seat belt on?" Beckett asked.

Madison did as he asked, turning away from the stench of alcohol. "Where do you work now, Mr. O'Reilly?"

"He's sloshed, hon. Let's just get him home."

As if on cue, Mr. O'Reilly slumped in the seat, his head conking the window.

She could feel the waves of tension rolling off Beckett. He must be embarrassed, though he had no reason to be. He wasn't responsible for his dad's behavior. She wondered if Beckett had talked to him about rehab.

A few minutes later Beckett turned onto his street, braking for a cat. It had gotten quiet in the car, and she thought Mr. O'Reilly had dozed off until he muttered something.

Beckett pulled into his drive and put the truck in park.

Mr. O'Reilly shot straight up. "Shhhhhhhhh!" His spittle hit Madison on the neck. "It's a shecret!"

"Dad! Wake up. We're home." Beckett got out, rushed around the truck.

Madison unbuckled Mr. O'Reilly and held him steady until Beckett had him.

"Need some help?"

"I got him."

Beckett half carried his dad up the porch and into the house, struggling through the door. The lights came on, and their shadows passed in front of the window.

Beckett returned a few minutes later, his jawline taut, his nose flaring. "Sorry about that."

"It's not your fault."

He started the truck and backed out. The night had gone downhill, and it wasn't over yet. She wanted to ask Beckett about his dad, but his words about Michael teased her. She wondered now if he'd still want to talk about it. She hoped he wouldn't leave her hanging.

A few minutes later he pulled into the parallel slot in front of the town hall. The mood had shifted drastically. Now the air was thick with tension, and she wasn't sure how to break it. Fortunately they didn't have to wait long.

Grandpa came out of the building, and Madison waved him over. His presence eased the tension as he regaled them with Bingo night stories. Before she knew it, he was getting out of the truck.

"Thanks for the ride," he said.

"Good night, Grandpa."

"'Night, Mr. McKinley."

After watching him go inside, they drove to Madison's house in silence. When Beckett pulled in the drive, she saw Lulu part the curtains with her nose. Madison reached for the handle, but Beckett stopped her with a hand on her arm.

She looked at him in the darkness of the cab. The light from a streetlamp trickled in, lighting his face. Worry lines creased his forehead and separated his brows. His chest rose and fell in quick, shallow breaths.

"Are you okay?" she asked.

He met her eyes. "I have to tell you something, Madison."

Everything inside her went still. Frozen still. And for a minute she wanted to stop him. Because the look on his face promised she wouldn't like it, whatever it was.

"Something about Michael?"

"Yes."

She drew a breath, tried to prepare herself for upsetting news. "Okay."

His thumb rubbed her arm, a nervous gesture, she thought.

"Madison . . . I've been trying to find a way to tell you . . . I was there that day. The day he died."

Her heart raced, making her own breaths shallow. She shook her head. Michael had been swimming alone.

"I was." His hand had gone still. His eyes became more intense. He tightened his grip on her arm.

She'd never understood how the accident had happened. Another person at the scene would explain everything, wouldn't it? She had to know the truth, but she had a terrible feeling something worse was coming.

She swallowed hard, gathered her courage. "What happened?" Even as the words slipped out, she wanted to pull them back.

"I was swimming at the river. Michael showed up. We talked a little, joked around, and—" He pinched the bridge of his nose.

She recognized the look now. The one that had come over his face. Guilt. She recognized it because she'd lived with it herself for so long.

Something welled up inside that crowded her lungs, made it hard to breathe. "What did you do?" Her voice had risen. Her eyes burned. "What did you do to him?"

He turned to her, taking her hand. "Let's go inside and talk."

She pulled her hand away. "I don't want to go anywhere with you."

"Madison. Please."

"What did you do to him?"

"I didn't do anything to him. Let me explain."

She waited, all out of encouragement. She crossed her arms over her stomach, a barrier that couldn't begin to keep out the hurt.

"Michael started talking about the cliff there at Turner's Bend. Wondering if it was true what they said—that it was too shallow to dive there. I told him I'd done it before. He didn't believe me . . . so I did it right then."

His Adam's apple bobbed as he swallowed. He was looking out the front windshield now, his face inscrutable. "Afterward, we were messing around." He stared out the window for a long time, his eyes fading away like he'd gone back to that day. Then he closed his eyes. "I told him it was his turn."

She shook her head. But the somber look on his face made denial difficult. Her heart squeezed painfully. She was almost afraid to ask, wasn't sure she wanted to know. "What happened next?"

Beckett shook his head. "Nothing. He said no thanks or something. He didn't want to risk it. I messed with him a little, then I left." He turned to her. "It never occurred to me he'd do it after I left."

Madison looked away because she suddenly wanted to look anywhere but into Beckett's guilty face.

He took her arm. "I swear, it never occurred to me—"

She jerked away. "Don't touch me."

"Madison—"

"All this time you knew . . . and you said nothing."

He winced, but she didn't care. Beckett was still alive, and her brother was dead.

All the ugly darkness from that day welled up inside, flooding through her. All this time, the wondering, the pain, the loss. All this time, it had been Beckett's fault. She knew that wasn't quite rational, but he'd been there. He'd teased her brother, and if he hadn't been there, Michael never would've jumped. Never would've died.

It was more than she could stand. She grabbed her purse and got out of the truck. She didn't want to see his face anymore. Didn't want to think about Michael being taunted by Beckett or feeling like he had something to prove. Some stupid, pointless act that led to his death.

She hurried across the driveway and up her porch steps.

"Madison, wait."

Her sight blurred with the sting of tears. Her lungs couldn't seem to keep up with her heart. Her heart. If felt as if it had gone through a combine; had been reaped, threshed, and winnowed in the space of five minutes. Just when she thought she was starting in the right direction, this. *It's more than I can handle, God. Beckett of all people. I was starting to think I—*

She'd managed to fit the key in the knob when he took her shoulders, turned her. "Please, Madison, I know I should've admitted this long ago. I'm sorry. You don't know how sorry I am. If I could go back and do it over—"

She pushed him away. "Well, you can't! He's gone. He's gone because of *you.*"

She thought of all the suffering his foolishness had cost. Not only hers, but her parents', her siblings'. She saw her mom weeping at the graveside, her dad crumpled on the floor of the barn when he'd thought he was alone.

She remembered her own grief, the dark days afterward when she couldn't crawl out of bed. The years of nightmares, the lack of sleep, and worst of all, the terrible emptiness inside from missing her brother.

Beckett was the cause of it all. And instead of coming forward, he'd left them wondering. He'd seen her suffering firsthand. Had held her in his arms as she'd wept. He knew exactly what he'd done. "You of all people . . ."

"I'm telling you now . . ."

She wiped the tears from her face in a jerky motion. "You should've told me sooner. You owed me that much. I thought you—" *Loved me.* She couldn't bring herself to say it. Couldn't bear to think it now, because his silence had been a betrayal.

"What can I do? What can I do, honey?"

She looked at him, telling herself she was immune to the endearment. Immune to the tears swimming in his eyes. Immune to the defeat in his slumped shoulders.

She swallowed hard and blinked back the tears. "You can go away, Beckett, that's what you can do. You can just go away and leave me alone."

Chapter Thirty-Five

THE NEXT DAY DRAGGED LIKE A BOAT RUN AGROUND. MADISON had too many hours to fill, too many unwanted thoughts. She ignored a voice mail from Beckett asking her to call.

Instead she cleaned her house from top to bottom, and when she finished she cleaned out the pantry and refrigerator. Still the clock ticked slowly. While tidying the living room, she found the prayer journal under a stack of medical journals. She picked it up, her mom's words from two days ago ringing in her ears.

What did she have to lose? She set down the dust rag and, heart in her throat, she retrieved a pen. The words came slowly, awkwardly at first as she edited her thoughts. But the longer she wrote, the faster the words came and the more honestly she expressed herself.

By the fourth page, tears streaked her face and kept coming as she articulated her anger at her loss and the pain of missing Michael. At the injustice of his death, of being cheated of years together. She wrote of her anger at Beckett for his role in the death.

She knew God was real. Knew He was omnipotent, ever-present, all that. Of course He knew her thoughts. Spilling them onto the page didn't make them any more real, but somehow doing so was a release.

You see all this, God? I'm a wreck, You know.

But He knew that too, of course. After writing almost an hour, she rested her hand on the journal. Her fingers hurt from clutching the pen, her eyes ached. Her heart felt bruised and battered.

I'm at the bottom here, God. I can't sleep, I can barely function, I'm losing my job. What do You want from me?

Just you.

The words fell quietly, a feather lighting softly upon her heart. Her eyes burned. *I'm not sure You want me, God. I haven't been very . . .*

A thought niggled in her mind until the memory surfaced. She'd been in the ninth grade, and Michael had found her after school, stretched facedown across her bed, crying.

The mattress sank as he perched on the edge. "What's wrong, Madders?"

She sat up, wiping her face. She could tell Michael anything. Even this, and he wouldn't feel any differently about her. That was the best thing about having him for a brother.

Nonetheless, heat filled her cheeks. "I got caught cheating today in biology."

He tilted his head. "You're the smartest girl in the class."

"I was helping Tricia Blevins cheat." Tricia was the It Girl, and Madison had only wanted her friendship. "I got a detention! Mom and Dad are going to find out, and they'll be so disappointed."

He gave a sympathetic smile. "Yeah, that'll stink." He nudged her shoulder. "But they'll know you're sorry."

"I can't believe I did that. For stupid Tricia Blevins!" She dashed the tears away.

Michael was quiet for a minute. "Everybody makes mistakes, Madders. But they'll forgive you, and so will God."

"What good'll that do? I'll still get grounded."

"Yeah, probably. But He'll take the guilt away. That's the worst part, I think."

He had a point. The guilt had eaten at her all afternoon. Her stomach was in knots. Michael wasn't like her though. He never would've done something so foolish.

"I don't think God wants to hear from me. I'm not like you, Michael."

"God takes us just like we are. He wants a relationship with us. Isn't that cool?"

Madison didn't know what that meant. It wasn't the first time he'd said it, but how did a person have a relationship with an invisible God? He wasn't here to hold her, to talk to her, to laugh or cry with her. Sometimes she didn't understand Michael at all.

Now the mantel clock chimed the hour, drawing Madison from the memory. Did God really want a relationship with her? What did that look like, exactly? She thought of her parents. They led ordinary lives, but she couldn't deny they had something she lacked. Was that the kind of relationship Michael had meant?

Madison began writing again. *I don't understand all this, God, but I want what they have. I've made a mess of everything, and I can't do this alone anymore. Take my anger, and help me through this. Forgive my sins and come into my life and show me what to do.*

Something began loosening inside of her, working free from a tight, tangled knot. She began writing again. By the time she set down the pen, pages of the journal were filled with words, and her heart was filled with a quiet peace.

The smell of garlic and oregano turned Beckett's stomach. Cappy's was almost full, chairs turned toward the various TVs, blaring the Reds and Cubs pregame. In the billiard room, a noisy game of pool was under way.

Beckett ordered drinks and settled into his seat. What a terrible day. He hadn't heard from Madison—not that he'd expected to. He felt like a jerk for telling her, felt like a jerk for *waiting* to tell her.

He'd thought it was the right thing. He should've done it long ago, but it was too late to fix that. Too late to fix a lot of things.

Across the restaurant, Layla was entering, her long-legged stride eating up the distance. She greeted friends on the way, then slid into the booth, the smile dropping from her face as she looked at him.

"Have you been watching *Old Yeller* again? 'Cause you can't say I didn't warn you about that."

He looked away, toward the TV, where a commentator was waxing eloquent about tonight's pitching lineup.

She touched his arm. "Hey, you okay? Is it Dad? Grandpa?"

"No."

"You and Madison have a fight?"

He had no desire to get into it. "Something like that." His thoughts went back to the night before. He remembered the look in Madison's eyes, couldn't seem to scour it from his mind. She'd felt betrayed, and could he blame her?

Layla tilted her head, studying him. "You really love her. It's written all over your face—and that's saying a lot."

He met her gaze, the truth of her words hitting him hard. He clenched his jaw. He did love her. So much. For so long. And yet look what he'd done. He'd hurt her. The weight of it pressed on his shoulders.

"Does she feel the same?"

He rubbed the back of his neck. "I don't know." They hadn't

gotten that far yet, and maybe that was for the best. Bad enough his own heart was broken.

He pictured the look on Madison's face, the hurt in her eyes. No, he wasn't the only one nursing a broken heart.

"I'm no good for her, Layla."

"That's not true."

He shook his head. He'd only hurt her. He'd been the cause of her greatest pain. She would never look at him again without remembering he was to blame for Michael's death. That he'd kept it to himself all these years.

Her family wouldn't forget either. Mr. McKinley would realize he'd been right about Beckett all along. He could see it now at the next family barbecue. *What did I tell you? That O'Reilly boy is bad news. You're better off without him, Madison.*

Layla grabbed his arm. "Stop it right now."

"What?"

"You know what. You're telling yourself you're not good enough again, and I won't have it."

"Let it go, Layla."

She shoved his arm. "You let it go."

She saw him through the rosy glasses of a little sister. He couldn't blame her for that. He hoped she never took them off, but *he* knew better. He knew what he'd done, and so did Madison. Her whole family probably knew by now.

"You're a good man, Beck. You'll make a great husband someday, a terrific father."

He gave a wry smile. "Because I had such a great example? Don't you ever wonder how many of Dad's genes we got? Even Mom's. Let's face it, we got gypped in the genetics department."

"We still have choices. We can choose to be the kind of people we want to be. You've always been there for me, Beckett. Even when we were kids. You'd show up at my volleyball games and track meets like you were my parent or something. You deserve someone special. If that's Madison, don't let her go."

He couldn't deny how much he wanted to believe those words. But Layla didn't know what he'd done. Didn't know the secret that had eaten at him all these years. Didn't know the pain he'd just caused the woman he loved.

He stuck the menu in the holder. "I'm sorry. I'm not hungry. I can't do this."

She grabbed his arm. "Beckett."

"I should get home. Make sure Dad doesn't pass out on the bathroom floor."

"Talk to her, Beck. Couples fight, it's a normal part of relationships. Don't stew on it—that only makes it worse."

There was nothing normal about this. He forced a smile as he stood, dropping a twenty on the table. "Get yourself the Whole Shebang. You can take home the leftovers—if there are any."

She frowned at him. "You're a stubborn man, Beckett."

"Only when I'm right."

Chapter Thirty-Six

Madison pulled into her parents' drive, her thoughts heavy. She'd called her mom that afternoon and told her about the journaling, about her decision. Madison also told her she wanted to talk to Pastor Adams about being baptized soon. She'd heard the tears in her voice when Mom responded.

The other piece of news had to be delivered in person though. If tears were shed tonight, they wouldn't be happy ones. She had an hour before the final dress rehearsal, time enough, she hoped, to break the news and leave them to digest it.

She wound her way up the winding gravel drive, taking the familiar turns without thought. It would be hard for her parents to hear how Michael had died. She hated to reopen old wounds, but they had a right to know.

Beckett.

Anger and hurt flooded through her in equal parts, followed by a trickle of sympathy. The look on his face, the quiver in his voice as he'd explained. She pushed back the memory and let the others rise high and fast. Anger was easier, more familiar, less vulnerable.

She pulled up to the house and spotted her parents on the porch swing, enjoying the last days of summer.

A moment later she climbed the wooden steps, searching for

words to soften the blow. After they greeted each other, Madison sank into an Adirondack chair. The familiar squeak of the swing comforted her.

"Beautiful evening, isn't it?" Dad said.

"It's perfect. Corn looks real good, Daddy. Getting high."

"It's been a prosperous year so far, thank the Lord. I love a good harvest." He gave her a smile. "Speaking of harvest . . ."

"Mom told you."

"I'm so happy for you, honey," he said.

"We both are."

"It was a long time coming." She knew she still had work to do. But she had God and the love of a supportive family. She had a lot working in her favor.

"I owe you an apology about Beckett," Dad said. "I was watching him with you when you were here the other night. I guess I misjudged him."

Madison sighed. He was going to feel differently in a few minutes. "Thanks, Dad."

"You hungry?" Mom asked. "There's pulled pork and sweet corn left over."

Her stomach turned at the mention of food. "Not hungry, but thanks."

Her parents, snuggled up on the swing, had obviously been enjoying a moment. They'd taken to the empty nest so naturally, Madison and her siblings had joked with them about being offended.

"I heard from Jade today," Mom said.

"You did?" Madison hadn't spoken with her since the regatta.

"She called the store. Sounded pretty good, I thought. It was so nice to hear her voice."

"Is she still working at the café?"

"That's what she said. I guess she's making good tips."

Dad curled his arm around Mom's shoulder. "I hope so, what with those city prices."

"She's still sharing a place with her friend, and they finally got a phone."

Madison took out her cell and plugged in the number as Mom cited it. "Makes me feel better knowing I can reach her."

"I know what you mean," Mom said. "She'll be fine."

"I miss her. The house feels so empty."

The swing continued its rhythmic creak. The wind rustled the leaves and made a shushing sound as it swept through the distant cornfields. A sound so familiar she could hear it in her sleep.

"Might as well spit it out, whatever it is," Dad said.

"Thomas."

"Well, something's eating at her."

"He's right, Mom." Madison picked at a fleck of paint on the chair's arm. "I just don't know where to start."

"Take your time, honey. We've got all night."

Madison looked them over. Her mom's small frame curled into her dad's side. Was she going to shatter their peace? She didn't want to hurt them. They'd been through so much.

She just had to say it. They were strong. Stronger than she'd ever been. And they had God to depend on. A priceless comfort, she was beginning to realize.

"I—I found out something recently that I have to tell you. It has to do with Michael. With his death."

Dad's lips fell to a straight line. The crinkles at the corners of Mom's eyes softened.

"I was talking with Beckett, and he told me he was there that day. Swimming in the river. With Michael."

Mom looked at Dad, and he squeezed her shoulder.

"I always wondered what made him jump. He wasn't a risk taker, you know? But now . . . now it all makes sense." She looked between them. "Beckett told me he dived from the cliff that day. He told me he—" This was the hardest part. "He told me he teased Michael because he wouldn't jump. I don't think in a mean way, just, you know . . ." Why was she making excuses for him? She snapped her mouth shut.

"Oh, honey . . ."

"Obviously I was very upset with him. I basically ended our relationship. I can't believe he never told us. Never told me."

"Jo . . . ," Dad said.

"I hate thinking of it, Michael there, all alone trying to prove something to himself, and just the sheer pointlessness of it all. All that's bad enough, but knowing Beckett knew, that he kept it from all of us, and kept it from me even when I was starting to . . ." *Fall in love with him.*

Starting to, Madison?

She closed her eyes, caught her breath. Okay. So she'd fallen. She was stumbling-downhill, head-over-heels in love with him. A hapless casualty of gravity. But none of that mattered anymore.

"Jo," her dad said, "we have to tell her." Her parents looked at each other, held eye contact for a long moment.

A thread of dread wiggled down Madison's spine. "Dad? Tell me what?"

Dad squeezed Mom's hand. He opened his mouth, then closed it again.

"Mom?" What could they possibly need to say? She could only imagine, and the dread of it stilled everything inside her.

The swing came to a halt. Mom leaned forward, set her hand on Madison's arm. "Honey, there's something you need to know. Something we didn't tell you."

Mom looked at Dad. He pressed his lips together.

"What? You're scaring me."

Mom's hand tightened on her arm. "Honey, Michael didn't die from diving off that cliff."

Madison frowned, her mind trying to make sense of it. "He had a concussion. From hitting the water. He passed out and drowned. That's what the autopsy said. That's what you told me."

Something flickered in her mom's eyes.

Her dad planted his elbows on his knees. "He did have a concussion. Sometimes that does happen from hitting the water wrong. But that's not what happened to Michael."

"I don't understand. What are you saying?"

"Honey, he had a condition."

"We didn't know about it," Dad said. "He'd never had any symptoms up till that day, but the autopsy found it. They said he died suddenly and hit his head on a rock when he fell."

"He didn't drown? What condition? Why didn't you tell us?"

"It's a metabolic disorder, but they said they'd never seen this particular kind before," Dad said.

"They identify new types regularly. But it was some type of what they call inborn errors of metabolism. And we didn't tell you because—" Mom looked at Dad.

"It's genetic. And since they couldn't identify the type, there was no way of testing for it."

"Honey, we didn't want you kids living in fear that you might just . . . drop dead one day."

"I could have it, you mean? And Ryan and PJ and Jade too? You should've told us." How could her parents have kept something so important from them?

"It's not likely that any of you have it, but there's a higher likelihood among siblings. Yes, I think now we should've told you, but at the time . . ."

"Everyone was already reeling," Dad said. "We were a mess ourselves, and it was just easier not to talk about it."

"You were having trouble expressing your emotions," Mom said. "And Ryan lost all that weight. PJ couldn't stop crying, and Jade wouldn't talk to anyone. We didn't want to add to your burden. It was all we could do to keep breathing."

Madison remembered well. It amazed her sometimes that people got through that kind of pain and went on to lead normal lives. Still, she wished she'd known. Maybe it would've helped her settle Michael's death, and maybe it wouldn't have. Maybe it would've only made her worry about her own mortality.

"And we can't be tested for it?"

Dad shook his head. "The pathologist hadn't seen anything quite like it."

"I'm sorry, honey, if we made the wrong decision."

"We never even discussed it, really," Dad said. "Just fell into the pattern of not saying anything. And by the time the grief had eased up, the *why* of his death didn't seem to matter."

"Except poor Beckett," Mom said. "He must've been carrying a world of guilt."

Beckett. Her conversation with him replayed in her head.

Madison groaned, resting her forehead on her fingertips. "I was so hard on him. No, I was awful, I told him—" That Michael's death was all his fault. That she wanted him to go away. She closed her eyes. She didn't want to think about it.

"We'll tell him the truth," Mom said. "It's our fault you didn't know, that no one knew."

Still, she could've given the guy a little grace. It's not like he intentionally harmed Michael. In fact, he'd done nothing wrong at all. Madison should've taken a few deep breaths instead of reacting.

But she hadn't, she'd lashed out. She, who knew what it was to bear a load of guilt. Who knew the kind of havoc it could wreak in your life, the way it could mess with your mind, with your focus, with your ability to make sound decisions.

Who was she to throw stones? She'd been so mean and unforgiving. Cruel.

"Thanks, Mom, but I think I'd better tell him."

"Of course, whatever you want. Let us know if we can do anything."

She had so much to digest, but she had to get this straightened out right away for her own peace of mind. Was Beckett still at Bible study? She checked her watch, but wasn't sure what time it ended. It didn't matter anyway, because she had final dress rehearsal in fifteen minutes and she couldn't miss that.

She'd stop by his house afterward, no matter how late it was. The hours between now and then stretched out like a long, deserted highway even as a question frayed the dark corners of her mind: would Beckett even want her back?

Chapter Thirty-Seven

Madison's mind spun all the way to the theater. Michael didn't drown. He died of a disease—what had her parents called it? Some kind of metabolic disorder? And she and her siblings could have it too.

What were the symptoms? Were there any changes she needed to make? And then it occurred to her. It had been ten years since his death. Ten years was a long time in medicine.

When she arrived at the theater, she tracked down Drew backstage and pulled him aside.

"I have a favor to ask."

He finished buttoning his costume. "Sure, what is it?"

"If someone had an autopsy ten years ago, would those lab reports still be available?"

His fingers stopped at the odd question. "Sure. Slides and tissues are usually kept for years. Why?"

"How can I get them looked at again? The cause of death was narrowed down to a metabolic disease, but they couldn't identify the type at that time."

"Your brother?"

Madison nodded.

Drew rubbed his chin. "I'm not sure how that works."

"Can you find out?"

"I worked with a pathologist in Chicago. Tell you what. I'll give him a call and see what I can do."

She squeezed Drew's arm. "Thanks, Drew. I owe you one." She hurried into her costume. She had to put this aside for the next couple hours and focus on the play.

They were rehearsing act 1, scene 3 when the alarm sounded. The intermittent signal blared through the theater.

Madison covered her ears. "Is that the fire alarm?"

"I think so," Drew said.

"Probably nothing," someone added. "It's an old building."

More of the cast filtered onstage in various stages of dress.

"Should we leave?"

"Should we call the fire department?"

Madison pulled her costume, a bathrobe, tighter, sniffing the air. "Hey, guys, I smell smoke."

Everyone seemed to notice at the same time. They scrambled backstage, gathering their belongings and the rest of the cast on their way.

Drew pulled out his cell phone. "I'm calling 911."

The smoke grew worse as they hurried through the backstage clutter. Ahead of them, Madison saw fire. An old mannequin went up in flames. She pulled her shirt over her nose. Despite that, the smoke burned her lungs. Sweat trickled between her shoulder blades as they skirted a burning stack of rugs.

"Did we get everyone?" Madison asked Drew after he hung up. "Where's Layla?"

"I saw her up ahead."

Madison coughed. "What about Elliot?"

"I don't know."

"We have to go back!"

"He probably went out the front."

They couldn't take that chance. She thought back. "I saw him on a ladder before the alarm went off, adjusting the overhead rig."

She spun back the way they came.

"Madison, no!"

She ran down the hall. The heat got more intense with each turn. She heard Drew's footsteps on her heels.

"We have to hurry!" he said.

They skirted burning props and a falling curtain before reaching the stage. Madison spotted the ladder and saw a form huddled at the base.

"There he is!"

Elliot's knees were pulled to his chest, his face buried in his arms.

"Come on, Elliot, we have to go!" Madison tugged his arm. He resisted, burying his face further into his arms.

"There's no time!" Drew scooped Elliot into his arms. "Hurry up!"

A wall of fire blocked the front of the theater. They'd have to go back the way they came. Madison coughed into her shirt as she scurried past the burning debris, checking behind her as she went. Elliot's slight body bounced with each step.

The air was filled with smoke now. Her lungs were on fire, and her eyes burned so much she could hardly keep them open. She could barely see a few feet ahead.

She didn't know how Drew was managing. She rounded the last corner and knew the exit had to be close.

Finally she saw light, and the smoke cleared as she stepped out the door.

"Oh, thank God!" Dottie said. "That's everyone."

Madison dragged in a lungful of oxygen and gave another long hack. She staggered to where the others had gathered in the potholed parking lot behind the theater. She sank to her knees, heedless of the pebbles digging into her flesh.

"Deep breaths . . . clear your lungs," Drew said. "Ambulance on the way."

"I'm fine. Check Elliot."

The young man was hunched over and coughing hard.

Some were making phone calls to loved ones. A few moments later the squeal of a siren split the night.

"There's the fire truck," someone said. It pulled to the curb in front of the building. Smoke rose from the back, but no flames were visible. The group caught their breath, watching as the volunteer firefighters entered the building. Madison watched Ryan go in and breathed a prayer for his safety even as she coughed. Dottie had gone out front to assure them everyone was out.

"What could've started it?" someone nearby asked.

"I saw Wayne O'Reilly backstage about an hour ago. He was smoking."

Madison turned to see who'd spoken. Gary.

"I was working on the curtain mechanism, and I smelled smoke. Turned around, and there he was. Drunker'n a skunk too. I told him to put the thing out."

"I'll bet that's how it started."

Behind Gary, Layla was taking it all in. Madison was sorry she'd heard the speculations about her dad. Layla said something to one of the costume designers and slipped away from the group, hurrying toward the front of the building.

"Why would O'Reilly come around here anyway?"

Gary shrugged. "Who knows."

"Probably didn't know what he was doing."

"He almost sideswiped my dad a few years ago, driving drunk. Oughta put that man in jail and keep him there before he kills somebody."

"I'll bet he dropped the cigarette."

"We'll know soon enough."

"Lucky no one was hurt."

"Did anyone see him leave?"

Heads shook.

Madison pulled her robe against the slight chill in the air, hacking until it felt like her lungs would explode. It was the last thing she remembered before everything went black.

~

Beckett scooped the burger from the skillet and set it on a bun. The smell of cooking beef usually perked him up, but tonight it only made him queasy.

He put the pan in the sink and squirted a generous dollop of mustard on the burger. He needed to eat, hungry or not. And he needed to sleep, badly.

The past twenty-four hours had been rough, Madison's face lingering in his mind like a sweet perfume. He'd dreamed of her the night before. She'd been in a sinking boat. He'd dived in from the shore and swum toward her. But the farther he swam, the farther away the boat drifted, and it had been sinking quickly. Just as she'd disappeared under the surface, he'd awakened.

He'd thrown off the covers, his heart beating wildly, and lain there afraid to go back to sleep, afraid the dream would continue, that he'd be unable to find her. That he'd lose her. He'd suddenly understood why Madison's nightmares had disrupted her life so severely.

Compliments of you, O'Reilly.

He'd half expected to hear from other McKinleys today, maybe her dad or Ryan. He owed them a debt he could never repay.

He took his plate into the living room and sat in his favorite chair.

Someone burst through the front door.

"Where is he?" Layla slammed the door behind her, not stopping for an answer.

Beckett jumped up and followed her.

She pushed open Dad's door. He was facedown on the bed in the dim room.

"What did you do, Dad?" She shook him. "Wake up and answer me!"

Beckett grabbed her arm. "He's out cold, Layla. What's going on?"

Even in the darkness, he saw something black on her face. Her eyes were shooting darts.

"I'll tell you what's going on. Our dad set the theater on fire!"

He stiffened. "What? Are you okay?"

"I'm fine."

"Wait . . . tonight, during rehearsals?" Madison . . .

Layla kicked the bed. "She's on her way to the hospital, along with a few others."

He froze inside. "Is she okay?"

"Smoke inhalation. They were giving her oxygen and taking her in for X-rays and stuff."

Beckett pulled her into the living room, his mind on Madison.

He wanted to be with her right now. Wanted to see for himself that she was all right.

"Sit down. Are you sure you don't need to go to the hospital?"

"I was one of the first out. I'm fine."

"And Madison . . . You sure she's going to be okay?"

"That's what Drew said." She paced across the room. "I can't believe him!"

"Why do they think he had anything to do with this?"

"How long's he been home?"

"'Bout half an hour."

"He was at the theater. Gary saw him smoking backstage."

Beckett pinched the bridge of his nose. Please, no. Hadn't his dad caused enough trouble? "Maybe it wasn't the cigarette. Was anyone backstage ironing or anything?"

"No, we were all rehearsing. It was him, Beckett, you know it was. It always is." She dropped into a chair and let out a long breath. "Why don't you go check on Madison?"

Beckett was the last person Madison wanted to see right now. "How bad's the fire?"

She shrugged, the fight seeming to have drained out of her. "I don't know. It seemed pretty bad. There sure was a lot of smoke."

"And you got checked?"

"Just by Drew."

"And you're sure Madison's okay?"

Layla tilted her head. "Beckett. Just go to the hospital."

He wanted to. He wanted to look her in the face, run his hands over her, know for himself she was okay. Then he remembered the look on her face when he'd told her the truth. The shades of pain and betrayal that had colored her expression.

Even if she could forgive him, it was still hopeless. Whatever made him think he was good enough? His dad had gone to jail just long enough to make Beckett forget his place. Somewhere down with the muck at the bottom of the river. That Madison had ever looked twice at him was a miracle. It had never been clearer that the two of them were on different playing fields.

"It'll be all over town by midnight, what Dad did," he said.

He was tired of living with the black cloud hanging over his head. He prayed no one had been seriously hurt tonight, but it was only a matter of time. A man could only get lucky so many times. Beckett was going to have to do something. Something drastic.

Layla quirked a brow. "We should be used to it by now."

He pushed the plate back on the coffee table and settled into his chair. He couldn't eat now.

Layla eyed the burger. "You gonna eat that?"

He handed her the plate. The girl could outeat a sumo wrestler. He wasn't sure where she put it.

"Anger makes me hungry." She bit into the burger with gusto. Beckett brought her a washcloth, and she wiped the soot from her face.

"Thanks. How long will he be out? So help me, I'm gonna have it out with him when he wakes up."

"Won't do any good. He probably won't even remember being there."

"What about liability? Good grief, if the building burns to the ground, are we liable?"

"Let's take one thing at a time."

She set down the burger and pulled out her phone, dialing.

"Who you calling?"

"Sara Beth. She's in the play with— Hey, Sara, it's Layla. How's it going over there? . . . Uh-huh. Yeah . . . That's good . . .

Yeah, I know what they're saying. He's fine. He's here at his house . . . Okay. Well, thanks, Sara. Go home and get some rest." She hung up the phone.

"They're still fighting the fire. She said it looks bad. A couple more of the crew were taken to the hospital just to be on the safe side."

"But of course Dad comes home unscathed."

"Of course."

Layla tucked into the burger again and Beckett turned on the TV. He didn't even want to think about tomorrow.

CHAPTER THIRTY-EIGHT

BECKETT PUT THE PLYWOOD ON THE TABLE AND SET THE saw's blade depth. He'd already marked the curve, now he just had to make the cut. The boat was coming along nicely.

The regatta prize money still sat in his bank account. He had big plans for his business, but he didn't feel right about taking the money. Hadn't felt right about it when Madison had given it to him, and he especially didn't feel right about it now.

He put on his goggles and turned on the circular saw. Rigsby scampered from the building. Beckett guided the wood, easing the blade along the outside of the line.

He'd slept restlessly until Layla had called him early and let him know Madison and the others had been released from the hospital.

The theater fire had been the talk of the town all day. The building had been reduced to a heap of smoldering brick. The disaster had been plastered over the front page of the *Chapel Springs Gazette*.

Word was also out about his dad's possible role in the fire, though the official report wouldn't be out until next week. Beckett spent the day lying low, as he always did in the wake of one of Dad's incidents.

He turned the wood, following the drawn-on curve. A shadow fell over the table, and he looked up.

Madison came to a halt a few feet away, one hand tucked into the pocket of her khakis, the other resting on Rigsby's head. The sight of her was like a sucker punch. She could be dead right now if things had gone differently. A lot of people could be. All because of Dad.

Beckett shut off the machine, removed the goggles. The sudden silence was sharper than the blade of the saw. He ran a hand through his hair, and sawdust flittered to the floor.

"Hi," she said.

"Hi there."

"Sorry to drop by like this." Her voice sounded husky. The smoke inhalation. She didn't seem angry, though she had reason. More than one.

"You're okay?"

"Yeah, I'm fine."

"I'm glad."

There was the understatement of the century. Layla's reassurances had only gone so far. Seeing Madison there in the flesh was balm to his soul. He looked her over, taking in the sweet curve of her cheeks, the delicate slope of her shoulders.

"It was a little scary."

"Freaked Layla out. Everyone's okay though, right?"

She nodded, scratched Rigsby behind the ears. The dog gazed up in half-lidded adoration. Lucky dog.

"Sad about the theater though," she said. "It was a fine old building. So much history."

"And the play?"

"There's talk of using the town square. Maybe next weekend. It won't be the same, but . . ."

He nodded. Speculation about his dad's part in the fire

hovered between them like a heavy fog, neither acknowledging it. No way was he bringing it up. Wished he could forget it altogether. That and so many other things.

"You have a minute?" she asked.

"Ah, sure." He looked around. This was no place to talk. Nowhere to sit. Dad was in the house. Beckett walked past her into the yard, where darkness had begun to fall. Twilight silhouetted the trees against a pink sky. He wondered if she was going to bring it up now, his dad's role in the fire. Maybe she didn't know he was aware of the gossip.

He gestured toward the picnic table. An empty beer bottle perched on the edge. He knocked it over, and it thumped onto the ground, silencing a nearby cricket.

He lowered himself onto the bench across from her. His first mistake. It put them face-to-face. He could smell her subtle perfume. Her bangs draped over her eyes, and his fingers itched to brush them back. He clenched his fist. Those eyes, wide and vulnerable, only made him want to take her in his arms. He swallowed hard.

"How are you otherwise?" he asked, remembering the painful night he'd put her through. That's all he really needed to know. All he'd wanted to know since they'd parted three days ago. He could get through this. He could lose her, if he just knew she'd be okay. But, man, she'd had a hard week.

"I'm good. I'm—I didn't handle the other night very well. I'm sorry."

She owed him nothing. "You had every right to be upset. I'm the one who's sorry."

She looked down, bit her lip. She began picking at a loose fleck of wood on the table. "I was going to come over last night after rehearsal, but then the fire . . . A lot's happened since we talked. I'm not sure where to start."

For some reason his mind went straight to Drew Landon. Maybe she'd hooked up with him again. Maybe she'd realized she could do a lot better than Beckett O'Reilly.

His gut ached at the thought. *He's a good guy, Beckett. Doesn't she deserve that? A man who isn't an embarrassment? A man who'd be a good husband someday, a good father?*

"I got some things straightened out with God, for starters," she said. "You were right about all that. I've been journaling the last couple days about stuff. I guess I have a lot of grieving I never really got out."

He didn't deserve any credit, but her decision warmed him on the inside. "I'm glad for you. That's great."

Her eyes flickered to his, then back to her fingers. "I have a long way to go, but it's a start."

No thanks to him. Since she was looking down, he took the opportunity to look at her, memorize her features. He loved her perfect nose and her little elfin chin. He'd seen it set before, so stubborn, but even then she was adorable. Love for her welled up inside, expanding until he felt he'd burst with it.

"There's something else . . . ," she said.

He was afraid to speak. Afraid if he opened his mouth, his love for her would spill out. He locked his teeth together.

She put her hand over his. Despite the warmth of the evening, it was ice-cold. He took it instinctively and warmed it between his own.

"Something you don't know," she said. "Something I didn't know until—" She closed her mouth, her eyes drilling into his. "Michael didn't drown, Beckett. He didn't dive off that cliff after you left. His death had nothing to do with you."

She wasn't making sense. Of course Michael had drowned. They'd dragged his body from the river.

He shook his head.

"He didn't drown. Michael had a medical anomaly, a metabolic disorder of some kind. That's how he died. It was in the autopsy report."

"But you said . . ."

"I didn't know. Not until yesterday. My parents never told us."

He had nothing to do with Michael's death? He tried to wrap his mind around it. "Are you sure?"

"My parents didn't know anything was wrong with him, and once they found out, after the autopsy, they didn't tell us because . . . they didn't want us to worry. It's genetic, that type of disorder, but they couldn't identify the specific type, and they didn't want us kids living in fear we'd just, you know, drop dead someday."

Drop dead? The words were a jolt of electricity. Did Madison have the condition too? "Are you okay? You need to get tested."

She shook her head.

"I mean it, Madison, don't mess around with this."

Her head tilted, her eyes softening. She squeezed his hand. "It was something the pathologist hadn't seen before. There's no way of testing for it that we know of. But that's not the point. The point is . . . you had nothing to do with Michael's death. I'm so sorry about the things I said, about the way I reacted. It was wrong of me, regardless of how he died."

He wasn't responsible. Michael wasn't gone because of him. It was beginning to sink in. He drew in a deep breath and let it out, letting himself savor the rush of air, the rush of serenity. It was a good feeling.

"Can you ever forgive me? I was so mean. I know I don't

deserve it." The smallness of her voice put a crack in his heart. Her eyes sparkled. She blinked, and a tear spilled over.

"Of course. Of course I do. You're fine, Maddy. All's forgiven."

He realized he'd just called her a pet name, that he was stroking her hand with his thumb. He let go, and her hand fell to the table. He shoved his own hands under the table where they wouldn't be tempted to touch her again.

He wouldn't lead her on when it was time to let her go. He was relieved to hear the truth, but it didn't change things between them.

A frown creased her brow as she pulled her hand back. Her brown eyes, like dark chocolate in the evening light, studied his face. "Well . . . thanks. I appreciate it. I . . . didn't know what to expect when I came over."

He read the hope in her eyes. She was waiting for him to reach over and kiss it all better. And God help him, he wanted to. So badly his heart was beating up into his throat, closing it off. He clenched his fists.

Help me be strong enough to let her go, God. To do what's best for her when I want nothing more than to—

"Beckett . . . ?"

He had to get out of there fast. He stood. "I should, ah, get back to my boat . . . I have a lot to do on it yet." *Stupid. She knows you don't have a buyer.*

A flash of hurt flickered in her eyes as she slowly stood and stepped out from the table. "Sure. Sure, I'll, uh, let you get back to it. Sorry I interrupted your work."

Rigsby nestled against his leg, and he set his hand on the dog's head. "You're not an interruption. Thanks for coming, for clearing things up." He winced at his formal tone.

"No problem. I . . . guess I'll see you later." Her voice cracked on the last word, and as she turned, he saw a shimmer of tears in her eyes.

He locked his jaw in place, stuffed his hands in his pockets, and turned away before he did something he'd regret.

Chapter Thirty-Nine

When the knock sounded at the door, Madison's heart froze. She set the spoon inside the half-empty cereal bowl and followed Lulu to the door. Her conversation with Beckett the evening before had filled her night with restlessness. Her eyes were heavy with lack of sleep and unshed tears.

But hope bloomed inside as she reached for the handle and pulled it open.

"Morning." Ryan stood on her stoop, holding two to-go cups from the Coachlight.

She opened the door, pushing back disappointment. "Come on in." He handed her the coffee. "Thanks."

"Your voice is still messed up."

"They said it would take a few days. Want some breakfast?"

He perched against the back of the recliner. "I'm on my way to meet Daniel. Just wanted to see how you were doing today."

"I'm fine, just fine." She forced a brightness she didn't feel into her tone and turned into the kitchen before he could look in her eyes and know she lied.

He followed her into the kitchen. "It's been a lot. The fire, the news about Michael . . ."

"When did they tell you?"

"Yesterday after I checked on you."

"Jade and PJ know too?"

He nodded. "It's so much to take in. That Michael didn't drown. That we might have some serious illness."

She dumped her cereal down the sink, rinsed the bowl, not hungry all of a sudden. "I'm looking into that, just so you know. Drew knows someone who can help, maybe."

He nodded. "That's nice of him."

She set the bowl in the dishwasher and shut the door. "I'll let you know what I find out."

~

Madison slipped her arms into the sweater and glanced in the oval time-speckled mirror. She wore a white skirt, a red sweater, and a year's supply of makeup. She sat at the tiny dressing table and began curling her hair. Dottie had opened up her home for the cast to ready themselves in.

Volunteers had worked hard all week to set up a makeshift stage. A group from church had worked to replace costumes and props, and art students from Chapel Springs High had come in after school and assisted with the new set. They'd had two rehearsals on their new stage, the last one running late into the night. The hoarseness had left her voice, and the only remnant of the fire was the heap of brick and ash.

She wound a strand of hair in the curling iron and noticed her hands shaking.

Nerves. She wasn't sure what was causing them: the imminent opening night performance or her conversation with Beckett the week before. She couldn't expunge it from her mind. The way he'd pulled his hand from hers. The way he'd stood, so abruptly the picnic table had tilted.

But inside she understood. He wanted someone without the baggage. Her life was messed up, she couldn't deny it. He'd seen her fall apart on her birthday, then days later she'd lashed out at him. She'd come unhinged twice in a matter of days, had practically lost her job. What man wouldn't be spooked?

She was on her way to becoming a healthier, happier person though. She was journaling every day and was starting to sleep better. She'd slept until almost nine this morning, unheard of. She hadn't had the nightmare in over a week, and she couldn't help but think she'd turned a corner. She was nearly fit to return to work. *Thank you, Jesus. For the rest, for the peace, despite the storms.*

One of the actors bumped her table as he scurried past her corner. "Sorry, Madison!"

The other actors dashed through the bedrooms, looking for props and wigs. Opening night began in thirty minutes, and she could already hear the buzz of the audience through the open window. The whole community was coming out to support the animal shelter. Even the nursing home was running shuttles. News of the fire had only spurred support.

Beckett would come, of course, to watch his sister. Knowing he'd be there made her nerves jangle more. It would be awkward, performing those intimate scenes with Drew, knowing Beckett was watching.

Stop it, Madison.

She couldn't be thinking of Beckett. She had to put him from her mind for the next few hours and concentrate on her part. She owed it to her fellow actors, to the audience.

She slipped a chunk of hair into the curling iron and wound it up. Her phone vibrated on the tabletop. She set the iron down and answered.

"Hi, honey," Mom said. "Just wanted to wish you luck."

"Break a leg," Dad added.

"Thanks. I'm starting to get nervous."

"You'll be great, as always," Mom said. "I'm so glad they were able to get the square set up so quickly."

"I know. It took a lot of people to make it happen."

"We'd better go, Jo," Dad said. "We're picking up your grandpa on the way," he told Madison.

"I'll see you at the party afterward."

Madison turned off the phone and greeted Layla as she dashed by in her lab coat costume. The opening night party for the cast and crew and their families was being held at the town hall after the play. Her parents and some of the other families had been preparing for it all day.

Drew squeezed her shoulder as he passed, ducking to meet her eyes in the mirror. "You ready for this?"

"Ready or not."

His pathologist friend from Chicago had agreed to look into the autopsy report, but he'd warned her these things could take awhile.

"You'll be great. Just don't forget that last bit of blocking we added in act 2."

"I've been going over it in my head all day." That and so many other things.

"Drew," Celeste Parker called. "I need help with this bandage."

"A doctor's work is never done," Madison said.

He patted his pager. "Tell me about it."

Madison's lips parted. "Oh, Drew, please tell me you're not on—"

"Just kidding," he said, eyes twinkling.

She swatted him as he walked away.

Chapter Forty

Beckett settled deeper into the metal chair as Layla appeared, the spotlight following her long-legged gait across the makeshift stage. She looked like a beautiful nerdy doctor in a lab coat and black-framed glasses. She delivered her lines with perfection and exited the stage. It was her third and final appearance.

A hush had fallen over the packed square as the play neared its end. The production had gone smoothly except for a curtain malfunction and a slight stumble by a minor character.

Beckett had arrived as the play started and slinked into a back-row seat. He was tired of the looks he'd been getting all week. Some sympathetic, some disgusted. He should be used to it by now. But this latest shenanigan of his dad's was worse than anything he'd done before. The cause of the fire hadn't been released yet, but this nonsense with his dad had to stop. Beckett was going to take action soon.

Seeing Madison onstage had been hard. He'd been over their last conversation so many times, he'd memorized it. And there was plenty he wished he could forget. Like the look in her eyes when he'd distanced himself from her. The way she'd caught her trembling lip between her teeth just before she'd left.

It had been hard enough tonight just seeing her, but watching Madison and Drew feign love . . . that was torture. He had a knot in his stomach that had nothing to do with the coming climax.

Maybe that's because they're so good together, O'Reilly, you ever think about that? Of course he thought about it. How could he help it, when the two had flaunted it all over the stage? If there wasn't chemistry between them, they both deserved Oscars.

The man beside him let out a soft snore. Beckett envied him the escape.

A few minutes later the stage lights dimmed as the scene ended, then came back up. Madison was sitting on a bed in a robe. Someone knocked at the door. She opened it to Drew. He wore a navy suit that looked as if it had been tailored for him. Their practice was evident in the easy delivery of lines and their natural movement around the stage.

Drew reached out and touched Madison's shoulder.

Beckett stiffened, the knot inside tightening as he recognized the dialogue. It was the scene they'd been rehearsing in the park when Beckett had rushed in like a raging maniac.

He forced himself to watch as Drew spun Madison around and pulled her into his arms. It was about that time that Beckett had landed his right hook. He clenched his fist, realizing with shame how good that would feel about now.

"I can't live without you," Drew said, leaning into Madison. "I know I don't deserve you, but you're my everything."

She stared into Drew's eyes for a long moment before shaking her head. "Don't say that."

"Don't you see, Eleanor? I can't let you go. Be my wife, and I swear I'll never make you regret it, not for a moment."

Beckett clenched his jaw.

"I want to say yes. You know I do . . ."

He tipped her chin up. "I love you. I'll always love you. Say you'll marry me. Say it, and make me the happiest man on earth."

Beckett was glad he was in the back where he couldn't see the tears that were no doubt glassing Madison's eyes or see her mouth softening at his words.

"I've loved you from the beginning. How could I say anything else?" Madison said.

Drew pulled her close and lowered his head.

Beckett fought the urge to look away. *It's only make-believe. It's not real. She doesn't love Drew.*

But maybe she should.

He forced himself to watch the kiss. He had to get it through his thick skull that Madison was not his, would never be his.

Mercifully, the lights dimmed and the curtain swept down. The audience cheered. The man beside him startled awake and began clapping.

Beckett stood with the rest of the audience, his mind on the final scene, on the kiss. He'd bet Drew had enjoyed it, had enjoyed all the rehearsals.

Much as he wanted to hate the man, he had no reason to. He'd heard nothing but good things about him. How could he deny that Drew was better for Madison? She deserved a man who could slide right into the McKinley family circle and never miss a beat. Drew wasn't dragging a dysfunctional family behind him. Drew didn't have a blemished reputation in the community or a father who drove drunk and burned the theater down. He wasn't carrying a cesspool of genetics to pass along to her future children.

The roar of the audience grew louder at the curtain call. Beckett watched as they applauded Drew. He gestured toward Madison, who took a bow to thunderous applause.

A moment later the curtain fell, and Beckett drifted away

from the crowd. He wanted nothing more than to go home, but Layla was expecting him at the opening night party.

He turned toward the town hall, following other family members, his gait slow. The streetlamps glowed in the darkness, and a light breeze scented the night air with something sweet. He passed the vet practice and wondered when Madison would return to work. Wondered if the nightmares were better. She'd gotten some things worked out with God, she'd said. He was glad. God would help her through everything that lay ahead.

God could even get Beckett through this. Though at the moment, the heaviness of losing her weighed on him. He told himself it was for the best. Letting her go was the loving thing to do. And if Drew stepped into his shoes, it would be good for Madison. Painful as all get-out for Beckett, but he'd get over her eventually.

Wouldn't he?

By the time he reached the town hall, the party was already under way. Families clustered under the dimmed lights, music flooded the spacious room, and colorful streamers hung in graceful loops from the high ceilings. The smell of coffee and popcorn permeated the air.

His eyes swept the room for Madison, though he knew it was unlikely she'd arrived yet. The rest of the McKinleys were gathered at a circular table near the back. An area to avoid.

A few minutes later he spotted Layla at the punch bowl on the far side of the room, opposite a makeshift dance floor. He wove through the tables toward her. She'd ditched her doctor costume for her usual jeans and finished it with a filmy white blouse.

He kissed her on the cheek, determined to shake off the melancholy. "Who knew we had such astounding talent in the family. What's next—Broadway?"

Layla emptied the ladle into her paper cup. "Oh, shut it. I had a whopping four lines."

"You were good. Totally believable. In fact"—he shifted to the side and lifted the hem of his shirt—"I've been having this pain right here—"

She elbowed him, nearly spilling her punch. "I have a pain too; need me to tell you where it is?"

He stifled a grin as he poured himself some punch. "I think I know."

Beckett handed the ladle to the next in line, then moved over to the brick wall, wanting to find a place in the shadows. A few of the cast had arrived and were starting a line dance to "Country Girl."

"Oooh, it's my song. Come on, Beck."

"Oh no. You're on your own."

"Party pooper. Hold my punch." Layla shoved her cup into his hand and joined the growing crowd.

Beckett stepped back against the wall, smiling as he watched his sister. She laughed with another woman as they botched the steps. She'd grown up to be a beautiful woman, remarkably well adjusted.

The crowd grew on the dance floor until space required the dancers to take baby steps. One of the cast set his hands on Layla's waist and pulled her against his chest as they moved to the beat.

Beckett straightened as Layla pushed the guy's hands off and tossed her long hair, completing a turn step. When the man turned the other way, Beckett relaxed against the wall again. Maybe she didn't need her big brother anymore. Maybe she could take care of herself. She was on the dance floor, living it up, and he was in the shadows, wanting to hide.

Beckett turned his back to the crowd and scanned the photo boards someone had tacked up, the cast and crew during play rehearsals. His greedy eyes soaked up photo after photo. Madison gesturing. Madison smiling. Madison laughing. He remembered that melodic sound and wondered if he'd ever hear it again.

A few minutes later he felt a hand on his shoulder. He turned and found Layla. Only then did he realize how much he'd been hoping it was Madison.

Layla reclaimed her punch and pointed at one of the pictures. "Oh, that's hilarious." A few of the crew had joined her.

Jessie Brooks, who'd designed the sets, came up on his other side. "Long time no see, Beckett."

He'd gone out with her a few times over the winter. She lived a couple streets over from him and taught French and art at the high school.

He nodded her way. "Jessie. Nice job on the set."

Her rosy lips curled upward and her green eyes sparkled. "Thanks! It's been pretty crazy this last week, getting everything ready." She pointed out some of the photos and launched into a story of how she'd salvaged the sunset background.

She was a nice woman. Patient, pretty, kindhearted. There wasn't a thing wrong with her.

Except that she wasn't Madison.

"I don't suppose you'd want to grab a bite somewhere?" Jessie was saying. "I missed dinner, and popcorn isn't going to cut it."

A commotion sounded across the room, and applause began slowly, picking up until it drowned out the music. Beckett turned and faced the incoming party just as Madison and Drew emerged, smiling as the fans clapped and whistled.

Even the crowd seemed to recognize them as a couple. Their

hair was the exact same shade of brown with a bit of wave. They were both slender, similar in height, and attractive in their trendy jeans. They'd make beautiful kids.

The thought put a knot in his throat. He swallowed hard, but it didn't budge. He wished he could move far away, where he wouldn't have to watch her falling for someone else. But he had his grandpa to look after, not to mention his dad to keep out of trouble.

He took in the sight of her, realizing there was something different about her. And then he figured it out. She didn't look tired. The dark circles had faded. Even her color looked better.

Having you out of her life has been good for her. See how happy and well rested she looks?

He told himself that was stupid. That the changes were a result of time, of rest, of coming to terms with God. But his heart refused to believe it ended there.

She was beautiful, her cheeks flushed with excitement, her eyes sparkling. Madison's eyes caught his across the room. She stopped, her smile wilting.

Yes, she was better off without him. If he'd doubted it before now, he didn't doubt it any longer.

Her lips curved up a little, just for him, and his heart gave an extra beat.

Drew set his hand on Madison's shoulder and leaned close to whisper something in her ear.

Beckett frowned. What was he doing? He was supposed to be letting her go. Instead he was gazing at her like a lovesick puppy.

He pulled his eyes from Madison and locked onto the first thing he saw. Jessie.

"So what do you say?" the woman asked. "Are you hungry?"

The thought of food turned his stomach, but the thought of escape—that held appeal.

"Ah, sure. Sounds good."

"Cappy's is still open. Let me grab my bag." She walked a few tables over.

Beckett got Layla's attention. "You don't mind if I take off, do you?"

"I guess not. The party just started though."

"You're in good hands."

"Beck, maybe you should hang around, talk to Madison."

A short distance away, Jessie shouldered her purse and smiled at Beckett, waiting.

"I don't think so. You have fun though." He started for Jessie, but before he took a step, Layla grabbed his arm.

Her eyes swung to Jessie and back to him. Her brows drew together. "What are you doing?"

He gathered his courage, looked her in the eye. "The right thing."

Madison watched Beckett escort Jessie Brooks from the party, the air leaving her lungs in a rush. She hadn't realized he'd be here, had frozen in her tracks when she'd seen him.

Then his face had softened. The music had faded and everyone else in the room disappeared. She'd felt a pull so strong it propelled her forward. She'd taken a step in his direction when he'd turned away. Toward cute little Jessie Brooks. Moments later he was leaving with the woman.

If there was any doubt before, after their last conversation, it was all cleared up now. He couldn't get far enough away from the mess that was her life.

"You okay?" Drew said in her ear.

She swallowed hard and put on a smile. "I'm fine."

Her family waved from a nearby table.

"Have fun," she told Drew, knowing she'd never be able to follow her own advice.

She kept the smile plastered to her face as she walked toward her family, dreading the long evening ahead. She'd just pretend her heart wasn't twisting like a wrung-out washcloth. She could pretend. Hadn't she just done so onstage in front of all Chapel Springs?

CHAPTER FORTY-ONE

TODAY WAS THE DAY. BECKETT ROLLED FROM BED AND headed for the shower, staying under the spray for an extra ten minutes, working the plan in his mind.

He'd tossed and turned the night before, despite an early night. He and Jessie had gone to Cappy's but he hadn't been into it, into her. He'd tried to hold up his end of the conversation, but she was no fool.

"You're still hung up on Madison McKinley," she said, halfway through the pizza.

He opened his mouth but closed it again. What could he say?

"It's okay. I mean, I'd hoped, but . . ." She shrugged.

He hadn't meant to lead her on. "I'm sorry. I shouldn't have come."

She gave a soft sigh and dredged up a smile. "Let's just be two friends eating a meal, all right?"

The night had gotten better after that, less awkward. They'd parted as friends, but Beckett had no intention of repeating the experience.

After drying off, he dressed and spent the rest of his morning doing research on the computer while his dad slept off last night's overindulgence. By the time Dad slinked from his room, holding his head, Beckett had finished the research and made a dozen phone calls. He'd called Layla when he'd found a place.

"I'm coming over," she said.

"No, let me handle this. He's going to get upset, things might get physical. I'll feel better if you're not in the line of fire."

She'd put up a fight but had finally backed down.

Now all he had to do was wait for his dad to down some ibuprofen and finish a cup of coffee. Beckett was determined, but he wasn't stupid.

He snapped open the newspaper, and the headline, big and bold, caught his eye: THEATER FIRE CAUSED BY FAULTY WIRING.

Beckett read the article, his heart pounding. When he was finished he set the paper aside, let out a deep sigh. The investigation was complete, and the results were a reprieve.

But that didn't change his mind about what he was going to do.

When Dad settled in the living room and snatched up the sports section, Beckett took a deep breath. "We need to talk, Dad."

"Later. My head's splitting."

"Later you'll be buzzed, then wasted. We need to talk now."

The paper rattled as his dad closed it and flung it onto the coffee table, muttering something about a man finding no rest in his own house. His eye caught the headline on the main section.

"Ah, now lookie there. What'd I tell you? It wasn't my fault after all, was it?"

Dad looked older all of a sudden. Bags under his eyes, permanent lines etched by years of hard living.

"Not this time."

His dad huffed.

"Things are going to change around here, Dad. I'm not doing this anymore. I made a few phone calls this morning, and I found a place that can help you."

"I don't need help."

"Here's the deal, Dad. You have a choice. Either I can take you to this facility where you can get help, or you can leave on your own. One way or another, you're out of here today."

His dad laughed, no humor evident. "You can't kick me out of my own home."

"It's *my* home. And I'm done sitting by while you ruin your health, risk lives—"

"It wasn't me!"

"Two choices, Dad. Which will it be?"

"You'd kick your old man out? I don't even have a job! How am I supposed to eat? Where am I supposed to sleep?"

"You have a problem, and I'm trying to get you help."

"I don't have a problem! When are you going to get that through your head? You were always the stubborn one!"

Beckett got up, plucked a suitcase from the hall closet, and headed toward his dad's room.

He'd begun emptying the first drawer when Dad entered the room and grabbed his arm. "Put that back!"

He shook his father off and faced him. Beckett had four inches and considerable mass on him. He didn't want to use it, but he wasn't doing this anymore.

He shot Dad a look of warning, then continued packing until the suitcase was full, ignoring his father's loud protests. When he was finished, he zipped the case.

"What kind of son are you?" Dad's voice shook. "I'll go to Layla's, stay with her. She won't turn me away!"

Over his dead body. "I have your car keys, and Layla won't let you in her house. I'll call the police if I have to and have you removed. Or you can get in my truck quietly and get yourself some help."

Dad's hair was spiked in every direction as if he'd run his fingers through it a dozen times. Fear lit his onyx eyes.

Beckett softened. "It's a good facility, Dad. I was on the phone with the director for an hour. You'll get good care, and it's not very far away."

"How can you do this to me? I'm your dad . . . I raised you alone after your mom left." His voice cracked as his eyes glassed over.

Beckett ached inside, but he was going to speak the truth. "Grandpa raised us, Dad."

His dad walked from the room, hitting the door frame on the way out. Beckett followed him with the suitcase.

Dad stopped in the living room, his hands on the back of the recliner, squeezing the cushioned back until his knuckles went white.

Beckett gave him a moment. It was a big decision. Life altering.

Please, God. Let him decide to get help. For his own sake. He has a lot of life ahead of him, but he'll never find his way like this.

He could hear his dad's shallow breaths, see the rise and fall of shoulders that used to seem much broader. He was Beckett's dad, but for too many years Beckett had been the caretaker. He was still taking care of him, doing the hard thing. Sometimes love meant letting go. He was learning all about that.

"What's it gonna be, Dad?" he said quietly.

His dad lowered his head, pinched his nose. It was the same gesture Layla teased Beckett about. He prayed that's where the genes stopped.

"You don't leave me a choice." His words were coated in bitterness. Beckett didn't care if they were coated in horse manure as long as Dad went to the treatment facility.

"Let's go then."

"I need a drink first." Dad turned toward the kitchen.

Beckett grabbed his arm. "No. We're leaving."

"Just one more," Dad said, his eyes frantic. "I need it."

"Now, Dad." He turned the man toward the door and grabbed the suitcase. It was going to be a long ride.

CHAPTER FORTY-TWO

THE OTHER SHOWS HAD GONE AS WELL AS OPENING NIGHT, but Madison was relieved to have the production behind her. She'd heard from the Kneeling Nanas that Beckett's dad had been admitted to a rehab somewhere in Kentucky. The women lifted him in prayer each morning, and Madison had added him to her own growing list. She was glad for Beckett's family. It would be a long road, but it was a good start.

The aroma of brewed coffee perked up Madison's senses as she entered the Coachlight Coffeehouse. A jazz tune played quietly through the speakers. Only a few patrons were scattered through-out the room. She spotted her honorary brother hunched over a tablet at a nearby table. Sometimes Daniel used the shop as his office away from home, though she hadn't seen him here lately.

She headed toward him. "It's not the same place without our girl, is it?"

He looked up, smiling, his dark hair falling into his eyes. "Hi, Madison." His eyes darted toward the corner stage where Jade had played her guitar for hours on end. "No, it's not. Have you heard from her lately?"

"No, but Mom did last week. She said she seemed okay. You want her number?"

"Ah, sure, if you have it."

He scrawled it on his tablet, then pushed out the other chair with his foot. "Have a seat."

"Oh, that's okay. I'm meeting Cassidy." She noticed he was writing in his journal and gestured to it. "I love mine, by the way. I've been using it a lot."

He laid his hand flat on the binding and tore the top sheet along the perforated edge. "Just finishing a note to my folks. They like letters—the old-fashioned kind." He folded the paper in thirds, making sharp creases with his thumb.

The neat folds flagged something in her memory. Or was it the perforated edges? She stared at the paper. The dimensions . . . the off-white coloring, gray lines. Just like her own journal, but there was something else . . .

An image flashed in her mind. A typed poem centered on that same paper. She should've recognized the paper before—it was just like her own journal—but she'd had her mind on other things.

She watched Daniel finish the folds and tuck the letter into the journal. Not an ordinary journal, the kind that could be snagged from the local shelves of the Book Nook, but a special-order item from Chicago.

Could it have been Daniel all along? She could hardly fathom it.

He was looking at her, his brow quirked, and she realized she'd been staring.

"It was you . . . ?"

She watched confusion flitter over his features, humor lighting his eyes. He shook his head. "What?"

"The paper is the same. The lines, the folding, everything. It was you . . . the rose, the cards, the notes . . ."

Gravity pulled at the corners of his lips, the humor fleeing. He grew somber. A thread of panic laced his eyes.

He'd been like a brother for so long, it was hard to imagine him thinking of Jade that way. He called her "squirt" and mussed her hair. He'd taught Jade her first guitar chords and defended her at school. Like a brother. Or like . . .

"Madison, I—"

"Sorry I'm late!" Cassidy threw her arm around Madison's shoulders. "Hello, Mr. Mayor."

"Ah, hi, Cassidy." His eyes never left Madison's.

"Have you ordered?" Cassidy squinted at the menu. "I'm seriously considering that new Peppermint Pattie thing. Probably has a zillion calories, but you only live once, right?"

She gave Madison's shoulders a squeeze and headed toward the counter.

Madison turned to follow. "Uh, I guess I'll see you later, Daniel."

"Madison . . ."

She turned at his worried tone and met his blue eyes. When had he grown from scrawny, awkward teenager to grown man with broad shoulders and a clean-shaven face? Into a man who was infatuated with her little sister? How long had he been fighting these feelings?

"Please," he said. "Don't . . ."

She felt a stab of pity. Jade had no clue how he felt. His name hadn't once come up in all their speculations.

She tried for an encouraging smile. "I won't."

The worry lines stretching across his forehead remained, as did the fear lighting his eyes, the tension in his shoulders.

"I promise," she said.

He swallowed and nodded once.

Madison joined Cassidy in line, ordering when it was her turn, her mind still reeling. "Venti decaf, please."

"Decaf?" Cassidy said. "You feeling all right?"

"I'm cutting back. Doctor's orders."

"Have you heard anything yet?"

Drew's friend, the pathologist, reread the slides from Michael's autopsy. Two years ago Michael's metabolic disease had been identified. She'd made a doctor's appointment the day she'd found out.

"Haven't gotten the results back yet," Madison said.

"PJ and Jade and Ryan are getting tested too?"

"Yeah. We should know soon."

When she and Cassidy had their coffee, they settled into a booth in the back corner of the shop, Madison's mind still on Daniel and his feelings for Jade. His table was empty now.

Cassidy caught Madison up on the goings-on at work, chattering a mile a minute. "You look good," she said when she came up for air. "Maybe you needed the break."

"That and a little interior work." She'd already told Cassidy about her step of faith. "I've been journaling about Michael and meeting with the Kneeling Nanas twice a week for their prayer circle. I'm sleeping better, thinking more clearly, and focusing better."

Cassidy tilted her head, her eyebrows raised. "But . . ."

"What makes you think there's a but?"

"We've been friends a long time. I know when my best bud's nursing a broken heart."

Madison sipped her coffee. She didn't want to think about Beckett. Every time she did, she remembered him leaving with

Jessie Brooks and felt that terrible ache in her middle, the sting of tears behind her eyes.

"What happened between you two anyway?" Cassidy asked, her voice uncharacteristically gentle.

"I told you already."

"I know, but it doesn't make sense. I know a lot's happened the past couple weeks, but there's no reason for him to lose interest just like that." She snapped her fingers.

"I'm telling you, I scared him off. You weren't there the night of my birthday. I was a blubbering psychopath."

"You were hurting. And he was fine after that, if you'll remember. He didn't get all weird till after he told you about being with Michael the day he died."

"Yeah, but he was wrong about all that." Madison finished her coffee and folded her arms over her stomach, trying to press the ache away. "The *why* doesn't really matter, does it? He's obviously done. He's going out with Jessie now."

Cassidy shook her head. "Uh-uh."

Madison shot her a look.

"Jessie brought Coco in today for her checkup. Something she said gave me the impression Beckett isn't over you. She seemed kinda bitter about it, so I didn't press for details."

Madison's heart gave an extra kick, and she told it to settle down. No sense getting her hopes up. "What did she say?"

"I told her I'd heard she was going out with Beckett—thought I'd do a little digging on your behalf—"

"Thank you."

"You're welcome. And she said, 'We're just friends. I guess he's still hung up on Madison.'"

She sucked in a breath. "He said that? That's he's still hung up on me? That doesn't make sense."

"Exactly what I've been trying to tell you. Did you see today's paper?"

"Today's—no, why?"

"There's an article—*someone* donated fifteen hundred to the sailing club for a scholarship in Michael's name." Cassidy raised her brows expectantly.

"Who?"

"It was anonymous. It wasn't your family?"

"No, I don't think so. They would've told me."

"Fifteen hundred . . . wasn't that—"

"The amount of the prize money. But he's using that to get his business off the ground." It couldn't be him, could it? That was a lot of money. He wouldn't just give it up. Would he?

Cassidy shrugged. "Who else could it be?"

Madison's head reeled. "Maybe he did it a couple weeks ago when he thought he was to blame for Michael's death. A guilt thing."

Cassidy shook her head, then scanned the coffee shop. She popped up, retrieved a paper from an empty table, and handed the section to Madison. "Right there."

It was just a paragraph buried in the metro section. Madison read it. "Monday, it says. Someone donated the money yesterday." She folded the paper and set it down. "I don't understand."

"See what I mean? You should talk to him, Madison. You said you arrived at the party with Drew Friday. Do you think the whole Jessie thing was to make you jealous? He did have to sit through that play, which, I might add, had a pretty steamy scene between you and Dr. Delight. Maybe he was jealous, and he just went all stupid."

Madison shook her head. "He's not like that. Besides, he was acting distant before." But if Jessie said he still had feelings for her, why else . . . ?

Cassidy gave a thoughtful frown. "Maybe . . ."

"Maybe what?"

"I don't know. I honestly don't, but, honey, you have to straighten this out. You love him, and he apparently still has feelings for you."

She remembered the way he'd pulled his hand from hers. The lack of emotion in his eyes. "You'd never know it."

"He remembers what you wore at some little high school dance eons ago. He's had a thing for you forever. Why do you think he waited so long to act on it?"

"I don't know. We never got around to discussing it."

"There's got to be more here we don't know."

Maybe Cassidy was right. She felt the stir of hope and squelched the desire to press it down.

"The question is, are you going to sit around nursing your broken heart or do something about it?"

Her heart was beating so fast, she wondered if she'd been given caffeinated coffee. But no, it was just nerves. She should confront Beckett. She'd taken the coward's way out since the night she'd told him how Michael had really died. He'd pulled away from her, and she'd been too afraid of rejection to ask why.

And then she'd felt discarded at the party . . .

Her mom's words from earlier in the summer came back. *"You've always been afraid of feeling, Madison. Sometimes those negative feelings are so strong, they're overwhelming, and it's easier to just not deal with them."*

That's what she was doing now, had been doing since Beckett

had pulled away. She was learning to face her feelings about Michael's death; she supposed she could find the courage to face Beckett—even if it only meant more heartache.

"I have to go." Madison stood and gathered her purse.

"Good luck," Cassidy called.

Madison's legs trembled as she left the coffee shop. She squinted against the bright evening light, got in her car, and headed toward Beckett's place.

Help me, God. I don't even know what I'm going to say. I just know I love him, and I have to know if he loves me too. She couldn't formulate more than that. But God knew her heart. He would answer her prayer one way or another.

A few minutes later she turned onto his street, her heart fluttering when she saw his truck.

You can do this, Madison. Be brave.

At the sound of her vehicle, Rigsby appeared in the window. Madison got out of her car, mounted the porch steps, and knocked. The dog gave an excited bark. She didn't see any lights through the picture window, but it was still daylight out. She knocked again.

Fear sucked the moisture from her mouth and made her hands shake. She stuffed them into her khaki pockets and told herself she'd live through this.

After a third unanswered knock she walked around back. Maybe he was working on the boat. But when she reached the backyard she saw that the outbuilding was closed up tight.

She strolled back to her car, a hollow spot opening up inside, spreading quickly. Where could he be? If he'd gone for a walk, he'd have taken Rigsby.

Think, Madison. Was it Wednesday, his Bible study night?

She'd had trouble keeping track of days since she'd been off work. But no, it was Tuesday. Where would he be?

She remembered something he'd said once and increased her pace. She hopped in her car, drove two blocks, and pulled into a diagonal slot. The park was empty, the swings swaying in the warm breeze. She headed past the slide, past the basketball court, and toward the wooded hillside.

It was where he liked to go when he needed to think or pray, up on the rock tower where he had a God's-eye view of the valley. She strode across the plush lawn, feeling the grass tickle the tops of her feet through her sandals.

She was going to do this no matter how hard it might be. No matter how much the truth—whatever it was—might hurt. Maybe she was afraid, but she was going to feel the fear and do it anyway.

Give me courage, God.

At the base of the hill, she kicked off her sandals and started up the path. The dirt was hard under her feet. Sticks poked at her soles and stones scraped the tender flesh. She still didn't like the way it felt, that hadn't changed. Life was full of discomfort and hurt. But pain wasn't fatal.

Her calf muscles ached at the steep parts. The darkness of the woods closed in around her. Her breaths grew shallow as she ascended, her mouth drying. Still she climbed.

When she neared the top, she spotted the tower of rock through the woods and climbed toward it. She stopped at the base, catching her breath, pulling in the scent of pine and earth. A bird gave a warbled call, and another tweeted in response.

She faced the tower, remembering the daunting climb. She opened her mouth, Beckett's name on her tongue, then closed it again. He was up there. She couldn't see him, couldn't hear him, but she knew he was there. She felt it clear down to her bare toes. She wanted to see his face when he heard her voice. Maybe it would tell her all she needed to know.

She began the climb, taking the first difficult steps. It was harder without Beckett's help, but she'd manage. Halfway up, she stretched for a hold and pulled herself up, her bare toes curling on a shallow ledge.

A breeze came and ruffled her hair, rewarding her effort, but by the time she neared the top, sweat beaded on the back of her neck. She eased herself up over the top, catching the most glorious sight.

Beckett, stretched out on the flat rock, arms folded under his head, eyes closed, Bible propped open on his stomach. The wires of earbuds dangled from his ears to his jeans pocket. She took a moment just to appreciate the view.

His lips were moving, and she wondered if he was praying or mouthing the words of a song. He sported a couple days' stubble, and his lashes, so dark, fanned his upper cheeks. She'd missed that face, those lips.

As if sensing her, his eyes opened and settled on her. There was something more than surprise in the look. Or was that only wishful thinking?

He sprang upright, pulling out the earbuds, catching his Bible as it fell. "Madison."

She shifted under his direct gaze. Her chest rose and fell as she caught her breath. "Hi. I was, uh, in the neighborhood."

Maybe she shouldn't have come, invaded his private time. Too late now.

He stared back, his expression an unsolved puzzle. "Have a seat."

She lowered herself to the flat rock, stretching out her legs.

"Where are your shoes?"

"Long story."

Her pulse raced, and her heart fought a losing battle with her ribs. Now that she was here, what did she say? She hadn't thought that far ahead. She pulled in her knees and clasped her arms around them. The sun had disappeared behind wispy clouds, turning the evening sky pink.

"Why are you here, Madison?"

Maybe she should pretend she didn't know he'd be here. That she'd just wanted to get away and remembered his hiding spot. But that wasn't true.

She gathered her courage around her like a cape. "Beckett . . . I need to know what happened. Between us." She looked him in the eye despite the heat rising to her cheeks.

Something flickered in his eyes. He looked away, then stood, took a few steps. But the rock ledge wouldn't let him go far. His shoulders rose and fell on a sigh. He cradled the back of his neck, his elbows jutting toward the sunset.

"You can tell me the truth. I'm not going to fall apart—well, I might, but not here."

He turned. She wished she knew what he was thinking, but he'd always been so hard to read.

"I don't want to hurt you," he said.

Her heart shrank four sizes. She gave a tremulous smile. "Too late."

He flinched, and she immediately regretted the words.

"Look, I guess I just wanted to tell you something, so I'm going to say it, and if that's it, then it just is. I'll—I'll get over it, okay? I just . . . I just need you to know that somewhere along the way, somewhere between the swimming lessons and the sailing and the really great kisses . . ." A lump formed in her throat, choking off the last words, and a burning started behind the bridge of her nose.

"Madison." Her name sounded etched in rock.

"I know I've been kind of a mess. All right, a real mess. But I'm working on that, and I just need you to be patient with me, Beckett, because I—"

"Madison, don't."

"Why? Why shouldn't you hear the truth?"

"There's no future here. How can you not see that?"

She pressed against the ache, but it was futile. "You don't love me."

He looked away, blew out a long breath. A shadow moved across his jaw. She could almost see the waves of tension rolling off him.

"Look," he said. "I'm not the one for you. You need to move on, maybe start going out with Drew again or—"

"Drew!"

"He's a nice guy, Madison, you should give him a—"

"You're pawning me off on Drew?"

His silence pretty much said it all.

She shot to her feet, her eyes stinging. "I don't love Drew. I love you, you idiot."

His eyes softened. Pity?

She hadn't thought she could feel worse, but guess what? "I thought you might love me too, but I guess I was wrong." So wrong. She turned to go, her vision clouded with tears.

"Wait, Madison."

"I got it, Beckett. Loud and clear." She took the first step down and slipped on the rocky slope. She caught herself, scraping her palm in the process.

"You're going to kill yourself." He leaped down, grasped her arm, turned her until she was eye-to-eye with him.

A tear escaped, rolling down her cheek. She dashed it away, but another took its place. She tried to shake him off, but he wouldn't let go, took her other arm too.

There was something in his eyes. Not pity, not indifference. "What am I going to do with you?" he said softly. He let out a breath. He looked skyward as if some answer might appear in the clouds.

"I don't understand any of this. I don't understand you. What do you want from me?" Her throat closed, choking off her last words, and more tears followed.

"Stop it. Just stop it." He pulled her into his arms.

Before she lost her will, she pushed at his chest. "No."

He held her arms, preventing her escape.

"You can't push me away and pull me toward you. You don't love me. I get it, now just let me go."

He tightened his grip. "I do." His eyes were fervent, his tone compelling. "I do love you."

She stopped her struggle, blinked to clear her vision. Were her ears playing cruel tricks on her?

His grip eased, his thumbs moved in a slow caress. "Look, honey. You're not the one who's messed up, all right? You're great. You've got a terrific family, had a solid upbringing. You're a wonderful woman, you'll make a great wife someday, a great mom, just like yours. What have I got? A mom who walked out, a dad who checked out . . . abandonment, divorce, and alcoholism—those are the tools I'm working with."

Madison frowned. "You're nothing like your dad."

"Genetics go deep, Madison, and I'm not willing to risk your future on the hopes that—"

"Risk *my* future? You don't get to make that decision, Beckett. That's my call."

"I'm trying to do what's best for you. That's what real love is."

"Real love is a choice. I choose to love you, despite who your parents are or what they did. I choose to believe that there's always hope, that with God all things are possible. Maybe you didn't have the best earthly father, but you have a heavenly Father, Beckett, and there's nothing He can't overcome. I'm only beginning to see that for myself."

He stared back, seemed to consider her words. "I'm a big risk . . ." He meant it as a warning. But something in his tone made the anger drain away.

Her lips lifted. "I'll take my chances."

She saw the struggle in his face, and her heart broke for him. For where he'd come from and what he'd been through. There were still old wounds, she saw that now. But somehow, in spite of it all, he'd become a courageous and godly man. It was nothing short of a miracle.

This was the man for her. She felt it way down deep inside where new seeds were being sown every day. "We both have things to overcome. But God's going to do big things with you, Beckett. He already has. And I want to be there, right by your side, watching."

"You don't know how badly I want that." His voice grated across his throat.

But she did. She saw it in his eyes, clear as the summer sky. "Then take it. It's yours for the taking."

A moment caught, suspended in time, stretching out until it was taut with tension.

Finally he framed her face, swept away the dampness with his thumb. "I love you, Maddy. Is that enough?"

"More than," she whispered.

He leaned in and brushed her lips, the tenderness of it making her ache. The good kind of ache that spread all through her, making her legs go weak with wanting. He pulled her closer, deepened the kiss, and she savored the taste of him. She touched his face, her fingertips tingling under the roughness of his jaw. She could get used to this.

When he broke the kiss, it was only so he could hold her. He tightened his arms around her, and she breathed in the scent of him. His body was warm and solid against hers, his heartbeat strong. It felt familiar and right and perfect, like starlit nights and barefoot summers.

Home. That's what it was. It felt like home.

Epilogue

THE SUN HAD DROPPED BEHIND THE OAK TREES, CASTING long shadows over the McKinleys' basketball court. Madison watched PJ put up a critical shot from three-point range. It swished through the basket, dropped down, and patted the concrete.

Beckett snatched up the ball, scowling playfully as Daniel and Ryan messed with him. With an H-O-R-S, missing this shot would make Beckett the second loser. Madison was already eating crow on the sidelines.

She clapped. "Come on, honey, you can do it."

Beckett took position, bent his knees, dribbled three times, and put up the shot. It sailed through the air in a beautiful arc, hit the rim, and bounced off, falling to the ground.

PJ strutted the width of the court, her ponytail swishing. "Oh yeah. Two down, two to go."

"You haven't won yet, hot dog."

"Just a matter of time, big brother."

"We'll see about that."

"How many letters is that for you again?"

"Shut up and miss a shot already."

Beckett joined Madison at the picnic table. "You could've warned me about her."

She lifted a shoulder. "Didn't do me any good."

Behind him, pandemonium broke out as Daniel sank a shot

from PJ's weak spot. Ryan laughed, and PJ bounced the ball against the back of his head.

"Hey!"

"Holy cow," Beckett said, turning to Madison. "You all must've been a handful growing up."

"What, us? Five little angels."

Beckett shot her a look as he took her hands and pulled her up. "Go for a walk?"

"Ready to leave the madness behind?"

"For a few minutes."

"We'll be back," she called over her shoulder.

"Take your time," her mom called from beside her dad on the porch stoop.

PJ let out a catcall, and Daniel's piercing whistle cut through the air.

Ryan chucked the basketball at his friend, and Daniel grunted when it caught him in the stomach. "Dude!"

Madison and Beckett headed down the drive, leaving the chaos behind. A few minutes later the only sounds were the gravel crunching under their shoes and the chattering of two squirrels playing chase on a thick oak. October had arrived, waving its magic wand over the trees, dusting them with gold and orange and red.

Madison inhaled the fragrance of early autumn: loamy earth, pine, a neighbor's wood fire. As much as she liked summer, she loved autumn the best. Roasted marshmallows, sweaters, and harvest. Colorful, cool, and fleeting. She was enjoying life these days. Enjoying work, and family, and yes, Beckett.

Something new and good had settled over her family since the secret surrounding Michael's death had come out. The news had shaken them all initially, but the results were well worth the fretting. The testing had revealed that none of them had the metabolic disorder. Their chances had been one in four, and of the five of them Michael had been the only one to inherit it.

"Heard from Dad today," Beckett said, breaking into her thoughts.

"Oh? How's he doing?"

"I was encouraged. He sounded different. Focused, more positive. He mentioned some changes he wanted to make when he came back, talked about opening a barbecue place someday."

"That's great." Mr. O'Reilly was in a ninety-day treatment facility. They hoped the longer stay would increase his chances of long-term sobriety. "You did the right thing in sending him there."

"I don't even remember him before he was an alcoholic. It's kind of like getting to know a new person. I'm hopeful for him."

"Speaking of dads, I saw you chatting with mine earlier." She nudged his shoulder. "I think he might be coming around."

Their hands swung between them. "Protective of his baby girl—can't blame him for that."

She'd noticed a lowering of her dad's guard each time she'd brought Beckett around. He'd initiated polite conversation with Beckett when they'd arrived tonight. She had a feeling her mom had been instrumental in softening him up.

"I know our families are different," Beckett said, "but I'm coming to peace with all that. My upbringing . . . I aim to do a lot better for my own family someday."

"I know you will. God used it to make you stronger. Maybe show you what you *don't* want for your own future."

He squeezed her hand. "And what I *do* want."

They traded smiles. He wasn't stingy with his affection. She loved that about him.

"I wasn't just chatting with your dad, you know."

"No?" She kicked a hickory nut, and it scuttled down the drive.

"I was asking permission."

She took three more steps, then stopped in her tracks. Dried leaves shuffled past on a soft breeze. His eyes had that look, the one she'd fallen into during that dance so long ago. The one that captured her heart each time he drew her into his arms, into the safety of his embrace.

"Permission?"

He took her other hand, facing her. The golden hour had arrived, softening the shadows on his face, making his eyes shimmer.

"I was going to wait," he said. "But I can't. I know it hasn't been that long, but I've never been more sure of anything."

His chest rose and fell on a breath even as her own froze, holding the oxygen captive. "I want you to be my wife, baby. I want to come home to you every night and hear your laughter. I want to build a life together with all the things that matter. I want there to be family, and sailing, and church, and work, and kids . . ."

Her lips trembled on a smile. "Five little angels?"

He squeezed her hands. "I was thinking we'd start with one and work our way up. What about it, Maddy—will you marry me?"

The world had narrowed down to the two of them. His words brushed the corners of her mind, the softest of caresses. His palms were damp against hers and there was tension in his arms, a question in his eyes.

He had to know—didn't he? How much she loved him, needed him? That she couldn't imagine a future without him?

The breath left her lungs, tumbled through the smile spreading on her face. "Oh yeah. You better believe I will."

He gathered her in his arms, crushing her against him. Close enough to feel his heart thumping against her sweater, close enough to smell his warm, spicy scent, close enough to hear the whisper in her ear.

"I love you, Madison McKinley."

And it was enough. More than enough.

Reading Group Guide

1. Which character was your favorite and why?
2. The Chapel Springs series is based on Jesus' parable of the sower. Read Luke 8:5. How was Madison's spiritual life like the seed that fell along the path?
3. Who were some of the people who watered Madison's spiritual seed to help her grow roots and flourish? Who are those people in your life?
4. Madison was experiencing a lack of peace that had begun to affect many areas of her life. When she became desperate, she set out on a journey to fix it. What are some things people do when they're looking for peace? What are some healthy alternatives? Have you ever struggled to find peace? How did you finally find it?
5. Madison learned that God could handle all her emotions. Have you ever felt that you had to hide your true feelings from Him? Why do you think we sometimes avoid being honest with God?
6. Sometimes bad things happen to good people. Madison struggled to understand why God had allowed Michael to die. Have you ever struggled to understand God's ways? How can you use what you've learned to help someone else through a similar difficulty?
7. Beckett and Madison both struggled with feelings of guilt.

Discuss the difference between healthy and unhealthy guilt. How would God have us handle our feelings of guilt?

8. When Madison lost Michael, she stuffed down her pain instead of dealing with it. Her mom helped her find the courage to face her feelings, to feel the bad stuff. Have you ever been afraid to "go barefoot"? How did you overcome it? How can trusting in God enable you to make the journey?

9. Life is a God-given gift, yet most of us feel entitled to a long one. Discuss why you think that is and how we can develop a spiritually mature view of death.

10. Beckett feared that his parents' failures would be replayed in his own life. He said, "Abandonment, divorce, and alcoholism—those are the tools I'm working with." What tools are you working with? What are some ways you can, with God's help, build a successful future in spite of or because of your parents' example?

Acknowledgments

Writing a book is a team effort, and I'm so grateful for the entire team at Thomas Nelson Fiction, led by publisher Daisy Hutton: Katie Bond, Amanda Bostic, Ruthie Dean, Natalie Hanemann, Jodi Hughes, Laura Dickerson, Kerri Potts, Ami McConnell, Becky Monds, and Kristen Vasgaard.

Thanks especially to my editor, Natalie Hanemann, who helped shape this story, notified me of gaping holes, and otherwise helped me fashion this into a more enjoyable read. I'm forever grateful to the talented LB Norton, who makes me look much better than I am!

Author Colleen Coble is my first reader. Thank you, friend! I wouldn't want to do this writing thing without my buds and fellow authors Colleen Coble, Diann Hunt, and Kristin Billerbeck. Love you, girls!

I'm grateful to my agent, Karen Solem, who handles all the left-brained matters so I can focus on the right-brained stuff.

I owe a debt of gratitude to sailing enthusiast Rik Hall, who helped me with all the details involving sailing and regattas. I'd have been lost without him! A big thanks also goes out to Dr. Ronda Wells for her tireless efforts in helping me with the facts related to inborn errors of metabolism. Any mistakes that made their way into print are entirely mine.

A special call-out to my small group. What a blessing you all

ACKNOWLEDGMENTS

are! Allen and Kristi Etter, Joy and Denny Geiger, Rod and Vicki Marquart, and Don and Wanietta Stuckey. You brighten up my week!

Thanks to my Facebook friends who helped me title this book and name my hero—y'all have great taste!

To my family: Kevin, Justin, Chad, and Trevor. I treasure and love you all!

Lastly, thank you, friend, for letting me share this story with you. I wouldn't be doing this without you! I've enjoyed connecting with readers like you through my Facebook page. Visit my website at www.DeniseHunterBooks.com or just drop me a note at Denise@DeniseHunterBooks.com. I'd love to hear from you!

Return to Chapel Springs in

Dancing
with
Fireflies

AVAILABLE APRIL 2014

The Big Sky Romance Series

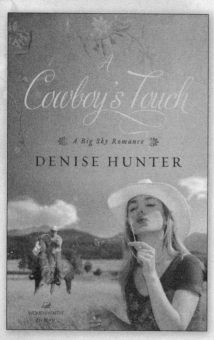

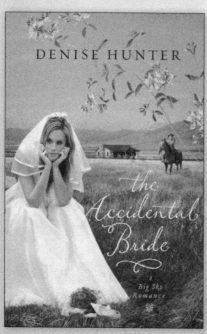

NANTUCKET LOVE STORIES

Four Women.   *Four Love Stories.*

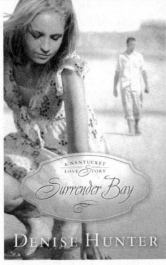

One Island.   *Escape to Nantucket.*

*S*he wished she could go back and change things . . . but life doesn't give do-overs. Could anything but good-byes be waiting on the other side of *Sweetwater Gap*?

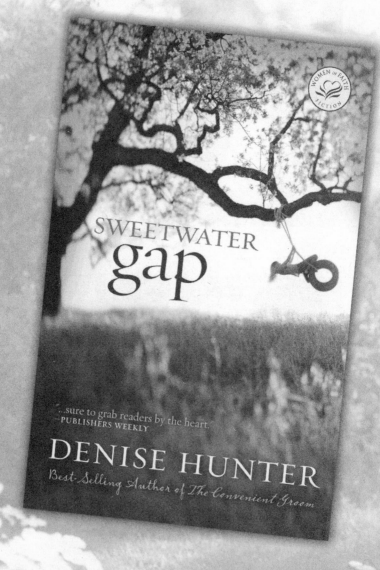

SWEETWATER
gap

...sure to grab readers by the heart.
—PUBLISHERS WEEKLY

DENISE HUNTER
Best-Selling Author of The Convenient Groom

Available in print and e-book

Love is on the way

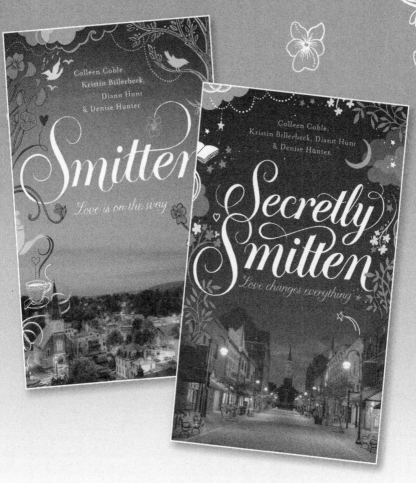

Available in print and e-book

Thomas Nelson
Since 1798

About the Author

DENISE HUNTER IS THE AWARD-WINNING and best-selling author of many novels, including *A Cowboy's Touch* and *Sweetwater Gap*. She and her husband are raising three boys in Indiana.

PHOTO BY AMBER ZIMMERMAN